This book is dedicated to my found family—
the people who have chosen to be my family
rather than being born to it. You know who you are.

FLARE UP

SHANNON STACEY

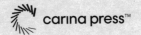

carina press™

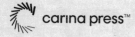

ISBN-13: 978-1-335-92459-9

Flare Up

Recycling programs
for this product may
not exist in your area.

www.CarinaPress.com

Printed in U.S.A.

FLARE UP

Chapter One

Grant Cutter had figured this was about as bad as a scene could get. The temperature with windchill well below zero. Their gear and lines freezing up. Stalactites of ice hanging from his helmet blocking his vision until he took the time to break them off with a swipe of his stiff glove. And the water was a hell of a lot more effective at turning the house and street into an ice sculpture than putting out the flames.

But he was wrong. It could always be worse.

The fire had not only jumped, but it jumped to an apartment building they couldn't confirm had been fully evacuated, so the incident commander was sending them in.

Canvassing a residential building that probably should have been condemned by the city before he was even born wasn't exactly the reprieve from the cold he'd been looking for but, after checking their gear, he and the other guys from Engine 59 and another crew went inside.

"Fast but thorough," Danny Walsh said. The LT led the way up the stairs since they'd start at the top and work their way down. The other crew would pound on doors at ground level and if all went well, they'd meet in the middle and get the hell out before it got bad.

The smoke thickened as they reached the top floor. A bare-chested, barefoot guy in undone jeans passed them on the stairs. He was coughing, but waved off their attempts to assist him.

"Is there anybody else up there?" Danny yelled.

"Dunno." The guy didn't even pause.

"Asshole," Scott Kincaid muttered into the radio, but Grant wasn't surprised. They'd responded to these buildings before and they didn't seem to attract the kind of residents who gave a shit about their neighbors.

They started pounding on doors, which was all they could do, but they didn't get any response until they'd worked their way down to the next floor.

"I hear something," Aidan Hunt yelled, pounding a third time on a door. "Something banged. Maybe coughing."

Grant was closest to him, so he used the Halligan bar to pop the door. Smoke billowed out, so dense they could barely see, and he followed Aidan in. The apartment was small—one room and probably barely legal— so it only took a few seconds to follow the coughing to the person on the floor near the window. While Aidan did a quick check of the bathroom and under the bed to make sure there was nobody else, Grant crouched down next to the person he was pretty sure was a woman, despite having a throw blanket over her head.

"Fire department," he said. "Let's get you out of here."

Her cough was so weak and ineffectual, he didn't bother asking if she could get up and walk. Instead he rolled her, intending to lift her and carry her out.

Then the throw blanket slipped away from a sleep-tangled mess of blonde curls, revealing dark blue eyes he saw in his dreams, and Grant's world stopped.

"Wren."

He hadn't seen her in five months, since she'd told him on the phone she didn't want to see him anymore and then ghosted. No explanation. No compromise. Nothing but five months of a broken heart that hadn't even begun to heal yet.

What the hell was she doing in this place?

Grant. Her mouth formed his name, though no sound got through her constricted throat. The grayish cast of her skin and lips terrified him, and he started to hoist her up.

Aidan was at his side. "I'll carry her out."

"I've got her." Despite the shock and pain from seeing her again, Grant wanted to hold her. He wanted to cradle her in his arms and feel that sense of contentment holding her had always brought him in the past.

There was no time for that. After draping her over his shoulder, he stood and headed for the door. It wouldn't be a comfortable ride for her, but the only thing that mattered right now was getting her out of the building and to an ambulance, where they could give her oxygen. Her body had gone totally limp by the time he reached the stairs, but he refused to consider the possibility she'd need medical care beyond that.

They'd gotten there in time, and that's all there was to it.

He heard voices in his radio and was aware Aidan stayed right behind him, but Grant didn't stop moving until he hit the clear, frigid air.

He paused to get his bearings and then headed for the ambulances on standby. Some of those voices in his radio must have warned them he was coming, because Cait opened the back of her truck and waved at him.

Cait Tasker was not only an EMT, but she was engaged to Gavin Boudreau, who was Grant's best friend and with the Ladder 37 crew. E-59 and L-37 were parked side-by-side in the firehouse and always rolled out together, so Gavin was on scene, too. And Cait knew Wren. The four of them had spent a lot of time together before Wren walked away from him and didn't look back.

By the time he reached the ambulance doors, he could feel her stirring. Not a lot, but she had to be breathing in order to regain consciousness and that was enough for now.

Because it was so damn cold and she was small, they didn't bother with the stretcher. He handed Wren up to Cait's partner, Tony, who turned away with her.

"Oh my God, Grant." Cait looked at him, her expression mirroring his thoughts. "What the hell was Wren doing living here?"

"I don't know. She'll be okay, right?"

"We'll take care of her. Are *you* okay?"

He didn't answer. As he watched Tony fit a mask over Wren's face, her eyes met his and, no, he wasn't okay.

Questions tumbled through his mind. Why was Wren living in this place? Why had she disappeared from his life so abruptly? How could she still be in the city and not miss him enough to at least send a text message?

Had she known he'd been days away from buying her a ring and asking her to spend the rest of her life with him?

"Cutter," he heard Walsh bark into the radio. "Where the fuck are you?"

He had a job to do and people's lives depended on him doing it. But as he started to turn away, his gaze caught Wren's again and he felt the impact all the way to his toes.

God, he'd loved her. And he didn't think he'd ever really be okay again.

The look on Grant's face—his expressive dark eyes going so flat and cold—before he turned and walked away almost finished what the smoke had started and killed Wren Everett.

Five months ago, she'd thought walking away from him would be the hardest thing she ever did. Seeing him again was harder. Even with her lungs filling with smoke and her eyes watering, in that unguarded moment he'd recognized her, she'd seen all the pain she'd caused him.

And as Cait's partner pressed a mask to her face and ordered her to breathe, she watched Grant's expression harden before he turned and walked away.

That hurt even more than her lungs trying to expel the smoke she'd inhaled.

"Wren, you can't cry right now," she heard Cait say. "You need to concentrate on breathing."

She hadn't even realized she was gasping harder and her vision was even more blurry until Cait told her she was crying, but it didn't surprise her. When she'd broken Grant's heart, she'd done a heck of a job on her own, too.

"Deep breaths," Tony said in a kind but firm voice. She tried, but she couldn't stop coughing.

"Were you living here?" Cait asked her while fussing over her, taking her vitals. Since she had a mask

over her face and was supposed to be breathing, Wren
nodded. "Why?"

All she could manage was a small shrug, and she was
almost thankful when another round of hoarse coughs
gave her a good excuse not to answer. Cait would have a
lot more questions. She'd been somebody Wren considered a friend and the feeling had probably been mutual,
but when she'd ghosted on Grant, she'd had to ghost on
Gavin and Cait, too.

"Save the questions for later, Cait." Tony looked at
Wren for a long moment before turning to his partner.
"I think she needs to go in."

Wren didn't even want to think about how much an
ambulance ride to the emergency room was going to
cost her, but when Cait nodded, she didn't bother to
argue. Cait was stubborn.

"You inhaled a lot of smoke and you lost consciousness," Tony explained. "The doctors will check out your
lungs and heart and make sure everything's clear."

"That sounds ominous," Wren said, her voice raspy
and muffled by the mask.

"Just a precaution," Cait said. "Did the smoke detectors go off? You should have had plenty of warning,
with time to get out."

"There were no alarms." It was all a little fuzzy in
her head, but she was sure the smoke detectors hadn't
gone off.

Tony swore under his breath—but not so under his
breath that she didn't hear it—and shook his head. "Asshole landlords, willing to risk lives to save a few bucks.
Hell, you can get them for free if you're not too lazy to
make a phone call."

"I remember hearing the sirens," she said. "But

it's not weird to hear sirens around here and I was exhausted, so I must have fallen back to sleep. When I woke up again, I was already coughing and the smoke was burning my eyes."

She'd panicked and her first thought was that her ex had found her. That the phone call that scared her and made her walk away from the life—and love—she'd found for herself hadn't been enough for him.

Cait set something on her lap. "When Grant picked you up, this was under you, so Aidan grabbed it on the way out."

She couldn't look down far enough to see it because Tony was holding the oxygen to her face, but she put her hand on the object and actually managed a small smile. The black, well-broken in leather wristlet hadn't cost her a lot, but her car keys, license and debit card were inside. They weren't much, but at least she wouldn't have to stand in line at the RMV for hours before she could even start rebuilding her life.

Once they'd secured her for the ride to the hospital and Tony was driving them away from the scene, Wren closed her eyes for a moment and tried not to think about Grant.

The last time she'd seen him in person, he'd knelt on the edge of her bed to kiss her goodbye before he left for work. He'd told her he loved her and that he'd see her later. Whenever the confusion and hurt in his voice when she'd told him on the phone they were done tried to fill her mind, she pictured that morning instead. It still hurt, but it was easier to remember the happy times with him.

She didn't want the expression on his face before

he walked away from her tonight to be her new last memory of him.

"As soon as we're released from the scene," Cait said, interrupting her thoughts, "I'll stop in and see how you're doing. I don't think you'll need to be admitted, honestly. And I have tomorrow off, so I can sleep in tomorrow if Gavin doesn't wake me up after his shift."

"You don't have to do that."

"So you already have somebody else who's going to help you out?" Cait folded her arms. "Who is it?"

"What? I don't…"

"Maybe I didn't know you as well as I thought I did, but if I had to bet, I'd say you'll be alone at the hospital and when they release you, you won't have anywhere to go, but you still won't pick up a phone and call any of us."

Since she'd plugged it in to charge before collapsing on her bed, Wren didn't currently own a phone, but she knew that wasn't the point.

"Am I wrong?" Cait insisted. When Wren refused to answer, she nodded. "That's what I thought. So I'm just going to show up."

Tears blurred Wren's vision again, but this time they had nothing to do with the smoke. She didn't deserve this kindness. She'd done a shitty thing to a man Cait considered family, but she still wouldn't turn her back on her. Maybe it was the EMT in her, but Wren could see the concern and caring in Cait's eyes.

"Thank you," she whispered.

"It's going to be okay, Wren. Whatever happened before and whatever's happening now, it's going to be okay."

She had to believe it would be okay. Maybe she was

just being paranoid. The building was a dump and she didn't need an expert to tell her it wasn't up to code. It could have been an electrical fire. Or a toaster mishap. There was any number of things that could have started the fire.

It didn't mean Ben had found her.

Chapter Two

The beef stew they'd reheated after leaving the scene filled the void in Grant's stomach, but it did nothing to warm him up. The hot shower once they'd returned to quarters hadn't helped, either. Nor would crawling into his bunk once they'd finished their delayed supper.

The chill from seeing Wren had settled into his bones and he couldn't shake it.

There wasn't a lot of conversation in the station's kitchen tonight, which didn't surprise him. They were exhausted and the rest of the guys—the guys whose chills could be cured with hot water and a warm meal—were getting sleepy. If they were lucky, the alarm wouldn't tone again and they could sleep until the next crew came in to replace them.

As tired as he was, Grant didn't think he could sleep.

What the hell was Wren doing in a place like that? That was the question that kept spinning in his brain, maybe because it was the least painful to dwell on. But there were others. Why had she left him? Why did it still hurt so much? And why did seeing her still make his pulse race and his mouth go dry?

On the table between Gavin and him, Gavin's cell phone buzzed, startling him out of his thoughts. It was probably important, since it was almost one in the morning, but he couldn't see the screen.

After several message exchanges, Gavin set his phone on the table and the look he gave Grant made it obvious whatever those text messages had been about involved him. "Was that Cait? What's up?"

"Yeah, that was Cait. She's finally home. And if I tell you, you have to promise not to hit me."

"Why do you make it sound like I go around punching things? I can't even remember the last time I hit anybody. Well, somebody who wasn't on skates, at least."

"Okay, good point. But if you were ever going to hit me, it would be now."

Grant wasn't sure things could get much worse than seeing Wren at the scene and he hadn't hit anything then. "Just tell me whatever it is you have to say."

"Wren's staying at my place."

He was still, trying to process that information without feeling anything. He knew he was wrecked emotionally at the moment and it would be too easy to get hung up on where loyalties should lie and say something he couldn't take back.

Gavin was a firefighter. Cait was an EMT. Helping people was in their nature. And Wren wasn't a stranger. She'd almost been family.

He nodded sharply. "Your place is a one-bedroom. Is she sleeping on the couch?"

"Tonight, yeah. For a longer term solution—you know, until she gets back on her feet—Cait suggested she stay with Cait's mom and Carter, in her old room because it's empty. She said Wren wanted no part of it, and she got really agitated when she suggested Danny and Ashley's, because they have a kid."

Grant connected the dots. "She's scared of something."

"Or somebody."

A new emotion coursed through Grant, so intense he sucked in a breath. Somebody wanted to hurt Wren. Somebody *had* hurt Wren, badly enough so she'd run.

She'd run from *him*.

"Okay, now he might hit something," Chris said, taking a step out of his arm's reach.

"I'm not going to hit anything." The person he wanted to hit wasn't here. He couldn't even be sure there *was* a person, though it felt like he'd found the missing piece of the Wren puzzle.

It made sense. Her reserve when they'd met. How reluctant she'd been to let him in. Why she'd felt the need to run.

There could never be an explanation for why she'd run from him, though, other than Wren not trusting him to keep her safe. To take care of her. That was never going to make sense to him.

"She can come stay with us," Derek said. "We live a little further from the neighborhood, so maybe far enough away from whatever the problem is. She and Julia really hit it off at the Labor Day barbecue. I know Olivia wouldn't mind."

Memories of Wren, her blonde hair shining in the sun as she laughed with Derek's daughter in Aidan's backyard, slammed into Grant's mind and they hurt. That day had been one of the happiest days of his life—watching the woman he was going to marry fitting right in with the people who were like family to him—and a week later she'd dumped him and taken off.

Rick was washing his bowl, but he looked over his shoulder. "If she wouldn't stay with Danny and Ashley because of Jackson, she's probably not going to stay with you. Especially since she *did* hit it off so well with your daughter."

"We need to find out what she's afraid of and take care of it," Scott said, and Aidan nodded.

"If she wanted our help," Grant said, "she would have asked me for it when I was her boyfriend. Obviously she doesn't."

Rick dried his hands and leaned against the counter. "Until we know what's going on, we don't know why she's doing anything she does. But we do know she needs help. You know we have your back, Cutter. If you want nothing to do with her, then Cait can set her up with the agencies who'll help her out and that'll be the end of it. It's your call."

"She's lost everything," Gavin said quietly. "And I'm guessing she didn't have much to begin with."

Grant wasn't surprised Gavin was the one pushing him toward helping her. Because they were best friends, he was the guy who'd spent the most time with Wren.

"If any of you can get her to stay with you while she finds a new place, I'm cool with that. And I have some of her stuff." He shrugged. "Not much, but there were some things she'd left at my apartment and since she didn't tell anybody where she was going, I couldn't give it back. And I couldn't just throw it away."

"She'd probably like to have it," Gavin said. "Even if it's not much, it's something. Because that fire was such a bitch, with the ice and all, there's not gonna be much to save in that building."

"It's in a bag. I can run home and grab it and…" He could give it to Gavin or leave it on the damn doorstep. There was no reason he had to see her. He waited, hop-

ing his friend would offer to swing by and pick it up,
but Gavin said nothing. "I'll stop by with it after shift.
See how she's doing."

It would hurt. There was no doubt about that. But
he hadn't been able to get her out of his head since he
saw her sitting in the back of Cait's ambulance, and he
knew it would only get worse when he went home to his
empty apartment and tried to close his eyes.

So he'd see her. He'd give Wren her stuff and see
with his own eyes that she was okay. And then he'd
walk away.

Wren sat on the edge of a couch that wasn't hers, wearing borrowed clothes after taking a shower and cleaning up with the spare toiletries Cait had given her. The
leggings were a little baggy on her and the lightweight
sweatshirt hung almost to her knees, but she was thankful for them.

Cait brought her a blanket and a pillow, which she
put on top of several throw pillows to keep Wren elevated a little. "Can I ask you something?"

She couldn't really say no, considering how generous
the other woman was being with her hospitality. "Sure."

"You were obviously running away from something,
so why did you stay in Boston?"

It was probably the last question Wren wanted to hear
because she didn't want to face the honest answer. "It
costs a lot of money to move."

Cait sighed and gave a slight shake of her head, as
if she knew Wren was lying to her. "Yeah, it does. Unless you're just packing what little you own in a car and
disappearing. One tank of gas could have gotten you
someplace a hell of a lot cheaper to live."

And someplace a hell of a lot farther from Grant. It had been stupid to stay in the city and she knew it. But she hadn't been able to bring herself to fill that gas tank and drive until she ran out of gas money. Her little car got good mileage and she would have gotten far enough away so she'd never see him again.

That was the thought that had kept her in the city, working her ass off to pay the outrageous rent on a crappy apartment while saving for something better. Even as she faced knowing he'd only be safe if she left, she couldn't imagine living the rest of her life without seeing him again. Maybe if she had a little time, she could come up with a way to make her problem disappear and then she could tell him everything.

Maybe he would have forgiven her and even loved her again.

Now she knew differently. The look he'd given her after handing her into the ambulance was seared into her memory already and it broke her heart all over again.

"I don't think you really *wanted* to leave Grant," Cait said in a low voice. "You should have talked to him, Wren. No matter what it was, you should have told him because he loved you."

Loved. Would there ever come a time that past tense wouldn't hurt?

"Okay, it's late," Cait said when Wren didn't have an answer for her. "Get some rest and things will look better in the morning."

Once Cait had turned off the lights and gone into her bedroom, Wren stretched out on the couch and pulled the soft blanket over her. She didn't expect sleep to come easily, especially with the coughing, but it had been a long, cold, scary night and feeling safe and warm knocked her out.

She woke up when the front door closed. It was light enough for her to see Gavin, and he closed the door as quietly as he could, but she'd been sleeping even lighter than usual in the months since she'd gotten the phone call from Ben.

He looked in her direction and winced. "Sorry. I tried to be quiet."

"I was awake anyway," she lied to make him feel better. Her throat was dry and scratchy, and her voice was hoarse.

"You doing okay?" He kept his voice low, probably to avoid waking Cait, so he walked closer as he spoke.

"I'm fine." That seemed to be her life now.

You doing okay?

I'm fine.

Nothing could be farther from the truth, but she knew if she opened the door to any of the people in Grant's life, they'd come charging through and she didn't want anybody else to worry about.

"Thank you for letting me crash here," she said. "I hope it didn't cause you any problems. With Grant, I mean. I assume you told him."

"I had to tell him. That's not the kind of thing I could keep from him." He shrugged. "It's not a problem. I mean, you aren't just some woman Grant used to date. You're Wren. We know you and we're not just turning our backs on you because…you broke up."

Because you turned your back on Grant and broke up with him in the most hurtful way possible. "Thank you."

The bedroom door opened and Cait poked her head out. "Hey, good morning."

To give Cait time to welcome her guy home, Wren got up and went into the bathroom. She didn't rush, giving them a few minutes to talk, so by the time she was done, the apartment smelled like coffee.

"Do you want some coffee?" Gavin asked while she folded the blanket and set it neatly on the pillow.

"Yes, please. Black is fine."

She could tell by the way Cait looked at her as she sipped that they'd talked about her while she was in the bathroom and they had something to tell her she probably wasn't going to like.

They let her have a few sips of her coffee—which tasted like heaven even if it was a little hot for her throat after the smoke and coughing—before Gavin broke the news. "Grant's going to stop by in about an hour."

"Oh." Wren set the coffee mug on the table because the liquid contents made it too obvious her hands were trembling. "I can be gone by then. I'll just—"

"He's coming to see you," he said. "Well, he's coming to drop off a few things you'd left at his apartment, anyway. Not much, I guess. But he thought you might want it."

So he wasn't *actually* coming to see her. He just wanted to return a few things, though at this moment, she couldn't remember anything she'd left at his place.

"I thought Cait and I would go get some breakfast somewhere. Give you two some privacy."

Privacy for what? Wren didn't feel strong enough to bear the weight of whatever anger and resentment Grant needed to get off his chest. Maybe he'd demand answers and she wasn't sure she was ready to give him any.

If Ben set that fire...

"Wren?" Concern practically radiated from Cait. "If

you're not feeling up to it, I'll stay. He can give me the stuff and go on his way."

"No, it's fine," she managed to say, despite feeling as if her sore throat was closing up on her.

If he had some things he wanted to say to her, she wouldn't run from him. He deserved that much after what she'd done.

Chapter Three

Grant knocked on Gavin and Cait's door, hoping the emotions churning in his gut didn't show on his face.

He wasn't sure what a guy was supposed to say to a woman who'd told him she loved him, too, and later the same day, told him they were done and she never wanted to see him again.

Why? That was the obvious question, but seeing her last night had been like reopening a wound that had barely begun to heal. It was still all tenderness and ragged edges and unexpected sore spots. And last night had ripped it all wide open. Right now he wanted to throw a bandage over it and pretend it didn't hurt.

When the door opened and Wren stepped back to let him in without really looking him in the eye, he felt as if that wound had been doused with salt water.

For a second, he was ready to toss the small duffel bag through the open door and run.

"Come in," she said, and the raspiness in her voice made him remember the feel of her limp, unconscious body draped over his shoulder last night.

He went in, walking past her to set the bag down on the table. "You left a few things at my place. Not a lot,

but I have that sweatshirt you…well, you said it was
your favorite, so I thought you might want it."

And he'd guessed right, judging by the way her face
softened as he pulled it out of the bag. It was obviously
old and had been washed a million times, but it was
a soft pink with a big, draping neckline and a long,
loose hem.

She'd liked to wear it with nothing but a pair of lace-
trimmed panties while they cuddled on the couch to
watch television.

He dropped it back in the bag as if it had scalded his
fingers. "There's some other random stuff, too. Nothing
big, but I figured you'd want the sweatshirt."

"Thank you for bringing it over. Cait warned me not
to expect to save much, if anything, from my apartment,
but I'll have my favorite sweatshirt. Thank you for not
throwing it away or tossing it in a donation bin."

He nodded because he didn't want to acknowledge
that would have been the typical thing to do. Or that
he'd tried and couldn't bring himself to get rid of her
things. Especially the sweatshirt. He hadn't slept with
it or anything, but he couldn't throw it away.

"Do you want some coffee or something? Gavin said
there's plenty of breakfast things and to help myself."

"No, thanks. I'm not staying." And yet he couldn't
bring himself to move toward the door.

"Okay."

Silence filled the apartment, heavy and awkward,
until Grant blurted out, "I want to know what's going on."

"Grant, I…I didn't *want* to hurt you. You have to
believe—"

He held up his hand to make her stop talking. He
didn't have to believe shit. "That's not what I meant. I

don't want to talk about feelings. I don't want to talk about us. I want you tell me what's going on with you right now."

"I don't know what you mean. If you don't want me to talk about us or why I left, what do you want to know?"

"If you'd gone off to some new great opportunity, it would be one thing. But you ghosted on me just to live in some shithole fire hazard, and that tells me you were running and I want to know what you were running from."

Her expression closed off and that kind of abrupt withdrawal wasn't in her usual nature, so he knew he'd hit a nerve. "It's nothing that concerns you."

"Bullshit. You're staying with friends of mine. That makes whatever you're afraid of my business."

"Then I'll leave."

Grant blew out a breath, forcing himself to take a minute before saying anything else. Even in the beginning, when she'd maintained a distance, she hadn't sounded *hard*. This kind of closed-off resolution was so unlike her, he knew something heavy was weighing on her. He needed to know what it was.

"It doesn't work that way, Wren," he said finally, in a much calmer voice. "You were mine and they're like my family. That means you were theirs, too. They've already proven that, no matter what went down between you and me, they're not going to turn their backs on you when you're down. They're not going to let you just walk away."

"They can't stop me."

He held her gaze, noticing the way her hair gave

away her trembling and how she blinked fast to keep tears from filling her eyes.

And even as he cursed himself for a fool, he stepped forward. He opened his arms, telegraphing his intentions and giving her the chance to turn away. To reject him. Instead, a tear spilled over onto her cheek as she moved into his embrace.

He tried not to feel anything. All he wanted to do was offer this woman comfort, but her body fit so perfectly against his. For months, he'd ached for her, and joy and pain ran through him like some kind of fucked-up emotional cocktail.

"I'm not trying to control you," he murmured against her hair. "Or threaten you or anything like that. I'm trying to tell you that, no matter what it is, we all have your back."

She whispered something that sounded a lot like *that's the problem*, which didn't make any sense.

Then she coughed, a harsh and ragged sound that reminded him that no matter how emotionally messed up this was, she'd been through a physical trauma.

"Let's sit down," he said, hoping that sitting together would not only ease her cough, but might seem less adversarial than standing facing each other. He'd been determined not to touch her at all, but that ship had sailed.

She didn't resist as he led her to the couch and pulled her down next to him. Rather than putting his arm around her, even though he knew she fit perfectly there, he laced his fingers through hers and squeezed her hand.

"I didn't want to make this personal, but I guess it can't be separated. Whatever this is isn't just hurting you, Wren. It ruined us. It destroyed me." He watched her face crumple as she closed her eyes, but he couldn't stop. "It stole the life I thought we were going to have together and I want to know what it is that had that kind of power over you."

"I'm scared to tell you. Like *really* scared."

He felt her body tense as if she was about to get up, and he put his other hand over their clasped hands. "Okay. Is it a something or a somebody?"

He didn't think it was some dark secret she was ashamed of or she wouldn't have bolted so suddenly. It was fear. He'd known from the night he met her that she had something in her past. Something that made her wary and slow to trust or open up. But when she had opened up to him, she'd been all in. Or so he'd thought.

"Somebody," she whispered.

Anger burned through him and he tightened his hands around hers. "An ex?" She nodded. "Ex-husband?"

"No." He watched her take a very deep breath, hoping it meant she was resigning herself to finally telling her story. "An ex-boyfriend."

"And he hurt you?" Again, the rage filled him, this time like a surge of energy he had to burn off somehow before it consumed him.

"Don't."

"Don't what?"

"I can feel your anger right now. You're squeezing my hand and your knee's bouncing and you're practically coiled up, wanting to strike at something."

"Did you think I couldn't keep you safe? Is that why you left me?"

"No. God, Grant. No." Her voice was hoarse from the smoke and raw with emotion.

"Then why? Why didn't you come to me instead of running?"

* * *

Wren could feel Grant's anger, almost like an aura surrounding him, but it was the hurt in his voice she couldn't bear.

She knew it was time to tell him, though. "I was afraid he'd hurt you."

"I'm not that easy to hurt, you know." She felt a pang of guilt when his fingers tightened again because they both knew he meant physically. Emotionally, she'd hurt him badly. "And I have friends. Resources. Contacts in law enforcement. We could have taken care of this guy and we wouldn't have let him hurt you."

"He didn't hurt me," she said, though her throat tightened up so it was barely a whisper.

"I don't understand."

"He didn't *hit* me. He…controlled me. He broke me down, I guess. He destroyed me without ever laying a hand on me." She swallowed hard. "My brother tried to tell me over and over again that he was bad for me."

"You have a brother?"

She heard the weird sound of distress she made and she tilted her head back, trying to control her emotions. She just had to get it out. "There was a lot. I don't want to relive it all, but I left Ben so many times. He was so good at getting me back, though, and then breaking me down again. And Alex—my brother—told me every single time that I was making a mistake forgiving Ben. Over and over, he told me that.

"The last time I left him, he came after me. And I finally told him no. I told him some of the things Alex had said about our relationship—about how it was unhealthy—and that he was right and I didn't want to see him again. That we were through."

She paused, taking a deep and shuddering breath that did nothing to ease the constriction in her chest. "He forced me into the car and then made me watch while he beat Alex so badly he was in the hospital for almost a week."

Grant let go of her hand and looped his arm around her shoulders, pulling her close. She resisted. She didn't deserve his comfort.

"He's okay, though? Your brother, I mean."

Wren nodded, feeling a fresh wave of pain. "But he never spoke to me again because he'd warned me. Over and over, he told me Ben was no good, but I didn't listen. It was my fault Ben hurt him."

"That's bullshit. The only person responsible for what Ben did was Ben."

"That a technicality," she said immediately, since she'd had this discussion with herself many times. "If I'd listened to Alex in the beginning, none of it would have happened."

"I can keep telling you it's not your fault, but I don't think you'll believe me, so I'm going to get you the name of the therapist Cait's mom sees because he's helped her family so much."

She tried not to focus too much on the fact he'd said he'd get her the name instead of just telling her to ask Cait herself. That implied Wren was going to see him again, or at least talk to him.

"What made you take off in September?" he asked, and his voice had changed. Hardened a little, as though hardening himself against the pain she'd caused him in the fall. "Is this guy in Boston?"

"I don't know where he is, but he called me. He

called my cell phone and said he wanted to see me so he could apologize and we could talk."

"When we met, you told me you left Virginia because you were bored there, but I assume that's where you lived with him?"

She nodded. "He pled down to misdemeanor assault and got sentenced to a year, but I didn't want to stay in Virginia anymore and the situation with Alex… It was just time for a fresh start. I'd been in Boston for almost a year when I met you and enough time had passed so I assumed he'd moved on."

"Didn't you get a new cell phone number when you left?"

"Yeah, but I gave it to a few people back home. He can be really charming, so he must have gotten it from somebody."

"So he called you and it scared you, and instead of telling me about this guy, you changed your number again and ghosted. And threw away what we had."

The flash of anger surprised her. "You make it sound like some guy I used to date called me and I ran away. You don't know, Grant. You didn't see what he did to my brother. I wasn't taking the chance he'd do that to you."

"I'm not gonna lie. It's a little hard to believe you dumped me because you were afraid some guy would try to beat me up."

"After I hung up on him, I kept imagining what he did to Alex, but with your face and… I couldn't live with that."

He stood and took a few steps away from her, shoving his hair back as he blew out a breath. "I can't talk about this right now. I really want to try to understand how terrifying that was for you and how it might have grown into a bigger fear than it needed to be, but right now I'm still pissed you didn't feel like you could come to me with it."

"I know you. You wouldn't have taken it seriously because you assume you could take him in a fight. But he's messed up and angry and dangerous, and that was *before* he went to prison. After all that, he still went to the trouble to get my number and call me, so he's still dangerous. I wasn't willing to take the chance he'd hurt you."

He gave her a sharp nod, but she could tell her explanation hadn't really helped. He couldn't accept that she'd reacted out of fear, not logic. "I should go. I know you have Gavin and Cait, but is there anything else you need?"

Honestly, she needed everything, but if she kept her focus on one thing at a time, maybe it wouldn't feel so overwhelming. "I know it was an exhausting night for you, but you guys didn't happen to notice if the cars parked on the street survived, did you?"

He winced and her stomach sank. "Is that what those ice sculptures were?"

"From the back of the ambulance, it looked like you guys hosed down the entire neighborhood. But my car was parked a ways down the street, so maybe I won't need a hammer and chisel to get into it."

"Tell you what. I managed enough of a power nap to get me through for a while, so why don't I take you out to breakfast and then we'll swing by and see if we can get your car. If it's frozen in, I can take you around to…work or to go shopping or whatever."

She shouldn't. It would be too easy to relax into the comfort of having Grant in her life, especially with the Ben situation looming over her. Was her apartment building burning related to the fact he'd found her?

And there was so much pain between her and Grant. The last thing she wanted to do was make it harder for him. He would take care of her, no matter what it cost him emotionally, because that's who he was. She shouldn't take advantage of that just because it made facing her day a little easier.

But she was weak and the doctor had warned her against strenuous activities or exposing herself to more germs than she had to. She honestly didn't have the strength to deal with public transportation today.

"You're going to have to accept help from somebody," he said. "If not me, than Gavin and Cait. Or somebody else. I'm here. I'm free."

Despite the many valid reasons she had for sending him on his way, her mind latched on the practicality of his words and decided accepting his offer was a good idea. "That sounds great. I'd appreciate it."

"Good. We'll start with breakfast because I'm starving, but no rush. Whenever you're ready. And dress warm."

The only things Cait had been able to find that Wren could wear were leggings and sweatshirts, but she'd make do. And she'd shoved her feet into her sneakers before she'd succumbed to the smoke last night, so she had those.

The loss of almost everything she owned threatened to crush her, but she took a slow, deep breath and forced herself to recognize how grateful she was to do so. And she had her car, her purse and friends.

And Grant. For today, at least, she had the man she'd loved—and walked away from—back in her life.

Chapter Four

The early morning air was like an icy slap in the face as Grant walked out of Gavin's building, and he felt an urge to back up and let it slap him again.

What the hell was he doing?

He could have given Wren the bag of stuff, made sure she was okay, and left. Hell, he could have given the bag to Gavin and not seen her at all.

Instead, he was holding the door for her because he was taking her out for breakfast. Almost like a date.

Not a date, he told himself in no uncertain terms.

He was just helping her out because she was a friend. Or had been a friend. He didn't know what she was now.

They didn't have to walk far to where his Jeep was parked, which was good. Wren had been reluctant to go into Gavin and Cait's closet, but Grant wasn't shy. He couldn't do much about the leggings and sneakers, but he'd found a heavy Boston Fire sweatshirt in Gavin's drawer and a parka of Cait's in the closet.

But he should have dug around for a scarf, he thought when the frigid air hit Wren's lungs and triggered a coughing fit. She winced and put the arm not covering her mouth over her ribs. They probably hurt not only from coughing, but from being carried down the stairs over his shoulder.

She slowed when she spotted his Wrangler. "Oh, you got the new wheels you wanted for it. The ones in the catalog on your coffee table. And those are new lights, right?"

"Yeah." He didn't want to talk about the money he'd put into the Jeep. If she'd blown him off a couple of weeks later, the chunk of cash he'd spent on the vehicle would have been spent and those wheels would have been the perfect diamond ring he'd chosen for her after months of trying to find the right one.

He wasn't going to think about that right now, he told himself. Sure, Wren had broken his heart and made him question whether he even wanted to stay in Boston. Life had been pretty empty since she left. But she'd almost died last night and she'd lost everything she owned— except, hopefully, her car—and he needed to help lift her up. Dragging them both down into the past would only make them miserable.

After hitting the button to unlock the doors, he opened hers. Even after five months, it was just habit to offer his hand so she could steady herself as she stepped up onto the running board and into the jacked-up Jeep. She smiled as she reached for her seat belt and, for a few beautiful seconds, it was if she'd never been gone.

Maybe it was simply self-preservation, but he avoided their usual breakfast spots and took her to a little place near the fire station that he liked, but was far enough from his apartment so they hadn't gone there together.

It didn't matter. He could have driven her to some random place in Vermont and once he sat down across the table from her and she smiled that soft, slightly shy smile at him, his heart would have beat a little faster.

This is what his life was supposed to look like.

"You left your job at the bookstore," he said, after they'd ordered omelets—his stuffed with veggies and hers with meats—and fixed their coffees. "What are you doing now?"

"I miss that job so much." She sighed, fiddling with her silverware. "But I'm working part-time at a market in the evenings and part-time as a receptionist at a hair salon a few days a week."

"Don't let them screw with your hair," he said without thinking. Grant loved her hair. Loved gathering it in his hands before tightening his grip and tilting her head back for a slow, deep kiss. He realized it had been a stupid thing to say, though, and cleared his throat. "Unless you want them to. It's, you know, your hair, of course. Are you supposed to work today? Or tonight?"

She shook her head. "I was already scheduled to be off at the salon and I called the market a few minutes before you got there and told the owner what happened. He said I could have tonight and tomorrow night off and that he'd still pay me."

"That's really decent of him."

"It is. It's not the best paying job I've ever had, but they're really nice people. They're an older couple and they thought it would be a family business, but their kids grew up and went off to have their own careers, so they're trying to slow down a little."

They made small talk until their breakfasts arrived. She talked about the salon for a few minutes, and then she asked about the people in his life. He caught her up and, once the food arrived, they talked in between bites. She ate slowly, chewing a lot and swallowing with some obvious discomfort.

"Have you been spending a lot of time at Kincaid's?" she asked after a while.

He wondered if that was her way of asking about his social life, and maybe whether or not he was dating. Kincaid's Pub was owned by Scott Kincaid's dad, and all of the guys from Engine 59 and Ladder 37 hung out there. Wren had been a few times, though meeting her had cured Grant of his need to be out on the town all the time. He'd much preferred quiet nights at home with her, watching TV or playing cards or whatever she was in the mood for.

"Not really," he said. "I hang out with Gavin and Cait sometimes. Or go out with the other guys once in a while. Hockey games and whatnot. I took a little time off and went home to visit my parents for a bit."

She looked down at her plate, but he caught a glimpse of her face before she did and he knew she'd guessed he'd gone home to his mom and dad after their breakup.

"So that's about it," he said with a light tone, wanting the smiling version of Wren back.

"I'm so glad Derek and Olivia got married. They're a nice couple, and I adored his daughter. She's a reader, like me."

"They almost didn't make it. They broke up for a little while." He stabbed a mushroom with his fork a little harder than was necessary. "But they worked through their issues and got through it. *Together*."

He heard her fork clatter on her plate. "Grant, I—"

"I'm sorry." He forced himself to look up at her. "I'm trying."

"I know. And I appreciate it. I really do, because

it's hard and I can't even imagine how much harder it is for you."

"Sitting here with you is harder than I thought it would be." He shook his head and laid down his fork because he'd lost his appetite. "I've missed you."

"I've missed you, too. Every day."

"I can't… I don't know what to do here, Wren. I can't just walk away from you." He blew out a breath as he shoved a hand through his hair. "But I can't forget what happened, either. I don't know what to do."

Forgive me.

That's what Wren wanted for him to do. Desperately. But it wasn't that simple and she knew it. She had to give him time to process what she'd told him today before she could ask him to let it go. And she could keep giving him the truth.

"I don't know if it helps any, but I wasn't afraid Ben could beat you up. I was afraid you'd…" She let the words die away because she didn't know how to explain it. And it probably *wouldn't* help.

"You were afraid I'd blame you like your brother did and throw you out of my life." Apparently her expression and the sudden film of tears in her eyes were answer enough because he sighed deeply. "I can't believe you thought I'd do that to you."

"I didn't really think at all. I just reacted."

He looked at her without blinking, his dark gaze locked on her with such intensity, she wasn't sure she could move even if she'd wanted to. "I'm not going to be able to stay away from you."

But… She was quiet, waiting for it.

"I cared about you too much to let you go through

this alone." There was that painful past tense again. "But I'm not okay. I don't know how to describe it any better than that. I'm not okay."

"I understand." She didn't bother to tell him she was a big girl and could take care of herself. He knew that, but he'd still be compelled to check on her. He took care of the people who were important to him.

"You were so reserved and, even once we got to know each other, I knew you were always holding something back. And now I know what it is and you don't have to hold anything back from me. I want to get to know the Wren who doesn't have any secrets from me."

His words were like a rainbow at the end of a long, rainy day. A faint rainbow, but there nonetheless. But there were still dark clouds in the sky, throwing a shadow across that little beam of hope.

"When I woke up and realized the building was on fire, I was afraid it was Ben," she said in a thin voice. "I'm still afraid he found me and he's coming after me. I need you to know that."

He nodded. "If he'd just been a controlling jerk with anger control issues, he probably wouldn't have called you when he got out of prison. Assuming he didn't call from inside."

"He's out. He was probably out before we started dating, but he either hadn't found me yet or hadn't gotten mad enough to look. I was able to find out he's definitely been let out of jail, though nobody official would give me any more information than that. And I was afraid to call any of our mutual acquaintances and give him more to go on if he was looking for me."

"Good call. After you changed your number, you got no more calls from him?"

"No. And now I'll probably get another number, since I don't have a phone anymore."

"We can pick one up today." He took a sip of his coffee, and she could tell by the way his eyebrows furrowed that he was thinking, so she kept quiet. "It's really unlikely he was responsible for that fire."

"I know that logically, but I guess fear isn't always logical."

"I doubt he could find you. I know the city and I have some connections and I couldn't find you, so it's unlikely he could. Not impossible, of course, but unlikely."

"I know. It's a big city and people tend to keep to themselves and mind their own business when it comes to strangers."

"Yeah, I guess Boston's as good a city as any if you're looking to hide."

She knew he didn't mean to insult her, but Wren heard the slight edge in her voice when she responded. "I didn't run to Boston to hide. I moved to Boston because I always wished I could live here and I realized, for the first time in my life, I didn't have a reason not to. My dad took off when I was young and Mom died when I was still in high school and Alex wouldn't speak to me anymore. There was nothing keeping me in Virginia."

"I'm sorry. I just assumed and…I shouldn't have."

"You don't have to take care of me, Grant." She said it firmly, looking him in the eye. "I have some money put aside. I have what I need to start over again and I have some friends. I don't need to be saved or rescued. Yeah, I'm scared of Ben, but I can handle that, too. I'm not a damsel in distress."

"I'm sure as hell not a knight in shining armor," he responded. "But I'd like for us to be friends."

"I'd like that."

"Although, I feel like I should point out I did, in fact, *literally* rescue you last night."

She laughed and he joined in until the laughing gave way to more painful coughing. And even though he didn't take her hand after he paid the bill and they walked out of the restaurant, like he would have five months ago, it felt good to laugh and recapture some of the happiness she'd given up.

And she told herself she wasn't going to let anybody take it away from her again. Maybe she and Grant could never go back to the relationship they'd had before, but she was done running.

Grant had his feet up and was about to nod off to a rerun of a cop show when his phone chimed.

Knock knock.

The caller ID said it was Rick Gullotti, which was weird.

Who's there?

After a few seconds, he got a reply.

What?

What who?

The phone rang in his hand. "What's up, LT?"
Though Rick was technically the lieutenant for Lad-

der 37 and Danny Walsh was *his* LT, they both got the nickname.

"Are you drunk?"

"Am I drunk? I'm not the one texting knock knock jokes at nine o'clock at night, and then screwing them up."

"It wasn't a knock knock joke. I want you to open your door."

"Oh. I would have known that if you'd actually, you know, knocked on the door."

"Open the damn door."

Grant tossed the remote on the table and walked to his front door to let Rick in. He was still standing in the hall with his phone pressed to his ear, and Grant laughed. "You can hang up now."

Rick cursed and shoved the phone into his pocket. "I'm too old for this shit."

"What are you doing?"

"Checking on you. Walsh called me. He was worried about you, but he said something about Jackson and terrible twos and Ashley having stuff to do. I didn't catch it all because the kid was screeching like he was on fire in the background. So I'm here to, I don't know. See if you're okay. Whatever. And somebody at the bar was talking about how young people don't knock anymore. They just text to announce their arrival."

"I'm not *that* young. And I'm fine."

"I left my extremely hot wife at home and put on pants and drove all the way over here."

"Okay, I can probably manage one beer's worth of not fine, just so you didn't put on pants for no reason."

Once they each had a can of beer and were sitting— Grant on the couch and Rick in the recliner because he'd moved faster—Grant started talking. He hadn't even realized how much he needed somebody to talk to until the words started coming out of his mouth.

He told Rick everything. About the asshole Ben from Virginia. Her fears. The way breakfast had ended. The trip to Walmart to get a *new life starter kit*, as she'd called it. Her finding out the apartment and everything in it were a total loss, but her car was okay. And her promise to spend another night on Gavin and Cait's couch while she decided what to do next.

"I don't want her living in another death trap," he said. "She might be able to get some assistance with a security deposit and whatnot for a new place, but I want it to be decent. And of course she won't let me give her any money."

"Okay, but how are *you*?"

Grant downed some beer before answering that question. "I don't know, really. I told her I've missed her and that I want to get to know her again now that she doesn't have any secrets. We're going to try to be friends."

Rick nodded before sipping his beer. It was tempting for Grant to fill the silence, but he resisted the urge. The older guy had gone to some effort to drive over and be a shoulder to lean on, so he could damn well do the work of offering the shoulder.

"Friends, huh?"

He was going to have to do better than that. "Yup."

"You okay with that?"

"I'm not okay with *not* being friends with her."

Rick pinched the bridge of his nose. "I don't know what that means."

"I don't, either, really. I'm not walking away from

her. But I also know our relationship before wasn't what I thought it was."

"Because she broke it off?"

"Because if the love between us had been as real as I thought it was, she would have trusted me to be able to handle an asshole ex-boyfriend."

"People do weird things when they're afraid. You know that. Hell, you've seen some of the crazy shit that happens on scenes." Rick shrugged. "On the other hand, I can see where you're coming from. It's hard to trust somebody who's hurt you like that."

"I need to solve the Ben problem."

The LT made a noise that sounded a lot like disagreement. "There's not a lot you can do about that guy without getting yourself in trouble. And it doesn't sound like he's the real problem, anyway. Even if that problem got resolved somehow, the emotional crap between you won't be magically healed."

Emotional crap. That was one way to put it. "Maybe not, but at least she'll be free to stop worrying about him and figure out what she wants."

"And if it's not you?"

Grant squashed the impulse to shrug off the question or give a wise-ass response. One, because he appreciated the two LTs checking on him and the effort Rick put into it. And two, because they'd put up with his shitty attitude and anger after Wren left, and they'd helped put him back on track before he threw everything away.

"I don't know if it'll be me or not. To be totally honest, I'm not sure if I even *want* it to be me. I'm still reeling. But if we're not meant to be together, I want us to go our separate ways with all the facts on the table and the knowledge that we both tried."

"Do you think you can move past the way she broke it off? Because you can't just say you forgive her. You have to accept it and let it go or it won't work."

"I don't know." Grant drained the last of his beer. "That's the only answer I have, LT."

"Then it's the right answer. You're not going to figure it out overnight. Just do yourself—and her—a favor and keep it in your pants until you *do* know the answer. Don't make it messier than it already is."

Messy was a good word for his life right now. His thoughts. His emotions. Everything was a mess.

"You know there's an option between walking away from her and diving back into the deep end right?" Rick set his can on the side table before leaning forward with his forearms on his knees. "Gavin and Cait can help her out. Hell, we'll all be there if she needs something, but you don't have to be involved."

"I can't walk away from her."

"Okay." Rick relaxed against the back of the recliner again. "Just be aware that we cut you a lot of slack when it came to your shitty attitude after she left."

"I know you did, and I appreciate it."

"You're going back in with your eyes wide open, so if you start that shit again, you'll have your ass handed to you."

"Understood." He didn't want to go back down that road any more than they wanted him to. "I just need to think with my head and not with my heart. Or my dick."

Rick laughed. "Jesus. You are so screwed."

Chapter Five

"Ohmigod, Wren! That is the worst!"

It was the third—and hopefully last—time she'd heard that since arriving at the salon. She was thankful they didn't open until ten each morning because she'd had a rough night of tossing and turning on Cait's couch. Her thoughts had bounced between how she was going to put her life back together and how she felt about Grant being back in it.

"Do you need anything? Like... I don't know. Anything?"

"Thanks, Kelli. I'll be okay, though."

She wouldn't say the women were her friends. She'd focused too much on just keeping her head down and doing her job to let that happen. But the owner and senior stylist, Sadie, along with stylist Kelli and Barb, the nail tech, were friendly enough and they were definitely distraught about the fire. But Wren was thankful when clients started showing up and distracted them so she could sit behind the reception desk and focus on the phone and appointment book.

Yesterday, while shopping with Grant, she'd bought a couple pair of black leggings with three tops and a pair of cheap ballet flats. She only worked three mornings a week at the salon, so those would get her through for a while. She'd also bought some jeans and casual shirts for her job at the market. Throwing in a winter coat had made her wince at the total cost, but it was February. She couldn't go without a coat.

Answering the phone and greeting clients were her primary job, so Wren had to drink a lot more water than usual to keep her scratchy throat from getting so dry she couldn't talk. Luckily, if she was fairly still and calm, she wasn't coughing as much.

During the downtime at the desk, she poked around online, looking at listings for apartments she couldn't afford. Some young women were looking for a roommate, but they were *very* young women and living with three college girls was pretty low on the list of options, as far as Wren was concerned. A better option than couch surfing or living in another apartment like the last one, but she liked quiet and she was afraid, even though she wasn't *that* much older, she'd become the house mom.

But most importantly, there was Ben to consider. Maybe he *wasn't* the problem she'd built him up to be, but she was leery to introduce three young women into the mix.

She might be able to find cheaper options outside the city. She could take the T to work and… Sighing, Wren closed the browser and leaned back in her chair. As much as she liked the couple who owned the market, neither of her jobs merited a commute into the city. If she couldn't afford to stay in Boston, she needed to move out of Boston. It was that simple.

Except it wasn't that simple. She loved Boston. Out of all the places she could have gone, she'd chosen to make Boston her home and she didn't want to leave it. And she didn't want to leave Grant.

No matter how awkward things might be, and whether or not he ever forgave her for leaving him the way she did, she didn't want to move away from him.

At two o'clock, she handed the desk over to the full-time receptionist and, after promising the women yet again she'd let them know if she needed anything, she switched the ballet flats for the sneakers in her bag and after wrapping the scarf Cait had lent her around her face to protect her lungs from the cold air, went outside.

Boots. She really needed boots. Grant had offered to buy her a pair, but she'd insisted the sneakers would be fine. And they would be if it wasn't unusually cold this week. She'd have to get a pair before snow showed up in the forecast again, but it was important to her not to take Grant's money.

She was halfway to where she'd parked her car when her cell phone rang. She'd had the inexpensive prepaid model less than twenty-four hours, so only a few people had the number.

Instead of the dread she'd felt ever since Ben had called, she thought of Grant, and she smiled when she saw his number on the screen and nudged the scarf down just a hair. "Hello?"

"Hey, you busy?"

"I just got out of work and I'm on my way back to my car."

"We've been invited to dinner at Patty's house this evening. You remember her, right? Cait's mom?"

We. They weren't really a *we* anymore. "I remember her."

"I know Cait already spoke to you about her old bedroom and—"

She cut him off. "And I told Cait it wasn't a good idea. It's still not. I don't want to drag anybody else into this, Grant. Can't you understand that?"

"Nobody's getting *dragged* into anything. Gavin and Cait filled Patty and Carter in on your situation and they're both on board."

She hated that everybody was talking about her business, but it wasn't as though it was idle gossip. They wanted to help her and it was time to let them in. Trying to go it on her own had cost her everything.

"Look, Wren. I know it spooked you when he called, but the fire wasn't arson. It was electrical. And some favors were called in and, thanks to a visual confirmation from the local PD, we know that asshole is still in Virginia, where he belongs."

The rush of relief almost buckled her knees, and she was thankful her car was in view. And she didn't have gloves on, so the fingers wrapped around the phone were starting to hurt.

"They actually saw him?"

"Yes. Ben Mitchell is in Virginia."

Wren unlocked her car and got in, switching her phone to her other hand so she could stick the key in the ignition. It would take a while for the car to start putting out heat, but at least she was out of the wind.

"Maybe I'm overstepping," Grant continued. "I probably am and I shouldn't be. But I know you, and you'll struggle quietly rather than ask for help. And you can do it. I know you can. But you don't *have* to struggle alone. You have friends."

"I don't know." But she was wavering. He was right.

She could do it. But he was also right about it being harder if she pushed away the people offering to help her.

"Gavin and Cait will be there. Just consider it a good meal with friends and we'll go from there. If you want to at least look at the room, that's great. But if you don't want to, that's your decision."

She had to do something. It was awkward, sleeping on the couch, but she hadn't been able to bring herself to reach out to the shelter offering space for the displaced residents.

"That sounds good," she said finally. "I'll talk to Cait and probably ride over with them."

"Good. I'll see you there."

As she dropped the phone in the cup holder and put her hands over the barely warm air coming out of the vents, she tried to focus on what she needed to do this afternoon and not the fact she'd be seeing Grant in a few hours.

We.

She liked the sound of that.

Grant practically jogged up the walk to Patty's front door. His mom had called as he was getting ready to leave and just hearing her voice settled him, so he'd spent a little more time on the phone with her than he should have.

He hadn't mentioned Wren at all, though. He wasn't sure what to make of the omission and he didn't have time to analyze himself right now.

Cait's younger brother opened the door as he lifted his hand to knock. "Hey, Grant. How's it going?"

"Good." He played basketball with the kid sometimes, since Gavin brought him to the Saturday morning pickup games. They'd tried to get him into hockey, but he couldn't skate for shit.

"So what's new in your life? Anything good?"

"Finally got my license," he said as they walked into the living room. "And I've been working, trying to save up for a car."

Patty laughed. "I told him I'd buy him a car."

"A 1970s Buick is a not a car. It's a boat on wheels."

"More like a tank," his mom said. "I wouldn't have to worry about you driving around this city as much."

"And you wouldn't have to worry about him getting into trouble anywhere," Cait added, "since he won't be able to *go* anywhere since he'll never find a parking space for a beast like that."

Grant laughed along with the rest of them, appreciating the easy humor between Patty and her kids. The family had hit a rough spot after the death of Carter's dad, but the vibe in the house was so much happier and more relaxed now.

Wren's laughter mingled with the others', and although it was softer and quieter, it caught his attention and turned his head. She was looking at Cait and her amusement had erased the signs of stress from her face.

The easy small talk continued through dinner. They all talked about work and teased Carter about what kind of car he should get. The conversation never got heavy and nobody asked Wren any hard questions, other than Cait putting on her EMT hat to ask about her follow-up with the doctor that afternoon, but Wren said everything had looked good and she should continue taking it easy until the lingering effects faded.

He did catch both Gavin and Cait giving them speculative glances now and then, and he didn't blame them. Seated next to each other, he and Wren had fallen easily into being a "couple." Easy banter. Her handing him the pepper without him asking. Him stealing a piece of ham off her plate because he liked the crispy edges. And her giving him a look because he knew he was supposed to trim that fatty edge off.

It was weird. He was aware of it, so he wasn't surprised his closest friends were aware of it, too. And while Cait kept her expression pretty neutral, Gavin would scowl slightly before turning his attention back to the group at large.

Grant figured it wouldn't be long before Gavin suggested they grab a beer and shoot some pool at Kincaid's, which would lead to a concerned grilling about what the hell was going on.

He didn't know.

When they were finished, Patty stood and started gathering plates. "Why don't you all go relax for a few minutes and let dinner settle before we have dessert?"

"Dessert?" Gavin groaned and put his hand on his stomach. "Warn a guy, would ya?"

"You always find a way," she said, her affection for her future son-in-law obvious in her voice. "Grant, why don't you take Wren upstairs and show her the room?"

He froze for a second. Sure, he knew which room it was. He'd helped out when they did a massive decluttering of the house and repainted the upstairs. But it wasn't his house.

But then he caught the look she gave him and realized Patty thought he was the one most likely to talk her into accepting the offer. "Okay. Sure."

Wren followed him quietly up the stairs and down

the hall to the small spare bedroom. He couldn't read her as he opened the door and waved for her to go in.

"It's small, but nice," he said, since that was pretty much all there was to say about it.

For a while, after Cait moved out, it had become something of a storage room. And then Cait had moved back in to help out after her stepfather died, living around the clutter. Once she'd moved in with Gavin, they'd redone everything and now it was a pretty typical guest room. Twin bed with a blue quilt. Bedside table with a lamp, and a small dresser. And a shabby floral armchair that had definitely seen better days, but Grant knew firsthand how comfortable it was.

"It doesn't have its own bathroom, but there are only two other people, so it wouldn't be hard to figure out the schedule."

"It's pretty," she said, still giving him nothing as far as her mood.

"I know it probably feels strange. But you like Patty and Carter. And it's a safe, comfortable place to live while you make up your mind about what you want to do next. This way you don't have to rush or keep sleeping on a couch."

"I've been looking around online," she said, running her hand over the quilt. "There's not a lot out there. And there's almost nothing decent in my price range."

"Patty would love to have you here. That's the truth."

"I could maybe use a mom in my life right now. Even if she's not mine."

He fought back against an urge to put his arms around her because it didn't feel like a friend offering comfort. It felt like a primal need to hold her, and that was too messy right now. He was supposed to be thinking with his brain, not his heart, he reminded himself.

"I'll rent the room," she said quietly. "I know she'll balk at that, but it's important to me. I'll pay room and board."

He knew Patty would definitely balk at that, but she'd give in once she realized Wren wouldn't do it any other way. "Okay. You two can talk about it. But you'll stay here?"

"I'll stay."

He smiled, and when she blushed, his body tightened in response. That was how it had started. A look. Her shy sideways glances. His smile. Her blush. Up until the moment he'd laid eyes on Wren, he would have walked away from a woman like her. He wanted company, not a challenge.

But she'd challenged him in a way he couldn't resist. He'd wanted to know her, and he'd moved slower than he'd ever moved before. He'd been patient and let her back away when she needed to. Eventually she'd started letting him in and the reward had been sweeter than he could have imagined.

Now, as her cheeks glowed pink and her gaze skittered away, he realized they were back where they'd started.

And maybe that meant they could get back what they'd had.

Chapter Six

"That didn't take long," Cait said, her hands on her hips as she looked around the room that was now Wren's.

"I guess there's a plus side to everything you own fitting in one duffel bag," Wren said.

Cait laughed and then covered her mouth, her eyes wide with horror. "Sorry. That's not funny."

"I said it to be funny. Laughing is better than crying, and feeling sorry for myself won't get me anywhere."

But Cait was right. It definitely hadn't taken long. Once Patty had reluctantly agreed Wren would be a boarder and not a guest and they'd had dessert, they'd gone back to Cait's for her belongings. Cait had insisted on returning to her mom's to help her settle in, which was pretty funny considering it had taken about five minutes to put everything away.

She barely got a chance to say goodbye to Grant. Since he'd driven over separately and it didn't take four of them to pack one bag, he'd gone home. Or out. Or wherever he'd gone. And she'd gotten little more than a wave and a *see you later* as he left.

Wren heard footsteps in the hall and then Patty poked her head through the open doorway. "How are you girls making out? Do you have everything you need?"

"I do. I'm all moved in." And she'd already asked them about their usual schedule, so she'd be able to stay out of the way. Not that Patty would mind, but she wanted to be as unobtrusive as possible.

"Make yourself at home, Wren. I mean it. Decorate the room however you want. And feel free to have friends over, if you want."

She wasn't really planning on staying there long enough to redecorate the room. And she hadn't had company over since the last time Grant visited her first apartment, so friends probably wouldn't be an issue. But she appreciated Patty's desire for her to feel welcome and smiled.

"Thank you, Patty."

"And let me know if you need anything at all."

"I will."

After giving her daughter a bright smile, Patty went back downstairs and Cait dropped into the armchair. "She's going to drive you crazy, you know."

"Or maybe I'll drive *her* crazy."

"I know you both well enough to tell you I'm right on this one."

Wren sat on the edge of the bed. "My mom was out cycling with a friend and got hit by a truck when I was sixteen. So while Patty might eventually drive me crazy, I think it'll be cool to have a mom figure for a bit."

"I'm sorry. I didn't know." After a few seconds, Cait's expression shifted from sympathetic to confused. "How did I not know that?"

"I got pretty good at saying a lot of words and deflecting and redirecting without people realizing I never actually answered the question." She smiled apologetically. "I'm going to try not to do that anymore, though.

There's no sense, because I'm not hiding anything, and I really want to be better about letting people in."

"What about your dad?"

Wren shrugged. "I don't really know. I know Everett is my mother's maiden name and our father's first name was Dave. Other than that, I know my mother decided *after* having two children with him that he was a no-good bum and that was the end of that. When my mom died, Alex was in college, so I lived with a friend's family until I was old enough to rent an apartment."

"Grant told us about your brother. And I know you probably hate that he did, but that's what we do. So you were totally alone in the world after your brother turned on you?"

She was about to correct Cait—it had been her own fault, not Alex's—but she didn't say the words. Having all of these people reaching out to help her after what she'd done to Grant had her doubting her conviction about that situation.

"I didn't mind it," she said. "I like a quiet, simple life and I didn't have to worry about anybody but myself."

"Then you met Grant."

"Yeah. Then I met Grant." Wren couldn't hold back the sigh when she thought of the first time he'd gone into the coffee shop where she worked. "It was the smile that did me in. I mean, he's hot, of course. And he's confident and strong and all that, but I was doing a pretty good job of resisting him, until he smiled."

"He didn't tell Gavin about you at first. That he liked you, I mean. He didn't want to be a *thing* before you were ready, and he knew you wanted to take it slow."

"Very slow."

Cait laughed. "He said he almost went broke going

to that coffee shop to see you and he doesn't even like fancy coffees."

"He did an amazing job of being patient and persistent at the same time," Wren said, but it took an effort to maintain the smile.

She'd really blown it. She'd let fear take over and she'd lost the best thing that had ever happened to her.

"We need a girls' night out," Cait said abruptly.

"What?"

"Fun. We all need a little fun. How about this Saturday? Do you have to work?"

"No, but—"

"No buts. You've been gone for months and now we've got you back and we're going to celebrate."

Wren chuckled, but it was a little more wry than amused. She needed a lot of things. Clothes. Food. A roof of her own. The last thing she should be doing was spending her money on a single meal and drinks, or whatever it was Cait had in mind.

"Don't do it," Cait said.

"Do what?"

"Your face is doing that closing off thing you do so well, and you're going to tell me no. Don't do it."

Wren didn't want to do the "closing off thing" anymore. And she didn't need to. There were no more secrets.

"I could use a night out," she confessed. "And something fun to look forward to."

"I'm going to text everybody." Cait had her phone in her hand before Wren could even speak. "And it'll only be women you know. No strangers, I promise. It's going to be so fun."

As she watched her friend sending text messages,

Wren thought about the fact she'd lost practically everything in a fire, almost died and didn't have a home of her own, and yet her life was *still* better now than it had been three days before.

She wasn't alone. She had friends and her jobs and Patty. And there was Grant. She wasn't sure what they had, but she didn't *not* have him, and that was enough for now.

Friday was a slow day. Clear skies and cold enough to keep people from running around too much, but not so cold as to present more problems. Grant didn't mind, since it meant they could work around the station and stay out of the cold, but it also left a lot of time for him to think.

And, sprawled in a recliner in the common room, the only thing on his mind was Wren.

That wasn't new. Wren had spent a lot of time in his thoughts since the day he'd met her. And he'd spent the last five months wondering where she was and if she was okay and wishing he could at least ask her why.

Now he knew where she was and knew she was okay and she'd finally told him why. Who she'd been running from, anyway. He wasn't sure he'd ever be able to wrap his head around why she hadn't come to him with it.

She said she hadn't thought, but had just reacted. But if she really loved him, wouldn't her instinct be to turn to him?

Something hit him in the chest, and once he was done flinching and identifying the something as a candy bar, he looked up to see it was Scott who'd thrown it. "What's this for?"

"You look like you need a pick-me-up."

"So you chuck a Snickers at me?"

"I was aiming for your head."

"Sucks getting old, don't it?"

The old Scotty would have lost his shit and, while he probably wouldn't have swung, he'd have blistered Grant's ears. This new, improved and in love version just grinned. "I'm getting better with age. I'm like wine."

Aidan had just walked into the common room. "You mean full-bodied?"

Scott flipped him off, but then he put his hand over his stomach, frowning. He'd only put on a few pounds over the last year, but he was sensitive about it and anybody but his best friend couldn't have gotten away with that crack. And Grant managed not to laugh. Barely, but he managed.

"Hopefully the women won't get up to no good tomorrow night," Aidan said as he dropped onto the couch.

That got Grant's full attention. "What do you mean? Which women?"

"Last I heard, the group was Cait, Wren, Lydia, Ashley and Jamie. Lydia and Ashley got Karen Shea to cover for them at Kincaid's. Olivia and Jess have something they're doing for the Village Hearts charity, so just the five of them that I know of."

"That's not a good idea." Grant didn't even think about the words. He just said them out loud.

And Aidan laughed at him. "No, telling those women they can't have a girls' night is what's not a good idea."

"Where are they going?"

"I don't know. Some club with fancy cocktails and a

dance floor and some shit. Honestly, I might have tuned out on some of the details."

"It doesn't bother you? Your wife going out drinking in some club without you?"

Aidan gave him a *what the fuck is wrong with you* look. "First, I don't tell Lydia what to do. Ever. People think Scott is the hardheaded Kincaid, but his sisters make him look like a puppy dog if they get pissed. Second, I trust my wife. And third, she works in a bar. Drunk guys hitting on her is just another day for Lydia. She can handle herself."

"Yeah, but—"

"Yeah, but nothing," Scotty interrupted. "You don't care if Lydia goes to a club. You want Aidan and I to try to talk our wives out of it so the girls' night out will fall apart and Wren won't be out at a club without *you*."

"No." *Fuck.* "Okay, maybe."

"Food's ready," they heard Chris yell from the kitchen.

Of course, once they were all gathered around the table, eating some of the finest pulled pork sandwiches in the city, Scotty made sure everybody knew Grant was tied up in knots about Wren going out on the town.

"How much trouble can she get into with those ladies? Oh wait…" Chris said, and then he laughed like he'd made the funniest joke ever.

Grant didn't laugh. "When a group of married—or as good as married—women go out with one single friend in a mix, they want to find her a guy. It's a thing they do."

"It's a thing they do?" Rick snorted. "I had no idea you were such a fountain of feminine knowledge, kid."

"They're probably going to buy some overpriced

pink drinks in tiny glasses and sit around complaining about their men," Gavin said. "Well, Cait won't. But the rest of them will."

They laughed when Danny, who'd been on his way to the fridge, cuffed him upside the head as he walked by.

"And least Lydia and Jamie won't be buying over-priced cocktails, since neither of them can drink. As a bonus, they've got the designated drivers covered," Scotty said with a chuckle.

Everybody looked at him like they were trying to figure out what he was talking about, except for Aidan, who elbowed him in the ribs. "Asshole."

"Shit."

"I just won twenty bucks," Danny said. "Ashley said Aidan would accidentally spill the beans first, but I knew it would be Scotty."

"Wait. Jamie and Lydia are both pregnant?" Rick scrubbed his hand over his jaw. "So we're getting a Kincaid baby and a Hunt baby let loose on the world at the same time?"

"About a month apart, give or take." Scott held up his hands. "And, no, it wasn't planned."

"Jesus, every elementary school teacher in the city's going to be doing the math to figure out how long they have to transfer or retire."

"And the hockey coaches," Rick added.

"We don't know if they're boys or girls yet," Chris pointed out.

Aidan laughed. "Shit, it don't matter. If you think either Scotty or I will have a daughter who won't throw a hard check, you haven't been paying attention."

"And you certainly don't know our wives," Scott said.

There were congratulations and jokes, but Grant

tuned most of it out. He was thrilled for the other guys, but hearing about the babies on the way caused a weird twinge in his gut.

One of the theories he'd come up with while lying awake in the dark in the time after Wren had disappeared was that she'd gotten pregnant and was upset and didn't want to tell him. It was an unlikely theory, not only because he always used protection, but they both wanted kids. Not immediately, of course, but children had come up in conversation and neither of them had ever said they *didn't* want to be a parent.

And because he'd been emotionally battered and his walls were down, he'd stupidly allowed himself to picture what that would look like. In his imaginings, she'd changed her mind and returned to him, and they'd had a baby together. A little girl with blonde hair, who looked like her mom.

The painful *what-if* thoughts hadn't helped him sleep at night.

"Hey, Grant," Gavin said as they started clearing the table. "Since they're having a girls' night out, we should hit Kincaid's and shoot some pool or something."

"Yeah, maybe."

Thoughts of Wren out at a club, dancing and laughing and having fun while guys tried to buy her drinks, were *definitely* not going to help him sleep tonight. Or tomorrow night.

The woman was hell on his REM sleep cycle.

Chapter Seven

Wren sipped her vodka and soda, straining to hear the conversation from the other side of the small, round table they'd crowded around. The bar wasn't very big—more of an upscale cocktail lounge, really—and they kept the music low, but the acoustics weren't great and the more people around them drank, the louder they talked.

She and Cait had chosen to take a Lyft over together, and when they arrived, she'd been greeted with varying degrees of warmth. Everybody was nice enough, of course, but she was aware that Ashley, in particular, was a little cool.

It was a well-deserved reminder that everybody at the table was Team Grant. She knew none of them would be here at all if he wasn't okay with it, but they also weren't going to magically forget what she'd done.

She wished Olivia was here. She'd only met her once—when Derek brought her to Aidan and Lydia's Labor Day barbecue—but she'd liked her. She was quiet, like Wren, though not shy.

Cait's knee bumped hers under the table in a way that had to be deliberate. When Wren looked up from her drink, Cait gave her a questioning glance so she smiled and tried to look like she was having fun.

Cait leaned close. "Do you want to leave?"

Apparently she wasn't a great actress. "No, I'm good."

The exchange got the attention of the other women, though. They'd been talking about baby stuff, since the news had broken that Lydia and Jamie were both expecting, and Wren had offered her congratulations, but she didn't have a lot beyond that to add. She didn't have a lot of experience with babies.

"How is everything at Patty's?" Jamie asked her. "Do you have everything you need?"

"I do. Just the bare minimum of course, but I don't need a lot." It was hard on her throat, talking loudly enough to be heard by everybody, but at least she wasn't coughing at the moment. "Grant took me shopping the day after the fire and I got what I needed to be able to go to work. And, you know, brush my teeth and stuff."

"And stuff to shave your legs?" Ashley asked and Wren blushed when the other women giving her expectant looks made the meaning of the question sink in.

"Well, it's February, so I don't really have to worry about it yet," she said. She'd thought about Grant when she was at the store with Patty, though, and had a moment of optimism. "But I did buy a razor, just in case."

More laughter, and then Lydia stood. "Enough sitting around, talking. Let's dance."

Cait groaned. "The dance floor is smaller than my bathroom."

"So we'll dance close," Lydia insisted. "Wren, let's go. It's time to have some fun."

Maybe heat from too many dancing bodies in a small space turned up the alcohol's effects, but Wren had a lot more fun than she thought she would. Even though she had to stop to cough now and then, she didn't want to sit. None of them could dance worth a damn, but they did it anyway, laughing and twirling and shaking their asses.

When her body needed a short rest, she went to the bar and asked for a soda water with a splash of cranberry—hold the vodka. Not only was it cheaper that way, but she had too much on her plate to deal with a hangover, too. Nor did she want to stagger, drunk, through Patty's house in the wee hours.

She was leaning against the bar, sipping her drink, when a man approached her. He was good-looking, she supposed. Dark hair and beard, with an okay build. A little thin for her taste, but he dressed well. And he was smiling at her in a bland, nonthreatening way.

"Hi," he said. "I'm Frank."

"Hi." She wasn't giving him her name.

"Is it your first time here?"

She wondered if that was his standard opening line or if he spent so much time here, he recognized the regulars. "Yes, it is."

"Cool place. Can I buy you a drink?"

Smiling in what she hoped was a polite, but tinged with fake regret way, she held up her glass. "I already have one, but thanks."

"I can buy the next one, then,"

He was persistent. She'd give him that. "I'm here with friends, actually. But it was nice to meet you, Frank."

"Nice to meet you, too." It actually seemed like he wasn't going to get pushy with her, which was a pleasant surprise. "Maybe I'll see you around another time."

She just smiled and he walked away, probably to find another woman not wearing a ring on her finger.

It wasn't the first time a man had tried to speak to her in the last few months, but he was definitely one of the more attractive of them—both physically and in personality. Not a single one of them had piqued her interest. She'd felt nothing since the day she left Grant, and had zero interest in dating or sex.

After Frank disappeared into the crowd, Ashley appeared next to her. After getting another drink—hers with vodka—she didn't walk away. Instead she took a sip and then looked at Wren.

"Having a good time?"

"I am, thanks. It's good to get out."

"That guy wasn't bad looking, you know. And he seemed really interested in you."

Wren snorted. "I think I'm one of the few women here not wearing a ring."

"And you're gorgeous, which doesn't hurt," Ashley added. "I noticed you didn't really give him the time of day, though."

Wren got the feeling the other woman wasn't making idle small talk. Tonight, they were all out as friends, but when push came to shove, Ashley was married to Grant's lieutenant. If Danny was the kind of guy who vented at home, Ashley might know just how hard Wren leaving was on Grant.

Rather than play coy, she just said it straight out. "When I left, it wasn't because I didn't love Grant. In that moment, I thought it was the best thing for him. I have absolutely no interest in dating anybody else."

"I hate you a little bit," Ashley said, her tongue no doubt loosened a little by the cocktails. "But I loved you two together. I loved who he was with you, so I'm rooting for you."

"Thank you."

Ashley slung her arm around Wren's shoulders. Definitely the cocktails. "I mean it. If you need anything, we're here for you."

"Wren!" This time it was Jamie, yelling to her. "Come dance, girl!"

They were determined she was going to have a good time, so who was she to say no? After sucking down the last of her soda water and setting the empty glass on the bar, she danced her way back to her friends.

Gavin crossed his arms and sighed. Again. "This is a really stupid idea."

Grant looked up at the neon sign with the fancy wineglass logo. Or maybe it was a martini glass. Hell if he knew. Frosted beer mugs were more his style. "That's like the tenth time you've said that."

"Won't be the last, either, because it's a really stupid idea."

"The place looks packed. They won't even know we're here."

"The place looks packed because it's barely bigger than our engine bay, and there are five women in there who know us. We're not going to be able to hide, they're going to know we're here, and you're going to look like a creepy douchebag."

"And you?"

"I'll just tell them I was trying to stop you, then I'll kiss Cait and buy them all a drink and they'll love me. You, though? They'll just think you're a moron."

"Okay, maybe it's a slightly stupid idea. We need a better one."

"I've got one. We go back to Kincaid's, have another brew and shoot some more pool."

"Maybe we could go in and you tell Cait you need her keys because you can't find yours and you locked yourself out, or something. Or maybe—" He stopped when Gavin waved to somebody. "Who are you waving to?"

Gavin nodded his head toward one of the windows, where Cait was waving back. With Wren at her side.

"Shit."

"I told you so."

The two women exchanged words and then laughed. A few seconds later, Jamie appeared next to Wren. She laughed and then yelled something over her shoulder. A moment later, they were all in the window, looking out at them.

Through the corner of his eye, he saw Gavin pull his phone out and send a text. "Who are you texting?"

"Cait. Trust me, I want to get out ahead of this."

Grant watched Cait read her phone and then burst out laughing. Naturally, her phone got handed off to Wren and then all the other women so they could all laugh. "What the hell did you tell her?"

"I told her you ate some bad seafood and I found you wandering the streets."

"Funny."

"They think so." He looked down at his phone again. "She said they voted and since we came all the way over here, we can go in for one drink."

"They have beer, right?" It didn't look like a beer kind of place.

"Let me get this straight. We left Kincaid's to come

all way over here so you could see Wren, but now you might balk because of the beverage choices?"

"I wanted to see Wren. She wasn't supposed to see me," Grant muttered.

"You know that's stalking, right?"

"Okay, yeah. In hindsight, this was a really stupid idea."

"If only you had a friend to tell you that."

"We should go."

Gavin laughed and gave him a shove toward the door. "Nope. You dragged me here to crash their girls' night and you're not backing out now. Face the dance music, my friend."

As soon as he walked through the door, Grant wanted to walk back out. The dance music wasn't obnoxiously loud, but it wasn't his thing. And there were a *lot* of smells happening. Good ones—perfumes and lotions and hair sprays or whatever—but enough of them so he felt an urge to sneeze. It couldn't be good for Wren, he thought.

But then he saw her and it didn't matter where they were. He was barely aware of Gavin joining Cait or the laughter that followed whatever he said to her.

Wren was walking toward him and she was smiling. "Bad seafood, huh?"

His cheeks got hot. "Really bad."

"That story smells a little fishy to me."

"Oh, Wren, no." He laughed with her, though. "How many have you had?"

"Just one, actually." Her eyes sparkled in the club lighting and he wanted to kiss her, but he held back.

He looked around and then steered her toward what

looked like a quiet spot. "I guess I should explain about tonight."

Her mouth quirked up at the corners. "I'm pretty sure crashing a girls' night is a huge no."

"It is. I know that. And Gavin already pointed out I'm a stalker, a creepy douchebag and a moron."

"That seems a little harsh."

"Maybe." He peeled off his jacket because it was about nine hundred degrees in the club. "I should explain, though."

"Okay." She tilted her head, waiting.

"I...don't really have a good explanation." He shoved the hand not holding his coat into the pocket of his jeans. "For months, I worried about you. I wondered if you were okay and where you were. Maybe, subconsciously, I still feel that, but I had the ability to answer those questions tonight. Where you are and if you're okay. Does that make any sense?"

"It does." There was a sadness around her eyes now, and he hated himself for chasing away the happiness. "I won't disappear again. I shouldn't have before and, no matter what, I won't run."

"Fair enough." He grinned. "I'll stop being a creepy stalker douchebag, then."

She laughed and put her hand on his arm. Heat flooded through him and he shifted his jacket, just in case. "You're not a douchebag. Gavin just got two beers from the bartender, so let's go sit down."

"You sure you should drink a beer after eating bad seafood?" Lydia asked, throwing a chip at him from one of the baskets of nachos on the table.

He caught it and popped it in his mouth, shrugging. It was going to take a while to live this one down, and rightly so. But all that mattered was that Wren was laughing again. The women who considered him a part of their extended family had obviously welcomed her back into the fold.

Fitting all of them around the table was tight, so Wren was pressed against his side. He could rest his arm across the back of her chair, but he resisted. He'd already made an ass of himself tonight. The next move was hers.

His phone buzzed and he pushed his chair back enough so he could fish it out of his pocket. It was a text from Lydia, and he looked at her questioningly.

She rolled her eyes and then looked down at her lap. A few seconds later his phone vibrated in his hand.

Did you follow us because you were afraid we were being mean to her?

And then the second text.

You suck at being discreet.

After making sure his phone angle would keep anybody—especially Wren—from seeing the screen, he responded.

She's the only single one, so I was afraid you'd try to find her a man. And I just needed to see her.

We wouldn't do that to you.

I know. I'm an idiot.

At least you're self-aware.

He snorted and shoved the phone back into his pocket to signal he was done with the conversation.

"Everything okay?" Wren asked as he scooted forward again.

"Yeah. It was nothing."

The dance music changed to a slower song, and Cait hauled Gavin to his feet. "You're going to dance with me."

"I love when she's bossy," he said, doing what he was told, and they all laughed.

Grant wanted to dance with Wren. He sucked at dancing, but he'd get to hold her for three minutes, give or take. But he'd already decided the ball was in her court, and he didn't want to push any more.

"Go dance with Wren," Ashley told him. Apparently she'd decided to run onto the court and hit the ball herself.

"That's up to Wren."

"You came all the way here," Wren said. "I guess I should at least dance with you."

She nudged him so he stood up and then gave her his hand. He'd intended just to help her up, but she didn't let go. Hand in hand, they walked to the small dance floor and then her arms were around his neck and his hands were on her waist. He didn't pull her any closer, but it was enough.

"So what were you and Lydia texting about?" she asked as they swayed to the music.

"I would be the world's worst secret agent, wouldn't I?"

"The absolute worst."

"She asked if I followed you guys here because I was afraid they'd be mean to you."

She laughed. "Since we're all adults, it makes more sense that anybody who didn't want to be around me simply wouldn't have come."

"And for the record, I didn't follow you here. Gavin pulled up the location of Cait's phone with his and it showed us you were here."

"Oh, that's so much less creepy, then," she said, and then she laughed loudly enough so heads turned, until it turned into a cough she muffled against his chest.

He felt his cheeks get hot and he decided not to say anything that would dig him a deeper hole. Instead, he just enjoyed dancing with her until the song came to an end and the music changed back to a fast, bass-heavy club mix.

"Okay, you two had your fun," Cait said when they got back to the table. "Time to go."

"You're really throwing us out?" Gavin tried to snake his arm around her waist, but Cait held him at arm's length.

"We really are."

"Thanks for stopping by," Ashley called out.

"I guess it's time to go," Grant told Wren. "I'll see you…soon."

"Thanks for the dance." She leaned closer. "You should go before they physically throw you out. *That* would be embarrassing."

Once they were out in the cold again, Gavin looked at him and shook his head. "Sometimes being your wing-man is a pain in the ass. You used to be cool."

"I seem to recall some less than smooth moves when you started dating Cait, dumbass."

"True. But nothing this lame."

Grant wanted to argue the point, but there wasn't really anything he could say, so he shoved his hands in his pockets. "Let's go shoot some more pool."

Chapter Eight

"You look happy tonight, for somebody who lost her home," Mr. Belostotsky told Wren when she showed up at the market for her shift on Sunday afternoon. "Don't you think so, Mother?"

Mrs. Belostotsky nodded. "She does. Did you find a new place to live, then?"

"Not yet, but I'm renting a spare bedroom from my friend's mother." Wren had no intention of mentioning Grant or the girls' night out.

"That's good," Mr. Belostotsky said.

She had no idea what their first names were. When she'd seen the Help Wanted sign in the window and gone inside, he'd introduced himself as Mr. Belostotsky and his wife the same way. And he called her Mother, and she called him Dearest. It was cute and always made Wren smile, even if it struck her as slightly old-fashioned. Neither of them had very strong accents, but strong enough so they were probably both first generation. They were kind and paid her on time. That's all she cared about.

"You'll tell us if you need anything?" Mrs. Belostotsky said.

"I will. You've already been so generous. I can't thank you enough."

"And you make sure you rest if you need to. You're a sweet girl. We like you."

Wren was slightly horrified to feel her eyes well up with tears, and she gave them a quick swipe before smiling at her employers. "I like you, too."

Then, before she could get any more emotional— Mrs. Belostotsky was a hugger—she headed for the back room to get started. The work wasn't hard, consisting mostly of doing the tasks Mrs. Belostotsky didn't want to do anymore.

She restocked items as needed, pulling the products forward on the shelves so they all lined up neatly. There was a small notepad for listing anything they were running low on. Expiration dates were checked and dust was taken care of. It wasn't a sophisticated system, but they'd been running their market that way since before Wren was born.

They closed early on Sundays because Sunday dinner was something the Belostotsky family didn't compromise on, but they always stayed at least an hour past locking the doors to clean. Starting fresh with a clean store was important to them.

Wren was filling the mop bucket when her phone buzzed in her back pocket. She could count the number of people who had her new number on her fingers, so she wasn't surprised to see Grant's name on the screen. Not being surprised did nothing to keep her pulse from quickening, though.

Are you free for dinner tonight?

He hadn't been blowing smoke when he said he wanted to get to know her again, then. She hadn't wanted to get her hopes up last night, since the compulsion to know where she was and that she was okay might have been nothing but a residual impulse.

I'll be done working in about an hour, but then I'm free.

Did you drive?

No. She'd taken the bus from Patty's because there was literally no place to park her car within a reasonable distance of the market. Before the fire had displaced her, it had been perfect because she walked.

I took the bus.

I'll pick you up. Text me when you're out the door.

Sounds great.

She texted the street address for the market and turned her attention back to the mop bucket.

"You have a young man?" Mrs. Belostotsky asked from behind her, and she almost slopped water everywhere as she turned. "I saw you texting and only one thing puts a smile like that on a woman's face."

"He's…" She sighed, and then smiled. "It's complicated, but he's kind of my young man. Maybe. But he's going to take me to dinner tonight."

"I can wash the floors if you want to leave early."

"Thank you, but he's going to be pick me up out front. *After* I finish cleaning up."

She would have preferred to go home and change first. Not that she needed to dress up, even if she had the wardrobe for it, but a quick shower or at least the chance to brush her teeth would be nice. But seeing Grant would be nicer.

As instructed, she sent him a text message when she was ready to walk out the door and not even a minute later, he pulled up out front. She was ready and climbed into the passenger seat when he came to a stop, much to the annoyance of the disgruntled driver behind him.

"Hi," he said as he accelerated again. "Sorry about the rush."

"No problem," she said, buckling her seat belt. "Parking's a horror show around here."

It felt surreal, Grant picking her up from work. Being in his Jeep. The way he smiled at her and the sound of his voice. It was too easy to imagine the nightmare of the last five months hadn't happened.

But it had, which was why he didn't reach across and take her hand or rest his on her thigh like he used to do.

"You in the mood for anything in particular?" he asked.

"Whatever has parking available," she said, and he laughed.

He navigated through the city, taking random side streets, until she was good and lost. Not that it was hard to do. It would take years before she felt confident finding her way around Boston, if ever. People joked about the original city planners being drunk, but she was pretty sure there hadn't been any planning at all.

"This place has good calzones," he said, pulling the Jeep into a parking space. "Or I can find someplace better if you want."

"A calzone sounds great. And I just got out of work, so I'd rather not go someplace fancy, if you know what I mean."

He looked at her as if he didn't, in fact, know what she meant. "You look perfect."

Rather than point out she had a coffee stain on her shirt and her hair needed more than the small brush in her purse, she accepted the compliment with a smile. "Thank you."

He got out and walked around the Jeep to open her door. "The sidewalk's a little slick, so be careful."

She took his hand as she stepped out and felt the muscles in his arm stiffen as he supported her. Once she was safely on the sidewalk, he closed the door and hit the fob button to lock it.

It was the kind of hole-in-the-wall place only locals knew about, but there was still a decent crowd. Grant led her to a table near the window and the server dropped two menus on it as she walked by.

"The service isn't quite as good as the food," he said as they sat down. "But the calzones are worth it. Fair warning, they're also huge."

After looking over the menu, they decided to split a buffalo chicken calzone and an order of fries, and they each ordered a soda.

"Thanks for agreeing to have dinner with me," he said.

"Thank you for inviting me."

"I guess you got home okay last night?"

"I did." She laughed. "Did Cait's phone not tell you where we were?"

"I'm never going to live that down, am I?"

She'd spent enough time with the other guys to know

the answer to that, and she grinned. "I don't know about never, but it's going to be a while."

Grant loved the way her eyes crinkled when she laughed at him. He'd be willing to do stupid stuff forever if it meant she'd look at him the way she was right now.

"Actually, that's one of the reasons I asked you to dinner tonight," he admitted. "To apologize again for last night."

"You already explained. You didn't need to feed me, too."

"I know I explained, but it was still weird. And everybody was watching us, which made it even worse." He paused while the server set down their drinks and walked away. "There's nothing worse than temporarily losing your mind with an audience."

"I think it's weird for everybody," she said quietly. "Me being back, I mean. Nobody knows how to act. Them. You. Even me."

"You just be you," he said. "And I'll try to be myself without the side of weird and possibly creepy."

"Okay, it's a deal." After taking a sip of her soda, she leaned back in her chair. "So catch me up on what you've been doing for the last few months."

He'd rather talk about last night than relive the last five months, but they'd happened. They couldn't pretend they hadn't. "I worked. Watched sports. Made a few trips home to see my parents. Worked some more. I covered a lot of shifts, when I could get them."

"And played hockey?"

He pressed his lips together for a few seconds, and then forced himself to relax. "I haven't been playing much hockey lately. I, um…it's not a great way to blow off steam if you've got anger issues."

The understanding washed the amusement from her features, leaving behind guilt and sorrow. "I'm sorry, Grant. You love playing hockey."

"I still hit the ice with the guys here and there. I just haven't played in the actual games." He shrugged like it was no big deal. "But I'll play again. Guys kind of go in and out all the time, as stuff happens in life. Danny didn't play for a while after Jackson was born. Now he's back. Stuff like that is pretty normal."

"I feel like you're saying that to make me feel better."

"I do want you to feel better, but it's also the truth." He reached across the table and took her hand. "Nobody's responsible for what I do but me. And now I want to hear what *you've* been up to."

"Working." She sighed. "That was pretty much it. It wasn't a great neighborhood, so mostly if I wasn't at work or at the library, I was in my apartment, reading."

"It breaks my heart, thinking about you being alone and shut away like that." It was so true, his voice was a little hoarse when he said the words.

"It was a choice I made." She looked out the window for a long moment, and then back at him. "It doesn't matter why, or how afraid I was. I made that decision."

"I know neither of us like dwelling on this, but can I ask you a question?"

"Of course."

"If not for the fire, were you just going to stay there? I know you're quiet and like to read, but under that quiet exterior, you're so…vibrant. If you were going to run, why not run somewhere you could be more free?"

"Cait asked me that, the night of the fire. Why I

didn't drive until I was someplace cheaper to live. But I didn't want to leave Boston. I was saving every penny and researching when I could, trying to figure out a way to make Ben go away."

He flinched on the inside when she said his name. "I don't want to beat a dead horse, but I'm compelled to point out again that the research would have been easier with friends helping you. Especially friends like firefighters and EMTs who know people, like the police."

"I know. By the time I'd found a place to hole up in and the panic started easing, I couldn't bring myself to make the call. I couldn't drag you into it after what I'd done." Her voice caught, and she swallowed some soda. "I think, deep down, I was hoping if I stayed in Boston and could figure out a way to solve the Ben problem, that maybe you and I... If I ran too far, there was never going to be any chance of seeing you again."

It was still there, churning in his gut. *Why the fuck didn't you just tell me?* He wanted to fling the words at her—to yell them from the rooftops—but he swallowed hard and kept them inside. He was never going to understand because he'd never felt the kind of fear and vulnerability she had, so the words would do nothing but inflict more pain and guilt.

The food couldn't have arrived at a better time, he thought as the server set the calzone and fries on the table. "You need anything else?"

"We're good, thanks," he said to her back as she walked away.

"You weren't kidding about the service," Wren said. "Does she know you? And really hate you?"

"Nope. That's just how she is. Her sister is the other server. She has the sweetest personality, but forgets everything you say about five seconds after it leaves your mouth."

Wren laughed, and he was relieved the black cloud over their dinner was lifted. "So you can have great service with a bad attitude, or a great attitude with bad service, but not both?"

"Exactly." He cut the calzone in half and shifted her portion to her plate. "But the calzones are always good."

"This looks amazing. And I'm starving."

He grabbed the ketchup bottle and poured a puddle onto the plate next to his half of the calzone. It wasn't ideal, but he remembered Wren didn't like ketchup on her fries, so he couldn't just pour it directly over the basket.

There were benefits to dating a woman for a second time, he thought. He already knew her dos and don'ts, and her weird little quirks. Not liking ketchup on fries was definitely weird.

"What are you thinking about that's making you smile like that?"

Busted. "I was remembering that you don't like ketchup on fries because you're weird."

"Paying for crispy, salty potatoes that you can't even taste because all you can taste is the ketchup is what's weird."

He laughed and dredged a fry through the puddle of ketchup before popping it in his mouth. They'd had this conversation on their third date, when he'd taken her to the aquarium. He'd bought fries from a street cart and, because they were walking around, he'd just poured the ketchup over the fries. She'd tried to be a good sport, but the grimace every time she took a bite gave her away.

They avoided heavy conversation for the rest of the

meal, much to Grant's relief. It hadn't been easy for him to reach out to her after last night, but he'd wanted to spend time with her alone. And now he was glad he'd worked up the nerve to send the text.

Once they were done eating, there wasn't a lot of point in sticking around. There was no dessert menu and Wren claimed to be too full to eat another bite, anyway. It was time to be a gentleman and take her home.

And because he was a gentleman, he didn't just pull into the driveway and let her jump out. He walked her to the front door, where she turned and looked up at him.

"Thanks again for the dinner."

"It was my pleasure. Thank you for the company." Because of his determination not to push, he didn't move any closer, even though his body felt as if it was a dowsing rod and she was fresh water.

Wren took a half step toward him, her face tilted up. "Are we really doing the awkward first kiss goodnight dance?"

"After last night, I made a promise to myself not to push you, since we're…on shaky new ground, I guess."

She tilted her head, her mouth curved into an inviting, sexy half smile. "Am I allowed to push *you*?"

"Absolutely."

She braced her hands against his chest as if she was actually going to push him, but then she ran them over his shoulders as she pulled him closer.

Touching his lips to hers felt like coming home. He was more content—happier—than he'd been in a long time as he finally claimed her mouth. Her fingers slid into his hair and his tongue danced over hers.

Mine.

It was the same thought that had gone through his

mind the very first time he'd kissed her. He leaned in, the kiss growing deeper and more possessive until her body was pressed to his.

Reluctantly, he pulled back, breaking off the kiss. They were both a little breathless, and a smile played with the corners of her mouth.

"Smiling's a good sign," he said, surprised by how rough his voice sounded.

"That was our second first kiss." The smile was bright, but her eyes looked a little misty. "Goodnight, Grant."

She opened the door and slipped inside before he could say anything else, so he just walked back to his Jeep, trying not to whistle like an old movie cliché.

Their second first kiss. And maybe, this time, it had been their *last* first kiss.

Chapter Nine

Working the reception desk for a salon on Valentine's Day should come with a bonus, Wren thought as she hung up the phone and picked up her water bottle, hoping to get a few sips in before the phone rang again.

It seemed as if their entire clientele, along with countless women just calling around for a last-minute appointment anywhere they could get one, had big plans for the evening. She'd been warned ahead of time that it would be a crazy day, and her coworkers hadn't been lying.

Sadie—who was not only their most popular stylist, but also the owner—paused as she passed by the desk.

"You doing okay, Wren?"

Other than her throat being extra sore from all of the talking, she had a handle on it. "I seem to be. Nobody's cursed at me, yet."

She laughed. "Some days that's all you can ask for."

Wren didn't mind being busy. It made the time go by and didn't allow her to dwell on things she'd rather not think about around the clock. Like the ongoing mental list of items she needed to replace that seemed to get longer each day. While she had the things she absolutely needed, things kept popping up. She didn't own tweezers. Or slippers. Or a coffee mug of her own.

Luckily, she'd lived rather frugally, except the rent, so she had some savings. Since she'd need a huge chunk of that to move into a new apartment when she finally found one, she was trying not to spend it. Each week, she planned to buy a few small things and start replenishing from her regular paychecks. In the meantime, she was just unbelievably grateful for Patty's generosity.

During a lull in phone calls, she checked her cell and saw a text message from Cait.

Call me when you get a break.

She still had another few minutes before Kelli would be free to cover the desk, so she sent back a thumbs-up emoji. A few seconds later, she took a call from a tearful woman who wanted to cancel her appointment because she'd found out where her boyfriend had made dinner reservations and apparently the cheap bastard didn't deserve her at her best.

"Are you sure you want to cancel?" she asked. "No matter where you eat, you might feel better if you look amazing."

"I'm sure. I'm going to leave my hair in a messy bun and wear my yoga pants just to prove a point."

After wishing the woman luck, which it sounded like she'd need, Wren scratched her name out and called the next client on the wait list.

When Kelli finally showed up to spell her, she was frazzled. "Sorry, I ran over with that last blowout. The woman would *not* stop talking. I only have fifteen minutes until my next client."

"I'm just making a phone call, anyway. No worries."

Once she was in the break room, which was really only a folding table in a corner of the storage room, Wren brewed a coffee and grabbed a protein bar from her bag. After she'd washed down a couple bites, she pulled out her phone to call Cait.

"Hey, Wren," she said when she answered. "Gavin and I are going to Kincaid's tonight. You should come."

She laughed. "Right, because nothing livens up a Valentine's Day for a guy like his best friend's ex tagging along as a third wheel."

"Shut up. It's not even like that. We're not really into the whole holiday thing. Mostly it's the fact we both have tonight off and a bunch of us are going to the bar to hang out. Lydia's making some special cocktail for the women, I guess. It's not like we're going out on a super romantic date and asking you along."

It did sound more fun than reading alone in her room. Patty had plans with some single women she knew and Carter would be doing teen boy things. "Are you sure it won't be weird?"

"I swear. It's more like a group thing, anyway."

She couldn't bring herself to ask Cait if Grant would be a part of that group thing. He hadn't mentioned it when they had dinner. That could be because it was no big deal and he hadn't thought of it. Or it could be that he was avoiding the implication of what spending Valentine's Day together might mean.

Especially after that kiss.

They'd only talked on the phone once in the few days since dinner, but there were a lot of text messages. Sometimes just a hi. He'd been busy with a charity thing and helping a friend work on his truck on his off days, but he'd kept in touch.

She honestly wasn't sure if they were a couple again. But they seemed to be kind of dating? But not for Valentine's Day, apparently.

Unless he'd never planned to go and had forgotten about it.

"It does sound like fun," she admitted to Cait.

"I have to drop off some stuff for my mom, so you can ride with us."

"Okay. And I can just grab a Lyft home."

"We'll make sure you get home. I'll text you when we figure out what time we'll be there."

Once she was off the phone, Wren glanced at the time and winced. Fifteen minutes wasn't very long, so she finished her protein bar and decided to take the coffee back to the desk with her.

"Oh, good, you're back," Kelli said, standing up as soon as she saw Wren. "I'm the worst at the desk, but I don't think I screwed anything up while you were gone."

"It was only fifteen minutes."

"Yeah, but I'm *really* bad at it."

A quick glance didn't show anything amiss, so Wren sat and took a sip of her coffee. The phones would slow down, she guessed, since people would know it was too late in the day to get a last-second appointment.

"Oh, Wren, I forgot." Kelli waved her next client over to the sink and then walked back to the desk. "While you were on break, some guy called and asked for you. He didn't leave a message, though."

Wren froze, her mind spinning. "He didn't leave his name?"

"Nope. Just said he'd try again another time." She

started to walk away, but then turned with a big grin on her face. "Maybe it was some dude working up the nerve to ask you out for Valentine's Day and he chickened out."

"Maybe." Wren forced herself to smile and then turned her attention to the appointment book.

The writing blurred, but she wasn't really reading it anyway. She just needed a moment.

Grant would have called her cell. So would Gavin or Carter. Even Mr. Belostotsky. She couldn't think of another man who would need to call her who wouldn't have her cell number.

It can't be him.

She couldn't see any way that Ben would be in Virginia, where he belonged, and know she was working at this salon. No, she wasn't using a fake name, but she also kept her footprint as faint as possible. Unless he hired a professional investigator, he probably wouldn't find her. And he didn't have that kind of money, as far as she knew. Especially after being incarcerated.

Maybe it had to do with the apartment burning, she told herself. She couldn't remember if she'd listed the salon on what had passed for a rental agreement. She'd already been told her unit had been fully engulfed and there was literally nothing left, but maybe she needed to sign something that said she officially no longer lived in the nonexistent apartment.

Not knowing who had called left her unsettled for the remainder of the busy day, but the paperwork theory at least let her focus on the phone and the clients, and then the drive home.

By the time Gavin's truck rolled up Patty's driveway and Cait ran in to get her and speak to her mom for a minute, Wren had talked herself out of thinking it could be Ben. And she was more than ready to relax with whatever cocktail Lydia had concocted and enjoy herself.

Grant tried to stay away. He'd gotten the text invite to Kincaid's from Gavin and declined. The only person he wanted to celebrate romance with was Wren and that was messy.

They'd had dinner together. They'd kissed. Maybe they were dating? He didn't want to see anybody else and he was confident she didn't, either, but he wasn't sure that officially made them a couple.

And he didn't know if he was ready for that step, anyway. As much as he couldn't resist having her in his life again, he also couldn't forget the sound of her tear-choked voice telling him they were done and she didn't want to see him again. They were supposed to be getting to know each other. Taking time.

But in the end, he couldn't stay away and he walked into Kincaid's about an hour after Gavin said he'd be getting there. It wasn't packed, since it wasn't exactly a Valentine's Day destination, but there were enough regulars to make a small crowd.

He forced himself to go straight to the bar without looking around, because he didn't want to look as if he was searching for Wren. It was dumb, he knew, but he was struggling to maintain a clear head and some distance between them while he sorted through his emotions.

"You want one?" Lydia asked him, holding up a very red cocktail garnished with cherries in a fancy glass.

There was something around the rim that looked like red-tinted sugar, but he wasn't sure.

"I'll take a beer." He was pretty sure if he drank one of those cocktails, he'd be pissing pink tomorrow.

After she handed him a frosted mug filled with normal-colored beer, he took a sip and looked around. It didn't take him long to spot Wren. She was with Gavin and Cait, laughing at something Aidan was saying.

God, he'd missed her. It had been a week and a half since he'd carried her out of her apartment and he felt as if he was just coming to grips with all that had happened.

Like the kiss. And the fact she was here separately because he hadn't invited her out on Valentine's Day.

There was a time he'd had game. He and Gavin had had no trouble with the ladies, but then Gavin and Cait had crossed paths. And he'd met Wren. His game was shot to hell.

She glanced his way and when she saw him, her face lit up. As always, the way she looked at him made the doubts disappear. Wren was his. He just had to let go of the shit that had gone down between them and let her back in.

He knew almost everybody in the bar, so it took him a few minutes to make his way to the pool table alcove where most of the E-59 and L-37 folks were milling around. And Wren.

"Hi," he said to the group at large, but he was looking at her.

"I didn't know you'd be here," she said. "But I'm glad you showed up."

"Me, too."

"You're not going to try one of Lydia's cocktails?"

She held up the red drink, which he was guessing wasn't her first.

"Nope. I've gotta show up bright and early tomorrow morning, and I'm driving," he said. "One beer is my limit tonight."

"For a bunch of us," Gavin said, holding up his half-empty mug. "The worst part is nursing it so you can put off switching to water or soda as long as possible, but not wanting it to get warm."

They made small talk for a while, as people shifted around and came and went, but he was never far from Wren. At one point, he lost track of her, and then she reappeared with a fresh cocktail.

She caught him scowling at her—Lydia was known for a heavy pour when it came to her friends—and winked. Then she licked the sugar from the rim of her glass. Slowly. Deliberately. Never breaking eye contact with him.

He sucked in a breath and then took a healthy swig of his beer, even though it wasn't going to do a damn thing to cool him off.

And she knew it. The look she gave him over her glass could have melted steel and he had to clear his throat before he stepped close enough to her to speak.

"How many of those have you had?"

"Are you counting everybody's drinks or just mine?" She smiled sweetly, but he heard the undertone. Basically, she was a grown-ass woman and it was none of his business how many cocktails she had. "Lydia's bringing out cupcakes soon."

"Cupcakes?"

"For Valentine's Day. She got them from a bakery for tonight."

"You wanna share a cupcake with me?"

"Share?" She considered it, pursing her lips in a way that got all of his attention. "I will share my cupcake with you."

Wren loved cupcakes, so sharing was a pretty big deal. "We should head that direction because I know this bunch. Cupcakes won't last long."

They timed it out perfectly. As they reached the bar, Lydia was opening a huge box of cupcakes. She slapped a couple of hands away and then started putting them on cocktail napkins.

"What flavor are those?" Tommy bellowed from the corner.

Tommy Kincaid had a place of honor at the bar, over in the corner, because he owned the place. And his best friend for decades, Fitzy, sat next to him. They were retired from E-59 and L-37, respectively, which was one of the reasons this place was like a second home to so many of them. And the fact Lydia, Ashley and Scott were his kids. And Danny and Aidan were his sons-in-law. Jamie was his daughter-in-law. It was literally a family hangout.

"Red velvet," Lydia yelled back.

"What the hell's wrong with plain, old chocolate?"

Lydia gave her dad an exasperated look. "It's Valentine's Day."

"So?"

She just rolled her eyes and kept serving. Since Wren's drink was still half full, Grant set his empty mug on the bar and grabbed one of the cupcakes. He wasn't a huge fan of red velvet cake and didn't have much of a sweet tooth in general, but Wren wanted one.

They moved out of the way of the others trying to

get to the bar, ending up near the wall, under the picture of Bobby Orr.

Hopefully nobody would break a glass and interrupt them. If you broke a glass at Kincaid's Pub, you had to kiss Bobby Orr—or, really, kiss your fingertips and press them to the glass—or bad things would happen. And the Kincaid family had the stories to back it up, so it wasn't really optional.

"Ladies first," he said, holding the cupcake out to her, with the napkin under it to keep crumbs from falling in her drink.

Apparently, the red velvet cupcake was good because she closed her eyes and made a low, throaty sound of pleasure that was so familiar, every muscle in his body tightened in response.

Her tongue flicked out, swiping at a bit of frosting on her lip. "Now you take a bite."

He did as he was told, trying to get mostly cake because he recognized the bakery's name on the box and their frosting was so sweet his teeth would ache for hours. His body was doing enough aching at the moment.

"I have to pee," she whispered once they—mostly she—had finished the cupcake and she'd drained her glass.

"Let's go." He held her hand and walked her down the short hall to the ladies' room. She gave him a bright smile before disappearing inside, and it took her three tries to lock the door.

He waited in the hallway, listening for anything that sounded like a woman falling down or passing out, but he didn't hear anything. He'd give her a couple more minutes and then he was going to knock. He wasn't sure what he'd do if she didn't answer. Call her? Get Cait? Kicking the door in probably wasn't a good look.

Then he heard the water in the sink running, followed shortly after by the thump of the garbage can lid.

Seeing him in the hall startled her and he grabbed her shoulders because it looked for a second like she was going to crash into the wall.

"Are you being creepy again?" she asked, giggling.

"I walked back here with you," he reminded her. "And I stayed to make sure you're okay. You've had a bit to drink."

Her eyes widened, and then she grinned. "I didn't mean to. But they're really, really good."

She stepped closer to him, and since his hands were already on her upper arms, they slid around her back. When she stretched onto her toes and her face tilted up to his, her intentions were plain.

Unable to say no to her, he lowered his face and touched his lips to hers. Wren wanted more and tightened her fingers in his hair. She tasted like sweet fruit and alcohol as he devoured her mouth.

"We should go to your place," she muttered against his lips.

That sounded like the best idea he'd heard in a very long time. He lifted his head and smoothed her hair back. "Not tonight, sweetheart."

"I know you want to. I can feel it."

Grant groaned and tried to put some distance between his erection and her body. "Of course I want to."

"And I want to." She traced his bottom lip with the tip of her finger. "I really, really want to."

"But we're not going to."

Her pout made him chuckle. "That's stupid."

"You're drunk."

"I'm not *drunk*." The same fingertip that had stroked his lower lip now jabbed his chest.

"Okay, you're not drunk. But you're also not sober." He captured her wrists in his hands so she'd stop touching him. "I don't want you to regret waking up in my bed tomorrow morning."

"But I don't want to regret not being in your bed tonight. I like being in your bed. With you."

She was killing him. "You'll be in my bed when I'm sure it's you telling me that and not the cocktails. Come on. It's getting late and Gavin and I have to work tomorrow, so it's time to head out."

He wasn't sure about her ability to not fall off a stool, so he had her stand at the bar and gave Lydia a look. She chuckled, but nodded to show that she understood Wren was not to wander too far alone.

Gavin was helping Cait into her coat when Grant found them. Since Cait was still talking to Jamie and another woman Grant didn't really know, he pulled him aside.

"I'm gonna need you to drive Wren home."

Gavin's eyebrow lifted. "Huh. I kinda thought she'd be going home with you tonight."

"Yeah. We had dinner Sunday night and we kissed, but…we weren't there yet, if you know what I mean. And the only thing that's changed between then and now is the alcohol."

"I asked Lydia what was in the drinks and then I got bored and wandered off halfway through the list. Wren isn't the only one who'll be sorry in the morning."

"Yeah." Tommy's daughter had outdone herself behind the bar tonight. "But I want to make sure the drinks are the only thing she regrets tomorrow."

"You know I'll get her home." Gavin gave him a hard look. "But they've been drinking red drinks all night and eating red velvet cupcakes. If either of them gets sick in my truck, *you're* paying to have it reconditioned."

Grant cringed. "You might want to steal a bucket from the kitchen."

After helping Wren get her arms into her coat, which was no easy task, he walked out to Gavin's truck with them. He helped her step onto the running board and into the backseat without falling, and then fastened her seat belt for her.

"You're so sweet," she said, running her fingers through his hair.

"I have to work tomorrow, but I'll text you and see how you're doing." He pulled her hand down because her fingers were tightening and tugging, and he didn't want to put on a show for the others. "It won't be too early, though."

"Okay."

He kissed her quickly and then slapped the back of driver's seat. "Good luck, man."

"You owe me," Gavin said.

Grant laughed and, after making sure Wren was totally in, he closed the door. He could hear the women singing as the truck pulled away and he knew Gavin was going to save that IOU until he came up with a doozy.

Once the truck was out of sight, he shoved his hands in his pockets and made the walk to his Jeep. Alone.

Chapter Ten

Wren woke up in her own bed with a headache, served with a generous side of mortification as memories of last night played in her mind.

Lydia made one hell of a cocktail. Not that it was the alcohol's fault. Wren had been having a good time and then Grant walked in and she…just lost track of how many drinks she'd had.

Thank goodness he was a gentleman. Not that she'd be sorry to be waking up in his bed this morning. Her desire for him hadn't been the alcohol talking. It had just made her a little more expressive about the entire thing.

But it would have been an awkward morning after.

And she would have questioned whether he'd actually been ready for this relationship do-over to move to the bedroom or if he'd just taken what was very freely offered to him.

Eventually Wren forced herself out of bed and into the bathroom, where she took a quick shower and gave thanks for the bottle of ibuprofen she found in the medicine cabinet.

Then she went downstairs, not expecting to find anybody in the kitchen. Patty would have already left for work and Carter would be at school.

But Patty was seated at the table, sipping coffee. "Good morning."

"Good morning." Wren poured herself a mug of coffee and carried it to the table. "No work today?"

"I guess I've reached that age where getting up early after a night out with friends isn't as easy as it used to be." She laughed weakly. "I called in sick and went back to bed for a little while. Want some toast?"

Wren took a triangle of raisin toast from the plate Patty pushed toward her. "Thank you."

"You guys were out late last night." Patty smiled. "I was surprised you weren't facedown on the couch this morning."

"I'm so sorry. I would tell you I tried to be quiet, but that would be a lie. The cocktails Lydia was making were delicious and, apparently, I'm a lightweight. Or I can't count. I'm still not sure what happened."

"Don't be sorry. It's good to let loose now and then, as long as you're with people you trust."

She could certainly trust Grant, though she didn't share that tidbit with Patty.

They nibbled toast and sipped coffee in silence for a little while, listening to the morning show playing on the TV in the other room.

"What are you going to do with your fake sick day?" she asked after a bit.

Patty laughed. "I don't know how fake it is. I'm feeling better now, but it was pretty rough when my alarm first went off. But I might do some housework. Or I might sit and watch Netflix all day. I'm not sure yet. How about you?"

"I have to work at the market at two, so I'm going to take it easy and hope my stomach and my head are recovered by then." She blew out a breath. "And next time I go to Kincaid's, I'm having one drink and that's it. Between going to the club and last night, I've had more alcohol in a week than I've had in the last year or more."

"You went through a lot, honey. Take your fun when you can get it." Patty got up and refilled their coffee mugs. "Oh, I have a couple of bags in the back of my car for you. I forgot all about them."

"Bags of what?"

"One of the tellers at the bank is built like you and she's always talking about needing to get rid of at least half of her clothes because she's always buying new ones and never donates the old. When I told her about you, she went through her closets and drawers and filled two trash bags. She said it's a mix of casual and work wear."

Wren's eyes welled up, but she blinked the tears away. She absolutely couldn't cry right now. Her head couldn't take it. "That's so generous of her. Tell her I said thank you, please."

"I will." Patty looked at her closely and then frowned. "You don't feel weird about it, do you? She was going to donate them, but she's a nice dresser, so I think you'll like them."

"I don't feel weird about it at all. I'm very grateful to her. And to you." She sniffed hard. "To everybody. I don't know how I would have gotten through this without you all."

"You would have gotten through it, one way or the other. But I'm glad we can make it a little easier for you."

Later, when they'd summoned the energy to bring the bags in from the car and they were side by side in the laundry room, sorting them into lights and darks, Wren found herself getting emotional again.

"Are you okay?"

She gave a wry laugh. "I think this is more clothes than I had before the fire. And nicer, too."

"I swear that girl blows all of her money on clothes. I tell her all the time she should be saving some of it." Patty poked her arm with her elbow. "But today, I'm pretty happy she doesn't."

Wren laughed. "Me, too."

She was getting ready to leave for the bus stop when her phone chimed with a text message from Grant.

How are you feeling today?

She felt her cheeks get hot and was glad he couldn't see her.

Not bad for somebody who obviously had too much to drink last night.

I'd like to see you tomorrow.

Before she could type a reply, another text came through.

We should talk.

That sounded ominous.

I don't work either job tomorrow so I'm free. Do you want to meet somewhere?

He took his time responding.

It might be easier to talk here at my place. But we can meet somewhere if you'd rather.

Your place is fine. What time?

Five? I'll order that pizza you like.

A sausage and mushroom pizza with the garlicky crust she liked from the place around the corner from him sounded less ominous.

Sounds great.

See you then.

She didn't have a lot to go on, but at least the question of how she should feel about last night wouldn't drag on for days.

Saturday afternoon dragged on like no other Grant could remember in a long time. He'd cleaned his apartment, which hadn't taken as long as he'd hoped it would. And he'd put clean sheets on his bed, but it was his usual day to do that. It had nothing to do with the fact Wren was going to be in his apartment for the first time in months.

He was trying very hard not to think of Wren and his bed in the same thought, but it wasn't easy. And taking a cold shower before she arrived probably wouldn't help any more than taking a cold shower when he got home last night had.

Sending her home with Gavin had been the right thing to do, but he'd spent half the night tossing and turning and yearning for her.

It was a dilemma, because he'd told her he wanted to get to know her again. To get to know the Wren who wasn't holding anything back from him. But his body already knew her and it ached for her.

The pizza was delivered at ten minutes of five, as he'd planned. It would stay warm enough and he didn't want the interruption after she arrived.

When she finally knocked on his door, he took a deep breath and opened it. She was blowing on her hands to keep warm, so he pulled her inside and closed the door against the cold.

"Why aren't you wearing gloves?"

"I left them at work yesterday because I was in a hurry and I didn't notice because it wasn't that cold when I left."

"You only have one pair?" When she gave him a look, he could have kicked himself. "Yeah, sorry."

It was a stupid thing to say to a woman who'd lost everything in a fire two weeks ago, so he was off to a great start.

When she shrugged out of her coat, he took it to hang it up, but froze when he saw the shirt under it. "What the hell is that?"

She frowned and looked down at herself. "What?"

"Why are you wearing a Giants sweatshirt? With *rhinestones* on it, for chrissake. Footballs don't have bling. Even in New York." The Giants logo and the football on her shirt were both covered in red and blue rhinestones.

"One of the women Patty works with passed on a

bunch of clothes to me and it looks like she's either from New York or has no loyalty. I'm not sure which. And after going through the clothes, she likes bling, regardless of the theme."

"And you chose to wear that to my house?"

She grinned. "You like football."

"I like *Patriots* football." The sound of disgust he made had her laughing at him again. "At least it's not a Jets sweatshirt."

"Are you still going to share your pizza with me?"

He pretended to think about it for a long moment before shrugging. "I kind of have to, since you shared your cupcake with me last night."

"I have very vague memories of a cupcake."

"I'm surprised you remember it at all." He nodded at the table, where the pizza sat. He'd already put out napkins and paper plates, too. And silverware, since he knew she preferred to eat pizza with a knife and fork.

"I should apologize for throwing myself at you the way I did." She frowned as she sat down. "In a hallway. Outside of a bathroom."

"Wanting me isn't something you should apologize to me for, honestly. I want you to want me." He loved that shade of pink on her cheeks. "I didn't send you home with Gavin because I didn't want you. Trust me."

"I'm glad you had Gavin bring me home. Thank you for that."

He opened the box and put a slice on her plate. "It seemed like the right thing to do."

"Just to be clear, though, I'm not thanking you because I would have regretted sleeping with you. I just would have regretted that it happened because I was drunk and not because the time was right."

"That's why I thought we should talk," he said, sitting down. He didn't pick up his slice yet, though. "I... don't know what we're doing, exactly."

"Me, either."

"I know I said I couldn't walk away from you and that I want to get to know you again now that you're not holding anything back from me." He struggled for the words to explain himself. "But now I don't really know what that means. I feel like we're falling into being a couple again, without actually being a couple."

"If it helps, you're the only guy kissing me."

He chuckled. "That does help, actually. You're the only woman I'm kissing."

"Are we having this discussion over pizza so you have something to look at besides me?"

He swallowed and washed the bite down with soda. "We're having this discussion over pizza because I wanted the privacy of my apartment, but a distraction from the fact we're not far from my bed."

"Fair enough, though the pizza's not *that* good." She took another bite, and he could tell by the way her brows were drawn in that she was thinking. "I would like for us to be a couple."

"I feel like there's a *but* at the end of that sentence."

"It's weird to be dating when we were...already past that. I think that's why we're having trouble with *what* we have. But I don't want to rush it. I hurt you, Grant. That didn't just disappear because you're happy to see me again."

"No, it didn't," he said honestly. "But knowing why helps, and I'll get past it."

"With time. And you rescued me—literally—and almost everything I have, I have thanks to you and the people in your life. I need a little time to feel like I'm back on my own two feet so we both know I'm not just with you because it was easy. And eventually we'll get back to where we were, but better, because I won't be hiding anything." She smiled. "Back to where we were sounds funny. We were dating. But we were further along in the process, I guess, so that's what I mean."

He opened his mouth, but then shoved pizza in it instead of speaking. He wasn't going to tell her about the ring. There was no reason for her to know they'd been far enough along in the process that he'd been planning to propose. It would only hurt her and make her feel more guilty than she already did.

And if the day came he did buy her a ring, he didn't want the first almost-proposal casting a shadow over the second.

"So we're a couple?" he clarified after he'd wiped his mouth. She nodded. "Good. Exclusive?"

"Of course. But we're not going to fast-forward through the dating even though we did it once. We're taking it slow."

"Agreed." He lifted another slice out of the box and offered it to her. When she shook her head, he put it on his plate. Then he gave her a long look over the rim of his soda glass before setting it down. "How slow, exactly? I'm just asking because the first time we dated, it was a *long* time before you let me round the bases, if you know what I mean."

She blushed. "You were very patient. I was impressed, actually. And judging from stuff I've heard, that was unusual for you."

"It was not easy. But you, I was willing to wait for.

And I'll wait again, if that's what you want. You're worth it."

Her expression softened. "I don't think either of us wants to wait this time."

"Hell, I didn't want to wait the first time." He winked at her. "I guess I should finish my pizza first, though."

She laughed and took another slice out of the box. "On second thought, I guess waiting a few more minutes won't hurt."

Wren took her time in the bathroom, trying to calm her nerves. It was stupid to be nervous. Grant had seen her naked a bunch of times, and she definitely didn't have to worry the sex would be disappointing. But she had the jitters and staring at herself in the mirror wasn't helping.

Because this was far from her first time in his bathroom, she knew he had a stockpile of toothbrushes in the bottom drawer of his vanity. Not because he liked to have them on hand for a string of overnight guests, but because every time he went to the dentist they gave him one, even though they weren't the kind he usually used.

"They're free," he'd told her the first time she'd stayed over and needed one. "You never know when you're going to drop one in a toilet or something."

After unwrapping one, she brushed her teeth and helped herself to his mouthwash. Spicy pizza with extra garlic in the crust was a great choice before making out with somebody, she mused, making herself chuckle softly.

When she left the bathroom, Grant was sitting on the couch with his feet on the coffee table and the remote control in his hand.

"I wasn't sure you were coming back," he teased.

"You don't have a window in your bathroom and you don't keep any food in there, so I would have come out eventually."

He lifted his arm when she got to the couch so she could curl up against his side. "All part of my master plan. It keeps people from spending too much time in my bathroom."

"Is that usually a problem for you?"

"No." He tapped his temple with his free hand. "Because I don't keep food in there."

She laughed, loving how right it felt being there. On the couch, with his arm around her and making really dumb jokes. One of the things she'd loved most about being with Grant was how low-key they could be together, just enjoying each other's company. That it hadn't changed was a huge relief.

His fingers trailed up and down her arm. She didn't even know what they were watching, and she didn't care. All of her focus was on the fingers stroking her arm.

It was distracting as hell and she decided to return the favor. Her hand had been resting just above his knee, but she ran her palm over the denim. Just small movements at first, but then she slowly started moving up his thigh. The muscle tensed under her touch and she smiled.

When his hand left her arm and plunged into her hair, she moaned—just a little—and turned so she could kiss him. His fingers tightened almost painfully in her hair as her lips met his. She kissed him softly at first, pausing to run the tip of her tongue over his lip before kissing him again. Gliding her fingernails lightly down his neck, she deepened the kiss, demanding more.

With a groan he hauled her onto his lap, turning her so she faced him. He tucked his hands behind her knees and tugged until she was straddling his erection. Then he ran his hands over her thighs and cupped her ass. She slowly rocked her hips and he dropped his head against the cushion.

But then he was kissing her again, one hand buried in her hair and the other grasping her hip.

Good lord, but she'd missed his hands. And his mouth. His eyes. His touch, his voice and the curve of his lips when he caught her eye.

She'd missed everything about him so damn much she would probably cry if he wasn't doing his best to distract her with those hands and that mouth. Rather than dwelling on the time they'd been apart, she closed her eyes and focused only on the now.

He tugged at the hem of her sweatshirt, trying to lift it. "Get this off."

She started to, but paused before giving him a glimpse of her white lace bra. "Do you really want me naked or are you just trying to get me out of this Giants shirt?"

"Two birds with one stone. I'm efficient that way."

She didn't even have it all the way off before his hands were on her breasts. After tossing the shirt aside, she put her hands on his shoulders and allowed herself a moment to revel in the heat in his eyes as he watched his thumbs running over her taut nipples through the delicate fabric. He made her feel beautiful.

When he slid his hands to her sides to pull her in, she arched her back to make it easier for him to close his mouth over her breast. His teeth scraped over the lace before he sucked hard enough to make her gasp.

Her fingernails bit into his shirt and she wanted to get it off him, but she didn't want him to take his mouth away from her nipple, either. Instead, she bunched the fabric in her fists as he turned his attention to her other breast, alternating between gentle sucking and the pinch of his teeth.

Her hips rocked, grinding against his erection until he grabbed her hips and forced her to stop. "You're killing me with that, Wren."

Her chuckle was low and husky. "And you think you're not returning the favor. I want this off you now."

He hauled the shirt over his head and flung it, then took advantage of the break in action to unclasp her bra. Inhaling slowly, he peeled the straps down her arms until it could join the pile of discarded clothes on the floor or the coffee table or wherever they were landing.

Then his mouth was on her again, his tongue gliding over her bare flesh. Wren ran her hands over his shoulder and down his arms, raking his strong forearms with her nails.

Then he sucked her nipple so hard, she whimpered, her nails biting into his skin. Before she could even catch her breath, he slid his hand between them and pressed hard against her clit through her jeans. Squirming, she rocked against his hand.

"We need to lose these clothes."

She totally agreed with that. "Are we really doing this on the couch?"

"Hell no. I'm just getting warmed up."

"I'm feeling pretty warm." And a little impatient to move things along, but she knew him. If he thought the pace was torturing her, he'd revel in it and slow things down until she wanted to scream.

"Trust me, I'm going to need some space to thoroughly enjoy you tonight. And time, too." She shivered in anticipation and he must have felt it because he gave her a wicked grin. "A lot of time."

Rather than risk a sex-derailing injury if he tried to stand with her in his arms, Wren climbed off his lap and extended her hand to haul him to his feet. She wasn't at all self-conscious about being naked from the waist up. This man told her she was beautiful with words, but also with his eyes and his body and that made her believe it.

"I can carry you to the bedroom, you know," he said, yanking her hips against his and grinning at her. "I'm a firefighter."

"I seem to recall you carrying me recently and it wasn't at all sexy."

"Yeah, but you'll be conscious this time."

She laughed. "Somehow I think that would make it even more uncomfortable."

When he reached down and scooped her off her feet, one arm under her knees and one behind her back, she squealed and grabbed on to his neck. "See, this is pretty sexy."

"Why didn't you carry me this way before?"

He chuckled. "Because we would have fallen down the stairs."

When he was almost to the bedroom, she ducked her head against his chest, which made him chuckle again.

"You don't really think I'd hit your head on the doorjamb, do you?"

"Not on purpose."

When he deposited her on the bed, she didn't let go of his neck. Instead, she kissed him again. He slid his body over hers and she reveled in the weight of him as his tongue danced over hers.

"We forgot to take our clothes off," she murmured against his mouth.

He pushed himself up onto his elbows to look down at her. "Are you in a hurry?"

Oh, she wasn't falling into that trap. "Nope. Just pointing it out."

His grin told her he wasn't buying it for a second. "I think you're impatient."

"I think you're wearing too many clothes."

He rolled off her and stood. Then, with his eyes on her breasts, he popped the button on his jeans and unzipped them. His sigh of relief was unmistakable. Then he slid the jeans and his boxer briefs to the floor, kicking them off, and she sighed, too, in appreciation. He pulled his socks off, and then leaned over the bed as she undid her jeans.

There was that grin again as he pulled and tugged her jeans down her legs. He tossed them aside and then her socks, leaving her in nothing but the white lace panties that matched the bra. "I like those."

"I thought you might." She knew he wasn't picky about her underwear. Lace or cotton, white or black. It didn't matter. He just liked that thin scrap of fabric to play with.

He lifted her leg and kissed the inside of her calf. Then behind her knee. Then he nipped gently at the soft skin of her thigh.

"Grant," she breathed.

He ignored her, kissing his way to the white lace. When his mouth closed over it, she hissed in a breath. Sucking her through the fabric, he made a low sound of appreciation that pleased her almost as much as the heat of his mouth through the lace.

When she lifted her hips, he used the flat of his hand on her hipbone to push her down against the mattress. Then he slipped his finger under the elastic so his knuckle brushed against her clit. She jerked and clenched the sheets in her fists.

Not until she was practically writhing on the bed did he lift his head. The panties joined the other clothes on the floor and he ran his hands up the insides of her legs. Wren held her breath as he pushed them apart so he could bury his head between her thighs.

His tongue slid over her clit and then delved into her, and she closed her eyes, savoring the sensation. When his mouth closed over her, sucking gently before his tongue dipped into her again, she curled her fingers in his hair, holding his head.

He didn't stop—licking and sucking and using his fingers—until her back arched off the bed and she moaned as the orgasm robbed her of coherent thought.

Only when Grant started kissing his way up her body again, stopping to give her nipples the same treatment he'd given her clit, did she open her eyes.

He lifted his head and smiled down at her. "You didn't think I'd forget how much you like that, did you?"

"I was hoping you'd remember."

"I could never forget anything about you. God knows I tried, but you're seared into my brain. Every look. Every touch."

She shivered under the intensity of his gaze, and then scraped her fingernails down his back. When she splayed her fingers over the curve of his very fine and muscular ass, the playful grin returned.

"As much as I want to make you come with my mouth again, I want to be inside you more." When she nodded, he ran his thumb over her bottom lip. "Maybe we can save that for dessert."

It was going to be a long, fabulous night, she thought as he stretched his arm out to his nightstand for a condom. It only took him seconds to put it on, and then he moved between her thighs.

Wren exhaled in a long, shaky breath as he entered her. Slowly. Excruciatingly slowly, which was both delicious and infuriating at the same time. She tried to lift her hips and take him all, but Grant anticipated that and used his hands on her hips to hold her back.

The smug curve of his mouth told her he knew exactly what he was doing to her, but the slight tremble in his arms and back let her know he was tormenting himself right along with her and it wouldn't take much.

"Please, Grant," she whispered, digging her fingertips into the cheeks of his ass.

He let himself go, filling her so completely it took her breath away for a few seconds. Then he started moving and the sweet friction made her whimper. She ran her hands up his back, feeling the muscles tense and ripple as he moved within her.

Lowering his head, he sucked first one nipple and the other with just enough pressure to make her gasp before reaching between their bodies to brush his thumb over her clit. He was trying to kill her, she thought as the sensations started building.

He quickened his pace, thrusting faster and deeper as he stroked her clit, until the orgasm shook her body and had her biting down on the side of her hand to keep from screaming out his name.

"You're so fucking gorgeous when you come," he said in a low, raspy voice. She barely heard him, as her body trembled and she tried to catch her breath.

His breath was almost as harsh and she fisted her hand in his hair, yanking his head down so she could kiss him. It was a hard, punishing kiss and he groaned against her lips, his hips jerking as he came.

When he collapsed on top of her, she wrapped her arms around him and hooked one of her legs over his, as if she could keep him there indefinitely. He kissed her neck and his breath blew in hot, rapid spurts against her skin.

All too soon, he reached down to secure the condom and rolled away from her. "Don't move."

She couldn't have moved if she wanted to. Her muscles were practically liquid and she was pretty sure if she tried to make a sound, it would just come out as a satisfied purr.

The second he was back in bed, he pulled her into his arms. She was pretty sure most couples spooned, but he liked her to be facing him so he could see her. He smoothed her hair back from her face and kissed her.

"I've missed that," he said. "So much."

"Me, too."

"It was the longest five months of my adult life," he said.

"Five months?"

"Trust me, jerking off in the shower is no substitute for having you in my bed. Not even close."

He said the words lightly, but even in the dim light coming from the living room, she could see the emotions behind them in his eyes. There had been nobody for him in the time she was away. She'd wondered a few times, but she didn't dare to ask out of fear of the answer. And she knew she didn't have the right to question what he'd done during those months.

She smiled and traced his lips with her fingertip. "I guess we'll have to make up for lost time."

Chapter Eleven

"You can't possibly intend to eat that much bacon."

Grant looked up from his plate to find Wren staring at it. "There's no such thing as too much bacon."

"There is. And it's on your plate right now."

"I worked up an appetite last night. I need to replenish myself." He grinned when she blushed and glanced around as if to see if anybody else in the restaurant had heard them. "And that's why people pay extra for the all-you-can-eat breakfast buffet. So they can have as much bacon as they want."

"You didn't get any toast."

"Toast is filler."

"You take that all-you-can-eat thing pretty seriously."

"It's all about the money. A lot of people think it sounds like a great deal, so they pay the extra and then end up with what they normally get on their plates. Their brains tell them that's breakfast, so very few go back enough to make it worth the cost. I only get the good stuff and I know I'll go back."

She leaned over and snagged a piece of bacon from his plate. "And I'll just eat my regular breakfast but steal your bacon. Since you're going back and all."

"You better not get my all-you-can-eat privileges revoked."

She laughed. "That's not a thing."

"It's totally a thing. Ask Tommy and Fitzy about it."

"You're joking."

He took a long swig of his coffee before launching into the story. "You can ask Marlene, the owner. Tommy and Fitzy have been eating breakfast here for decades, but they're not allowed to have the buffet. Years ago, when they were both still on the job, they'd come in and Tommy would get the buffet. Fitzy would always claim he wasn't very hungry and he'd get a coffee and an English muffin. Fitzy would just eat off Tommy's plate, and Tommy would keep going back until they were both full. Then they'd split the total cost."

"And they got caught?"

"Marlene didn't believe a guy like Fitzy—and a fire-fighter, no less—was getting through to lunch on an English muffin, so she started paying attention. Legend has it she *literally* kicked Fitzy in the ass on the way out the door when she threw them out."

"She must be tall," Wren said, her skepticism obvious.

He shrugged. "Or flexible."

"But she allowed them to come back?"

"The food is amazing and there aren't many places with coffee this good, so Fitzy calculated how many times he'd eaten off Tommy's plate and brought in a brown paper bag of cash to make it up to her."

"No, he didn't." Her eyes widened when he nodded. "And it worked?"

"She let them come back, but they can never have the all-you-can-eat buffet again." He pointed his fork at her. "So stop stealing my bacon."

She laughed and dug into her mushroom omelet. They ate in silence for a few minutes, but he didn't mind. His leg was rested against hers under the table and whenever their eyes met, she smiled.

He would have liked to keep her in his bed all day, but she had to work at the market. And because she hadn't intended to spend the night at his place, she had to go home first. But he'd talked her into having breakfast. And then he'd talked her into letting him follow her to Patty's so she could change and leave her car, and then he'd drive her to the market. Extra time with her.

She hadn't budged on taking the bus home after work, though. That fell under the *going slow* thing, apparently. She wasn't going to spend two nights in a row at his place, and she wasn't going to have him driving all around the city just to drop her off and go home alone.

This was nice, though. As he went back to the buffet to get more of the good stuff, he marveled at how much his life had turned around since the night of the fire.

It had been grim when she left. He'd gone through a lot of stages—shock, denial, grief—but the most potent one had been anger. He'd been angry with everybody over everything at first. Then it had mellowed to just a shitty attitude in general. Some of the guys had suggested he try dating again, but he'd had no interest in letting another woman into his life.

He'd pretty much come to terms with the fact he was going to end up a lonely, angry old man who yelled at kids who hit baseballs into his yard. Someday, when he actually *had* a yard.

And now here he was, happier than he'd been in months, and sharing breakfast with the only woman he'd ever loved.

He was going to have to tell his parents. He'd put off mentioning Wren because he wasn't sure what exactly to tell them about what was going on. But now that they'd defined their relationship and were going to work on building a future together again, that phone call needed to be made.

To say his mom wasn't Wren's biggest fan would be an understatement.

"You can't be serious," Wren said when he slid back into the booth.

"What? I didn't get any more bacon."

She stabbed one of the sausage links with her fork and transferred it to her plate, and then laughed when he made a big show out of looking over his shoulder for Marlene.

But if there was anybody he'd be willing to risk his all-you-can-eat buffet privileges for, it was Wren.

As she pulled into the driveway, Wren realized she had no idea what to say to Patty. She hadn't gone home last night. Was that a problem?

Grant pulled up to the curb as she was getting out, so she waited for him. "Do you think I should have called Patty last night?"

"I think it would have been a little weird, considering what we were doing."

She laughed and slapped his arm. "You know what I mean."

"I… Crap. I don't know. I mean, she's not your mom. But she's also not just a landlord."

"She seems like the kind of woman who would worry when she didn't hear me come in."

"*But*, you did tell her you were going to my place,

right?" When she nodded, he shrugged. "She's a smart lady. She probably figured that one out."

"I'm not sure how I feel about that." They started up the walkway, side by side, and he captured her hand in his. "I don't know what the expectations are, but it would be super awkward to ask."

"You're a grown woman. Yes, she'll worry about you, but I don't think you're expected to check in with her." He paused before they went inside. "When you think about it, you were being a courteous tenant by not trying to sneak in late and waking everybody up."

She laughed. "Good point."

Patty didn't seem at all put out when they walked into the house. She was sitting in the living room, but she got off the couch at the same time Carter walked out of the kitchen.

"Oh good, you're home and you brought Grant," she said. "I've been waiting for a nice, strong man to stop by."

Carter rolled his eyes. "Thanks, Mom."

"*Another* nice, strong man. It's a two-man job and yes, you'll be one of them."

"I'm going to run up and get ready for work," Wren said. And then, since she had no idea what Grant was in for or how long it would take, she added, "Grant's driving me today."

"Oh, don't worry," Patty said. "It won't take them long. They'll probably be done before you are."

On her way up the stairs, she heard them talking about the snowblower, but they went out the back door before she found out what the specific issue was.

She took one of the fastest showers of her life and put on clean clothes. It took forever to dry her hair, so she decided to skip that step today. Makeup was on her *replace someday maybe* list, but she had moisturizer and lip balm, which she made liberal use of.

She'd just finished putting her hair into a ponytail when her phone rang. That was weird because everybody sent text messages. Except Mrs. Belostotsky, who actually used a landline. Frowning, she flipped it over.

Unknown.

She jerked her hand away from the phone and took a step back, her heart hammering in her chest.

You're being ridiculous, she told herself. It could be anybody. Maybe it was somebody looking for the previous owner of the telephone number. They'd probably leave a message because she hadn't personalized the greeting with her name or her voice. It was just a generic robot reading off the number and inviting them to leave a message.

She waited, staring at it as it rang. And once it stopped, she kept staring and waiting. Eventually it became obvious whoever it was hadn't left a voicemail. There was just the missed call notification.

That was a disappointment. She'd been hoping for a "hey, wrong number" or "we're trying to reach so-and-so" so she could put it out of her mind. Instead it was just…unknown.

She was wound so tight, the text message chime almost made her scream.

You about ready?

She'd forgotten all about Grant and work and everything but her phone. After double-checking herself in the mirror, she picked up the phone and cleared the missed call notification. Then she flipped the switch to silent and slid it into her back pocket before going downstairs.

They were all in the living room, though it was obvious Grant was trying to work his way toward the door.

"Sorry," she said, keeping her voice light. "I lost track of time."

"I don't want to rush you, but we'll be cutting it close if we don't leave soon."

"I'm ready."

"Drive careful," Patty said. "And thank you again, Grant."

"Anytime." He practically pushed Wren out the door.

"We're not cutting it *that* close," she said.

"No, but she started talking about a few things she needs done around the house and I don't mind helping, but the more she talked, the more things she thought of."

"What did she need you to do today?"

"Oh, the snowblower had a flat. It wasn't so much a two-man job as a job she didn't think Carter knew how to do but needed to learn. Gavin said she's been telling Cait lately how concerned she is about Carter learning to do all the guy stuff with his dad gone and not around to teach him."

"Luckily, his sister married a firefighter and now he has a bunch of big brothers."

He grinned. "Pretty much."

She was trying her best to shake off the residual fear, but she must not be doing a good job because after she got in the Jeep, he didn't close the door. Instead, he looked at her more closely, frowning. "What's wrong?"

"Nothing." He just raised an eyebrow and waited. "Okay, I got a weird call on my cell phone."

"How weird? Who was it?"

"I didn't answer it because it said unknown on the caller ID."

"Okay." He thought about it for a few seconds. "That could be anybody, really. A wrong number. It doesn't really mean anything."

"I know. That's why I wasn't going to say anything. It just spooked me, I guess. Sometimes I forget about him and then—*bam*—something like that happens and I'm afraid again."

"I don't like you being afraid."

"Me, either." She laughed, though it was high-pitched and nervous. "I asked once about a restraining order, but he's never really done anything to me. Which sounds horrible, but when it comes down to actual facts, he's never even threatened me."

"Will you be okay at work?"

She forced herself to calm down. "Yes, of course. It's like you said, it could have been anything. And screw him. I'm going to live my life, dammit."

He grinned and kissed her mouth. "I like that philosophy."

After closing her door, Grant walked around the Jeep to get in and Wren tried to use that brief time to center herself. Sure, it was a nice philosophy, but it was a lot easier to say than it was to believe.

Chapter Twelve

Monday night brought snow, which meant Tuesday brought fender benders and hydrants needing to be shoveled out.

Luckily, the residents of Boston were pretty kick-ass about shoveling their hydrants out while clearing their driveways and sidewalks. Social media helped, with streets competing with each other to see who could do the best job. And as they drove around, clearing any that hadn't been cleared, they'd stop and chat with kids who were shoveling the hydrants, or who already had.

There was still a lot of seat time in the truck and a lot of hand shoveling, which were pretty low on Grant's list of things he liked about being a firefighter.

But there was chili in the slow cooker, and there were crackers to crush in it and a fresh bag of shredded cheddar to go on top. Sometimes it was the small things that made it a good day.

"Danny, Chris, Derek," Scott said. "You guys have kids. I know when women are so pregnant they look like they have beach balls under their shirts, you're supposed to go out in the middle of the night to get them ice cream or whatever, but you can't even see that Jamie's pregnant yet and she got up in the middle of the night to make hard-boiled eggs."

Chris laughed. "As soon as the pee stick has a plus sign, it's on."

"I woke up this morning and thought we had a gas leak. It stunk up the whole place."

"I wouldn't complain about it," Danny said.

"Nope." Derek shook his head. "Keeping your mouth shut about weird smells is pretty much your life until the kid's out of diapers."

Scott scowled. "Women on TV always want ice cream. I get the wife who wants egg salad at two in the morning."

"At least you had the eggs," Chris said. "Going out in the snow at two in the morning to find a dozen eggs is worse."

"I had it the worst," Derek said, and they all groaned. "No, seriously. When she was pregnant with Isaac, even the faintest smell of bacon made her very sick."

A hush fell over the room, and Scott laid down his spoon. "That's a thing? That can really happen?"

"We had no bacon in our lives for months."

"You went out and found yourself some side bacon, right?" Aidan asked. "I mean, a guy's got needs."

"I did not. I loved my wife and didn't run around with bacon behind her back." He chuckled. "And we ended up divorced anyway, so I should have had the damn bacon."

They all laughed, except for Scott, who looked as if he was still in shock over the concept of going months without a food because Jamie couldn't tolerate the smell.

"Cheer up," Grant told him. "Maybe it'll be vegetables she can't tolerate."

After they'd cleaned up, they got a little downtime before they'd be out on the streets again. Some of the guys hit their bunks and a couple went into the workout room, but Grant chose to chill on the couch. He wasn't surprised when Gavin joined him, taking the chair closest to where he was sitting.

It had been a while since they'd talked one-on-one. He supposed that was natural. Gavin had Cait now, and Grant had Wren. More or less. But the wingman days were definitely over.

"Catch me up," Gavin said. "Cait's being surprisingly close-mouthed about any gossip she may or may not be privy to."

That was a surprise. Grant had just assumed Gavin knew everything that was going on, since he thought Patty would tell Cait and Cait would tell Gavin. That's how the relationship chain was supposed to work.

"Not much to tell, I guess. We're a couple. We're working on it."

"I'm kind of surprised you haven't moved her into your place."

Grant gave him a sideways glance. "It's only been a couple of weeks."

"This time. But you were together before. Five months ago, you were as good as engaged. If you're just going to go back to where you were, you were getting ready to do that, anyway."

"We're not doing that." Gavin gave him a skeptical look. "Going back to where we were, I mean. We're getting to know each other again, but without stuff between us."

"But you're going to end up in the same place."

"You think it's a mistake."

"I didn't say that. I like Wren. You know that. I know how happy you guys were together, but I also remember how wrecked you were when she took off. It was rough, man, and I worry about how you'd come through if she does it again."

"She doesn't have any reason to do it again."

Gavin nodded but he wanted to say more. Grant could see it on his face. "What?"

"Nothing. If you're happy, I'm happy for you, plain and simple."

"Just spit it out."

"Okay, fine. When you get right down to it, she didn't really have a good reason to do it the first time."

"No, she didn't. But she thought she did."

Gavin nodded. "I guess I can see that. As long as you're good, man. That's all I really care about."

"I'm good." The words rolled off his tongue, but this was his best friend. "Mostly. She got a call on her cell from an unknown and it spooked the hell out of her."

"She think it was that Mitchell guy?"

"She doesn't know. But not knowing scares her, too. And when she gets scared, I get… I pull back, I think. Not a lot, but it's a reservation. It's there. Know what I mean?"

"You just told me *she* thought she had a reason to take off, and we're supposed to accept that. But it sounds to me like you're afraid she might think she does again."

He didn't want to admit to that—to say it out loud—so he shrugged. "The difference this time is that I know about him. I know what she's afraid of. I'm hoping that's enough. And she *did* tell me about the phone call this time."

"I hope you're right." Gavin leaned forward, leaning his forearms on his knees. "And I hope she knows you're not the only one she can depend on. We've all got her back if she needs us."

"I appreciate that. And I'll keep telling her that until it gets through her head."

"We need to go out sometime. The four of us, like we used to do. We haven't done that in a while."

Grant nodded, feeling his spirits lift. They could definitely use a night out with friends.

Waking up to snow meant a slow day for the salon. Between women who were nervous to drive slushy streets and those who just didn't want to clean off their cars, there was a flood of cancellations left via voicemail. The phone was ringing nonstop as they opened the doors, which meant rescheduling became a complicated puzzle that made everybody want a drink.

It also left a lot of time for socializing, though they did most of the talking while doing busy work. Polishing mirrors. Disinfecting things. Arguing over which *Real Housewives* franchise was the best.

"Hey, Kelli," Wren said during a lull in the television debate. "The other day you said a man called when I was on break and asked for me by name, and he said he'd call back another time. Has he, that you know of?"

"I don't think so. Nobody's said anything and, honestly, you're so private about things that a guy calling here twice for you would be gossip. No offense."

"None taken." Gossip at a hair salon wasn't really a surprise. "I have a favor to ask all of you, though. I have…an ex in my past who wasn't really nice and I'm pretty sure he's in the rearview mirror, but I'd appreciate it if nobody gives out any info on me. Everybody I want to talk to has my cell number."

Kelli's eyes widened. "Oh no. Do you think that was him?"

She didn't want to scare them into taking away her job. She just wanted them to keep their mouths shut. She'd told Mrs. Belostotsky the same story last night, knowing she'd share it with her husband. Not a lot of details, but enough so they'd be suspicious of anybody asking about her.

"It was probably somebody from the building management about the fire," she said. "But since it was weird, I just thought I'd mention my ex. That's all."

Sadie, the owner, gave her a thoughtful look. "How nasty are we talking?"

"He never put his hands on me," Wren answered truthfully. "But he's been violent before and...he's just really awful. I'd rather he not know where I am."

"Okay." After a short silence, she spoke again. "Do you have Facebook at all?"

"Nope." It's not as if she had a lot of family to keep in touch with.

"When you started here, there's a thing we do. Just a post saying 'hey, welcome Wren Everett to the reception desk' kind of thing. We didn't post a picture of you, but it's not like your name is Jane Smith."

Cold seeped through Wren's body. She wasn't exactly sure how Facebook worked, but she was pretty sure anybody searching for her name would be able to land on the salon's page. "Okay."

"I'm deleting it right now," Sadie said as she scrolled through her phone. "I'm sorry. It never occurred to me it might be a problem."

"I'm sure it's not connected at all." She wasn't sure of anything, but she didn't want to panic them, either. Or herself.

It was a relief when a client walked through the door and Wren had an excuse to end the conversation. She didn't want to share a lot of details about her life—past or present—with her coworkers. She just didn't want them giving out her information to any random person who asked for it.

There had been no more calls to her cell phone, so she'd managed to convince herself the unknown had been a wrong number after all. But it didn't hurt to be cautious and the fewer people who could or would give out information about her, the better.

When she left the salon after her shift, she checked her phone and saw a missed text message from Grant.

Gavin said we should double date soon. Like we used to.

Her mind turned the phrase over and over as she walked to her car. *Like we used to.*

She knew she should be thankful Gavin and Cait had forgiven her enough to welcome her back into their lives. If they wanted nothing to do with her, her relationship with Grant probably wouldn't survive in the long run. They were his family and what they thought of her would matter to him, even if it was on a subconscious level.

But it was also vaguely unsettling. Part of the reason she and Grant were taking things slow and getting to know each other again was to give them time to work through what had happened. Going back too quickly to *like we used to* could hinder that process and she didn't want that, either.

There was no way she could say no that wouldn't be awkward, though.

Sounds fun.

At home, she'd just finished a load of laundry when Patty got home from work. She looked exhausted as she sank onto the couch next to the clothes Wren was folding.

"What a day," Patty said, and then she groaned as she put her feet up on the coffee table.

"Everything okay?"

"Oh, sure." She waved her hand. "Just feeling old today. I wore new shoes without testing them out first and they weren't a good choice for standing all day."

"Ouch. Do they need to be broken in or are they just not comfortable?"

"Let's just say they'll be perfect for a sit-down dinner."

Wren laughed. "I'll tell you what. I make a pretty decent spaghetti and you've got all the ingredients. How about I make dinner tonight?"

She could tell Patty was about to say no, but then she hesitated and sagged against the couch cushions. "That actually sounds wonderful. You're not going out with Grant tonight?"

"He's working today."

"Oh, that's right. I swear, keeping up with everybody's schedules is beyond me." Without lifting her head, she turned it so she was looking at Wren. "How are things going with him?"

"Good. Things are good."

"I'm glad to hear it. I hope you know you can always come to me if you need somebody to talk to. And it'll stay between us. I know it seems like, because Cait's my daughter and she's marrying Grant's best friend, lines might be fuzzy, but you really can talk to me."

Wren's throat tightened with emotion. "Thank you. I hope you know how much you mean to me. Letting me stay here has given me a chance to rebuild my life without scrambling or settling for a bad situation. And it gives Grant and me the space to work on things."

Patty reached out and squeezed her hand. "I love having you here. Carter and I are in a good place now, but he's growing up and doing his own thing. Or hiding in his room. It's nice to have company sometimes."

"I'm going to go put my laundry away and then I'll start the spaghetti."

After texting Carter an ETA for dinner so he could plan his video gaming accordingly and hanging up her clothes, Wren went to the kitchen. Patty, of course, tried to help because she couldn't help herself, but she very firmly sent her back to the couch to relax and rest her feet.

The spaghetti and garlic bread were good, but the company was even better. It had been a long time since Wren had felt like she was part of a real family, sitting around the table and talking and laughing.

But tonight she did, and she was thankful for it.

Chapter Thirteen

"Gin."

Grant groaned when Wren fanned her cards out on the table and did a little victory dance in her seat.

He didn't care about the victory. The dance, though, was killing him. Her favorite pink sweatshirt, which she'd put on after a quick shower, was *really* killing him. It slid down her shoulder no matter how often she pulled it up, showing skin he wanted to kiss in the worst way. And the hem would ride up, showing off the lacy pink panties she had under it and more skin he wanted to kiss.

When Gavin had shot him a text suggesting they meet him and Cait at Kincaid's, they'd thought about it, but decided they'd rather have a quiet night in at his place. He'd ordered pizza while she jumped in the shower, and now she was kicking his ass at cards because all he could think about was sliding his hands up under that soft, thin fleece.

"How was work today?" he asked, desperate to distract himself from that line of thought.

She'd gathered the cards and was shuffling, so he noticed the slight pause. "It was okay."

"Wren?"

Sighing, she stared at the cards in her hand for a long moment, and then looked up at him through her lashes. "I don't want him here with us tonight."

There was no more thought about kissing her skin as every nerve in her body seemed to go on high alert. "What happened?"

"Nothing happened. But Sadie told me something today that means he could actually know I'm in Boston."

He relaxed a little. Anything but the guy actually being in Boston could be dealt with. "What did she say?"

"I guess she did a post on Facebook welcoming me to the salon and it had my name, so it is possible he knows I'm in the city and I work there. She deleted it today, but *if* he searched for me, it might have come up." She shrugged one shoulder, making the sweatshirt's loose neckline slip again, which brought his thoughts back to kissing her skin.

He was pretty sure it was ridiculous for a grown man to be turned on by a woman's bare shoulder, but there it was. After clearing his throat, he forced himself to focus on the subject at hand, although he *really* didn't want to. He was tired of Ben Mitchell being a part of their lives, especially since he wasn't sure they'd be able to really move forward until they knew for sure he wasn't an issue anymore.

"You must have started working at the salon after the last time I searched for you," he said, and she looked up from the cards she was shuffling. "What? You're surprised I looked for you?"

"I...I don't know. I guess maybe I thought you'd be too angry."

"I was pissed. But I was also scared because, even if you wanted to break things off with me, the way you did it seemed so out of character for you that I wanted to make sure you were okay. So yeah, I tried to find you." He paused to take a swig of his beer. "But it was painful and eventually I told myself if you'd wanted me to know where you were, you would have told me, and I stopped looking."

"I'm sorry."

He hated that pained expression on her face. "I know, and I didn't mean to drag it all out there again. Since you know there's a chance he knows you work at that salon, just be vigilant. If you get scared, call me. If you think something's wrong, call 9-1-1 and then call me."

"I'd feel stupid if it was nothing."

Grant reached out and grabbed her wrist as she went to deal the cards so she'd look at him. "I can tell you with one hundred percent certainty that the police would rather respond to a false alarm than get there after the fact because the victim talked herself out of calling. I mean it."

Her gaze locked with his and he knew she meant it when she nodded. "I promise, if I feel unsafe *at all*, I'll call 9-1-1. And then I'll call you."

"Good." He let go of her wrist and blew out a breath that turned into a wry chuckle. "Do I know how to suck the fun out of game night or what?"

"Stop." She dealt the cards, and then glanced at him. "It's kind of sexy, having you worry about me like that."

"Really?" He liked the sound of that. "How sexy?"

She gave him that slow, sensual smile that made everything else fade away until it was just the two of them, just the way he liked it. "Everything about you is sexy."

"Wanna play strip gin rummy?"

Her musical laugh drove the lingering shadow of her ex away as she shook her head. "One, I don't know how you would even score that. And two, you're fully dressed and I'm wearing two articles of clothing."

"It's easy to score. If I win, I get to choose which article of clothing you take off. And if you win, *you* get to choose which article of clothing you take off."

"You suck at gin, so—" She stopped when what he'd said sunk in and he laughed. *"Hey!"*

In the end it wouldn't have mattered if she'd agreed to the stripping or not because he didn't win a game. He didn't care, though. Wren was more competitive than he was, and he got a kick out of watching that victory shimmy, and she was pretty good at trash talking for a woman who didn't watch a lot of sports.

When she got bored with beating him, she got up and carried the paper plates from their pizza to the trash. He watched her go, admiring the way the hem of the sweatshirt flirted with her thighs and wished like hell she'd drop something and have to bend over to pick it up.

But she didn't, and then she started puttering around the kitchen. He couldn't let her do that alone, so he pushed back from the table and walked over to her. His intention had been to stop her from trying to wash the few dishes sitting in his sink, but when he got there, he couldn't stop himself from putting his hands on her waist and dropping his mouth to that bare shoulder. He kissed her there, nipping at the skin lightly, as she dropped her head to the side to give him access to her neck.

"I won more games than you tonight," she said in a breathy voice. "You know what that means."

Shannon Stacey 141

"It means I get to take off your clothes now?"

She laughed, and then sucked in a breath when he caught her earlobe between his teeth. "Since I won, that means later you get to strip for me. But that's after the movie."

He groaned and dropped his forehead to her shoulder. "I was hoping you forgot about that."

"It's a comedy, Grant. I don't think anything blows up, but it's not about women traveling to find themselves, either. You can do it." When he started kissing her shoulder again, his hands sliding down to the hem of the sweatshirt, she sidestepped away from him. "And no, we're not watching it naked because I actually want to see the movie."

He poured them fresh drinks while she flipped through the on-screen menu to find the movie he'd agreed to watch. If they'd already decided on gin rummy, he never would have agreed to the wager. If they'd played chess tonight, which *she* sucked at, she'd be baking him snickerdoodles right now.

But once they were settled on the couch, his feet up on the table and Wren snuggled against his side, he had to admit he didn't really care who won what because the real prize was having her with him. It didn't matter if they baked cookies, watched movies with no action or washed the damn floor. Any day she was with him was a good day.

"Did you tell Gavin we're up for going out?" she asked during a lull in the movie.

"Yeah. Cait's going to look at her schedule and then she'll probably get with you and you two can figure it out. She wants it to be a real date night, I guess."

"Good." She smiled up at him. "I like real dates with you."

"We could have gone out tonight if you wanted."

"No, these are my favorite dates with you. But it's nice to go out sometimes."

"These are my favorite dates, too." He slid his hand into her hair and closed his fingers, tilting her head back so he could kiss her.

He was about to haul her into his lap when she pulled her head back. "You're watching this whole movie, Grant."

"If I can stay awake," he muttered, letting go of her hair.

"If I miss any of the movie because I can't hear it over you snoring, I'm leaving you here on the couch."

He laughed, but then she shushed him because apparently the movie had come to a good part. It seemed like it was still a bunch of people just talking, but Wren laughed, so he tried to pay attention.

All he had to do to stay awake was think of all the things he was going to do to her when that sweatshirt finally came off.

Wren didn't mind driving in snow, but she hated freezing rain. Especially the light mist that didn't look like much, but turned the city into a skating rink.

Mrs. Belostotsky had called her shortly before she left the salon to tell her that business would be slow in the bad weather and they didn't want to worry about her being outside or on a bus in the ice.

With unexpected time off that, sadly, didn't coincide with Grant having the day off, she was heading home to relax for a while and maybe surf the job listings online.

Now that Grant was back in her life again and their lives were full of friends, she'd been thinking it might be time to revisit her employment situation. Not only because of the travel annoyances with the market, but because she'd rather work one full-time job with regular hours than two part-time ones that barely added up to enough.

Maybe she'd even get lucky and find a Monday through Friday day job, so she would only have two nights of sleeping alone and an otherwise normal schedule.

You're getting ahead of yourself, she thought. Changing jobs for practical reasons was one thing. But changing jobs to suit a life she wasn't living yet was putting the cart before the horse.

She was almost to the fire station, which she passed on her way home, when a light ahead turned red and the car in front of her started sliding. One second everything was fine, and the next, she was looking at the side of the compact car as it went sideways under a red light and into the intersection.

The impact of the pickup driving into it was so jarring, Wren hit her brake too hard and her car started to slide. She let off, letting it correct itself, and then gently brought it to a stop. Luckily, she didn't get rear-ended and, after turning her four-way flashers on because there was nowhere to pull out of the way, she got out of her car.

Another woman was already running toward the wreck and Wren could hear her yelling into her phone. Since 9-1-1 had already been called, she went to the car, which had been shoved into a pole and was sandwiched between it and the crumpled grille of the pickup.

The driver was awake, his eyes wide as he raised his hand to the gash on his forehead. "What happened?"

"You were in an accident. Are you hurt anywhere else?" Not that she could do anything about it, but maybe if she had answers by the time the ambulance showed up, it would save time if he *was* hurt.

"I don't think so."

Other people were talking to the driver of the pickup, so Wren craned her neck to see into the backseat. It looked as if he was alone in the car, which meant it wasn't as bad as it could have been if there were kids in the backseat.

She heard sirens and looked over the hood of the sedan to watch cars trying to get over enough to let the firetrucks through. She'd been expecting an ambulance, but her heart jumped when she recognized E-59 and L-37 fighting their way to the intersection. It was probably overkill, she thought, but they responded to accidents and they always responded together.

"Help's here," she told the driver. "Just be still and they'll get you out in a few minutes, okay?"

"I should call my wife." He looked around and he seemed a little confused still. "My phone. It was on the passenger seat."

"They'll get it for you." As much as she knew he probably wanted to hear his wife's voice, she wasn't about to go fishing around in broken glass for his cell phone. If he'd been more severely injured, she would, but he was going to be okay.

"Wren!"

She heard Grant shout her name and looked to where the firetrucks had stopped. He was running toward her and she was so afraid he was going to slip on the ice, she gave him a thumbs up, hoping he'd slow down. He didn't stop until he reached her.

"Are you okay?" he asked, grabbing her upper arms and looking her over.

"I wasn't in the accident," she said, left a little breathless by how fierce he looked. "My car was behind his. See?"

He looked over her shoulder and then back at her. "You're not hurt?"

"I only got out to see if he was okay."

She could feel the tension ease in his grip and then he wrapped his arms around her, smothering her with his bunker coat. "Seeing you… I don't know. Even though you were on your feet, it scared me."

She was aware of the other guys moving around the accident scene, checking on the drivers. Another siren in the distance meant the ambulance was on its way, but Grant didn't seem to be in a hurry to let her go.

"She okay?" Wren heard one of the guys ask. She thought it was Chris, though she couldn't see because her face was against Grant's coat.

"Yeah, she's a bystander." He let her go, then, and took a step back.

She was about to speak when he looked at something over her shoulder and his expression changed. Not quite a frown, but more like an instant of intense concentration. "What's the matter?"

"Nothing." He looked back at her and then shook his head. "I don't know. Some guy was looking at me and I feel like I've seen him before, but I can't remember where."

She turned, but there were a lot of people standing around, watching the goings-on. "Where?"

"He walked away. It's probably nothing. I see a lot of people in this job, plus there are always people fascinated by accident scenes. It's a little gruesome, but whatever. You should go sit in your car while we clear the scene. It's freaking cold out here."

She didn't want to. Now that she knew everybody was okay and help had arrived, she was having a bit of a delayed reaction and she wanted to stay with Grant. But he had a job to do, so she nodded and backed away.

The ambulance finally managed to pick its way through the cars and Wren stopped when she realized it was Cait and her partner, Tony. She'd never actually gotten to see Grant or any of their friends in action, and she took the opportunity to watch them.

Cait did a double take when she saw Wren, but she waved to let her friend know she was okay. And then she saw Grant talking to her as the firefighters stood by. They hadn't tried to open the doors or get the driver out, and when she saw Cait putting a collar around the man's neck, Wren realized why.

The police were there, too, and they slowly managed to get cars moving through the intersection, weaving around the accident with some guidance from the officers. After filling out a quick police report, Wren got back in her car and turned off onto a side street when they waved her through, but when she found a parking spot, she took it and walked back to the scene.

They were loading the driver of the car into the back of the ambulance, which she hoped was just precautionary. And the driver of the truck was standing next to his vehicle, his hands waving in the air as he tried to explain to the police officers what had happened.

It looked as if the firefighters were getting ready to

leave, but she spotted Grant. He was standing near the crumpled car, looking at something or somebody in the distance, that same look on his face as before.

She tried to follow his gaze, but he turned and saw her before she could pinpoint where in the crowd of on-lookers he'd been staring.

Smiling, he started toward her, at a walk this time. "You came back?"

"It didn't feel right to just drive off. I felt like I should wave goodbye, at least, but you were busy. Did you see that guy again?"

"I'm not sure. But it doesn't matter. Sometimes people get a little too interested in watching us work and they listen on the scanner and show up where we do. I don't really get it, but there's nothing we can do about it." He tugged at the strings of her hood, drawing the fake fur trim around her face. "Are you warm enough?"

"I'm okay. Are you guys leaving?"

"Yeah, and it won't be long before we get toned out for another MVA. How far away is your car?"

"Just around the corner." She smiled up at him. "Since nobody got badly injured, I guess it's okay to tell you it was really cool getting to see you guys work."

He laughed. "I opened a car door. I don't know about cool."

Grasping the front of his coat, she pulled him closer. "I thought it was sexy."

"Really?" Amusement sparkled in his eyes. "Just me, though, right? None of the other guys were sexy."

"Just you." She tilted her face up for a quick kiss and then let go of his coat. "You should go. And I'm on my way home since they told me not to bother going into the market."

"Stay inside, out of the weather," he said. "And think of me."

"Oh, I'll definitely think of you." She laughed when he made a sexy growling sound and then gave him a little shove. "Go. Do your job."

"I'll call you later."

Once she was back in her car and very carefully finishing her drive home, Wren couldn't help smiling at the memory of him running to her. He'd been scared, which wasn't a good thing, but his need to get to her was going to keep her thinking of him until he called and she could hear his voice again.

Chapter Fourteen

It was almost two weeks before all four schedules aligned and they could finally go on a double date. A nasty stomach bug seemed to being going around the fire department and, though Gavin and Grant avoided getting it, there were a lot of shifts that needed covering.

The guys had floated the idea of just hanging out at Kincaid's Pub for the evening, but Cait had checked the sports schedule and told them there was no chance in hell that was happening.

We're not going to sit and watch you two stare at a hockey game on the screen all night, she'd sent in a group text message. There had been multiple exclamation points and a red frowning face after that.

Kincaid's was *definitely* out.

Cait ended up making them reservations at some trendy new spot, which meant clothes that had to be ironed. Khakis. A shirt with buttons and a collar. Grant grumbled about it for hours, but it was all worth it when he walked into Patty's house to pick up Wren.

She looked gorgeous. A soft blue sweater over slim black pants and black boots that made her legs look incredible. Her hair was gathered up in a bun and she was wearing sparkly blue earrings that matched the sweater.

"You are so beautiful," he whispered as she moved into his arms for a hello kiss.

"Thank you. You're looking pretty good yourself."

The kiss hello turned into a kiss he never wanted to end and if she didn't live with Cait's mom, there was a chance they wouldn't have made it out the door. But Patty's car was in the driveway, and Gavin and Cait would be waiting for them, so he reluctantly let her go.

"I'm just going to say goodnight to Patty and then I'll be ready," she said. Then she handed him the bag she'd had slung over her shoulder. "Can you hold this?"

"It weighs a ton." And now that he thought about it, it wasn't the kind of purse that went with her outfit. It was more like a tote bag.

"It's my overnight bag." She arched her eyebrow. "Okay?"

"Definitely okay." It was so okay, he almost wished they could pile into one vehicle, do a fast-food drive-thru and call it good.

By the time they drove to the address Cait had sent and found a parking space, Gavin and Cait were waiting on the sidewalk out front. They couldn't have been there long, since they weren't shivering yet.

"Wow," Grant said, looking over the fancy front facade. "This looks expensive. What the hell *is* a gastropub, anyway?"

Gavin snorted. "It just means the food costs double and the beer has hints of citrus and bergamot or some shit."

"What is bergamot?"

"It makes the beer cost more."

"Stop it, you two," Cait snapped. "New rule. For

every four nights we hang out at Kincaid's, *we* get one night out at the place of our choosing."

Grant winced. "That could add up to a lot of bergamot."

"Every six times," Gavin countered. "And any times just Grant and/or I are at Kincaid's don't count. Every six times we're there as couples."

"Oh, you're good at this," Grant muttered.

"She's smart. Keeps me on my toes."

"That sounds reasonable," Wren said.

Cait narrowed her eyes. "Fine, but it's dependent on your attitude tonight. If all you guys do is bitch and moan about being here all night, it goes back to four. Or maybe two."

"Done," Gavin and Grant said at the same time.

"And neither of you says bergamot again."

It turned out to be not as bad as Gavin had feared. The beer was good and so was the food. Or maybe it was the company. There was something about the four of them sitting around a table together that felt right. He hadn't gone out with Gavin and Cait as often during the months without Wren because he'd felt her absence so strongly. And he'd never gotten to the point of looking for a woman he might like enough to bring instead.

"So we've got everybody out of the car, but the mom's a hysterical mess and the older kids are trying to calm her down," Gavin was saying.

Grant groaned and grabbed another herbed potato croquette, which he'd been thrilled to discover were simply expensive tater tots. "You're going to tell this story forever, aren't you?"

"Yup. Or at least until you top it." Gavin pulled the appetizer sampler plate out of Grant's reach. "So anyway, LT has to handle some stuff, so he hands the baby to Grant. You should have seen his face."

And then Gavin mimicked holding a baby by the armpits at arm's length, with a look of mock horror on his face. Both women laughed and after a few seconds, Grant reluctantly joined in. Having a screaming baby shoved at him wasn't something he'd trained for.

"So Eriksson yells at him to hold the baby properly and to bounce him to comfort him," Gavin continued. "So Grant's bouncing up and down and the baby stops crying long enough to puke all over the front of his gear."

Wren laughed so hard she had to dab at her eyes with her napkin. "I can so picture that. Was that back when you were a rookie?"

Grant clenched his jaw, so Gavin answered. "It was two months ago."

While they were busy enjoying themselves at his expense, Grant reached across the table and stole the fancy tater tots back.

The entire meal passed too quickly. There were stories and laughter and sports talk. Wren and Cait discovered they'd both recently read and loved the same book, so they talked about that.

It was one of the best nights Gavin could remember having in a long time, and he would have been sad to see it end if not for the fact Wren had packed an overnight bag.

They were parked in opposite directions, so they parted ways outside the restaurant, after agreeing they'd do it again soon. And he really hoped they would, Grant thought as he took Wren's hand in his and walked back to the Jeep.

* * *

"No more, Grant. Just…" Whatever Wren had been about to say didn't get said when Grant clamped his lips over her clit and sucked hard.

He knew what she wanted. But he wasn't going to give it to her until he was good and ready. He'd suffered through overpriced beer and tater tots while thinking about that overnight bag all evening, so she could suffer through one more orgasm before she got his dick.

He had her on her knees at the edge of his bed so he could stand behind her and enjoy the view while he got his fill of her. She'd started on her hands and knees, but after the first orgasm, she'd dropped her head to the mattress and she'd damn near ripped the sheet off the bed with her fists.

When she finally came again, it was with a growl that sounded a lot like a mixture of pleasure and frustration, and it made him even harder. Impatient-to-be-fucked Wren was one of his favorite versions of her.

Before she could catch her breath and start calling him names, he rolled on a condom and pulled her back so she had one knee still on the bed and one foot on the floor.

He slid into her with a groan he felt to his toes. She was hot and slick and he didn't torment either of them anymore. He drove into her with enough force so she had to bend and brace her hands on the bed to keep from falling.

"Yes," she said, the word little more than a breath.

Every thrust was hard and deep, and watching her fingers curl in the sheets was almost enough to send him over the edge. He reached around and stroked her clit, and then chuckled when she slapped his hand away.

Since that was too much, he slid his hand up her stomach, pressing hard enough to force her upright. Bending his knees a little, he pulled her back against his chest and rolled her nipple between this thumb and finger. Then he ran his hand up her neck and cradled her jaw in his hand. He tipped her head sideways and bit the soft skin of her neck. Not hard enough to leave a mark, but enough to make her gasp a little.

The sound did him in. Releasing her jaw, he pushed her back over the bed so he could grab hold of her hips. She came almost immediately, with a harsh cry as her body pulsed. He kept thrusting, faster, until he came so hard he thought his dick might explode.

"Holy shit," he breathed as he pressed his cheek to her back and tried not to pant. His knees were weak and he wasn't sure he could get them both on the bed without falling on the floor, so he grasped the condom and slid free.

Wren crawled across the middle of the mattress before she collapsed, and after wrapping the condom in a tissue and dropping it in the basket under the night table, he was able to crawl up beside her.

"Holy shit, indeed," she whispered. "I think I'm going to drag you to gastropubs more often."

His laugh was ragged and still a little breathless, and he kissed her shoulder. "We're sideways on the bed. And you pulled the top corner of the fitted sheet off the mattress."

"Don't care."

He slapped her ass and she yelped. "We can't sleep like this."

"I can."

"My feet are hanging off the side of the bed."

She shrugged, though some of the effect was lost because she was lying on her face. "There are times it's good to be short. This is one of them, I guess."

Once her breathing started to slow and he realized she really didn't care that she was sideways on a partially unmade bed, Grant forced himself to get up and walk around to the other side.

She groaned when he yanked on the sheet because the jerking kept her from sleeping, but he was able to hook the elastic corner back over the mattress. Then he picked her up and turned her the right way. It wasn't graceful, but he got her head on her pillow and was able to stretch out next to her.

"I was almost asleep," she said. "Now I'm awake again."

"I've been thinking about something."

She screwed her eyes shut and did a horrible version of a fake snore.

"Very funny. I'm serious."

Sighing, she opened her eyes again. "Okay. What have you been thinking about?"

"Let's go to New Hampshire for a couple of days. Visit my parents. Get away for a bit."

She lifted herself onto her elbow so she could look down at his face. "Really? You were thinking about your parents?"

"Well, not just *now*. Before. My mom's been after me to visit and if you go with me, you can relax. Like *totally* relax, you know?" He didn't spell it out for her because he didn't think he had to. There was nothing— or more importantly *nobody*—to fear in his home state.

"When would you want to go? And for how long?"

"I get that you don't want to miss a lot of work right

now, so what if we went up Saturday morning and came back Sunday night?" Long enough for a nice visit with his parents, but not so long it would drag on for Wren if she wasn't totally comfortable.

He knew his parents would make her welcome, no matter what their thoughts on the relationship were, but Wren was sensitive and she might pick up on any weird vibes his mom was putting out.

"I guess that means you've told your parents about me?"

"Of course." She didn't say anything, but he didn't need a psychic to tell him what she was waiting for. "They just want me to be happy. I promise my mom won't put anything awful in your food."

"Don't you need to sleep Saturday morning?"

He couldn't tell if she was concerned about that or just flailing for reasons not to go at all. "I've always gotta play that part by ear. I'll probably be fine to go, but if it's a busy night, I might need a quick nap before we head out. It's only an hour and a half of driving."

"If you're sure they won't mind me coming with you."

"They won't mind." He chuckled. "I should tell you up front you'll be sleeping in the guest room, though. And not the same guest room I'll be sleeping in. Not that they're really old-fashioned, but…uh, it's just a thing."

Wren laughed and slapped her hand on his chest. "There's a story there. I want to hear it."

"Nope." When she pinched his nipple, he yelped and grabbed her wrist. "Ow!"

"Tell me or I'll start twisting."

"You're so mean." She also had a painful pinching grip for somebody with such small hands. "Fine. The first time I went home, I brought a girlfriend with me and we crashed in my room because my parents didn't care. But, in the heat of the moment, I said something and I said it too loud, so my mom heard. She yelled 'Grant, that's disgusting' and woke everybody up. Breakfast was awkward as hell, believe me."

At least laughing at him made Wren let go of his nipple. "What did you say?"

"Honestly, I don't even remember. I swear."

"And now your girlfriends have to sleep in the guest room forever?"

"Yeah. Not that it would matter. I haven't been able to get an erection in that house since."

"Is that a challenge?"

"No." He rolled her onto her back, ready to go again. "I get plenty of erections in my own damn house, thanks to you."

Grant wanted to take her home to his parents.

The anxiety helped keep her warm while she worked in the milk cooler, checking expiration dates and re-stocking. They were going through half and half a little faster than usual, so their customers must be hitting the coffee and hot chocolate hard in the cold weather.

Going to New Hampshire with him felt like a big step. She'd met his family, of course, but this would be her first time staying in their home. Perhaps it was weird to think that was some kind of a milestone in a relationship, but she couldn't help it.

"Wren, you are going to freeze in there." Mr. Belostotsky had opened the cooler door from the store side and was peering at her through a gap in the milk jugs.

"I think it's warmer in here than it is outside."

"True. But Mother is worried about you being in there so long."

They were so sweet. "I'll be right out."

Now that they'd brought it up, she did feel chilled and her fingers were definitely cold. Luckily, the cold didn't make her cough anymore, but that didn't mean she should linger in it. She finished up in the cooler as quickly as possible, and then stepped out into the warm storage room. After making sure the big metal door was secure, she added a sticky note about the half and half to the ordering sheet.

"Oh good, you're done in there." Now it was Mrs. Belostotsky checking on her.

They never slowed down and she saw no signs they really wanted to. Wren was convinced they hadn't *needed* to hire any help. They just missed their grown children and wanted somebody around to fuss over. And she didn't mind it at all.

"We don't want you getting pneumonia before you go away with your young man, do we?"

Wren was fairly sure you couldn't get pneumonia from being in a walk-in cooler, but she appreciated the sentiment. "No, we don't."

When she'd asked them about having both Saturday and Sunday off, she'd been racked with guilt. They'd been so generous after the fire and there was the Sunday cleaning to do. But when she told them *why*, they'd been so excited for her, she might have felt guilty if she didn't go.

They left the storage room together, Mrs. Belostotsky telling the story of the time they'd taken their young kids on a drive up through New Hampshire to see the

White Mountains during foliage season. They were hoping to do it again soon, with their grandchildren.

It was almost closing time, so Wren started running through her mental checklist of things to do while Mr. Belostotsky went through the process of closing out the register for the day.

The bell over the door rang and Wren looked over from the coffee machine she was prepping for the morning brew. Hot coffee and fresh baked goods were one of the ways they rewarded their loyal customers.

Grant stepped through the door, his hair and shoulders coated with a light dusting of fresh snow. He smiled when he saw her, but he didn't approach her until she smiled back and waved him over.

"We'll be closing in a few minutes," Mr. Belostotsky said.

"He's with me," Wren said.

"I was in the neighborhood and thought I'd see if Wren would like a ride home," Grant said.

Mrs. Belostotsky popped out from the back room, where she'd probably been keeping an eye on the security camera screen. She hated when her dearest was doing the register at the end of the day because it made her feel vulnerable. They'd been robbed seven times over the decades and they'd never been hurt, but she never stopped worrying. "Is this your young man?"

"Yes, this is Grant." She introduced them and wasn't surprised they instantly seemed to adore him.

It only took her a few minutes to finish up and Mrs. Belostotsky practically shooed them out the door. "Go! Have fun with your young man."

"I should warn you, it's a bit of a walk to the Jeep," he said once they were outside. "Especially in this weather."

The wind was biting, so they walked quickly and didn't bother talking. It wasn't as bad as he'd made it sound, though, and within a few minutes, they were inside and soaking up the heat from the vents.

"What did you just happen to be doing in the neighborhood?" she asked once they were on the road.

He gave her a sheepish smile. "I was in the neighborhood to see if I could give you a ride home."

"You have to work tomorrow."

"Yeah, so I'm going to have to *actually* take you home, which is kind of a bummer." He squeezed her hand. "But I get to see you before I go to bed, so it's worth it. I hope you're not upset I showed up at your work, though."

She turned to look at him. "Why would I be upset?"

"I don't know. You're a pretty private person. I don't know if you tell people anything about your personal life." He chuckled. "If you hadn't looked happy to see me, I was going to buy a candy bar and leave."

It hurt that he thought she wouldn't be happy to see him, to the point he had an exit plan if she turned away. Had she been *that* closed off before? "I'm not holding back this time. Or hiding anything. I told you that."

When he stopped the Jeep and took it out of gear, she realized he'd driven to some kind of park. It was dark and cold, so they were alone.

"You don't think I'm going to have sex with you in this Jeep, do you?"

He laughed. "I don't think either of us are that flexible, though it might be fun to try sometime. Maybe with the top off when it's not twenty degrees." His thumb drew circles on her hand. "I just thought we could talk for a few minutes and it's quiet here."

"Okay." He sounded more serious now, which made her nervous.

"I figured I should ask you about New Hampshire again now that you've had a little time—*not* naked in my bed—to think about it. I don't know if it'll be hard for you."

"You promised me your mom wouldn't put anything in my food. I'm going to hold you to that."

He chuckled. "I'm not worried about you and my parents together. But it occurred to me if I was estranged from my family, it might be painful being around somebody else's."

"I've met your family, Grant. Several times."

"Good point. I guess the situation hasn't really changed, other than I know about it now." He sighed. "I don't want to push you, that's all."

"Not having a relationship with Alex anymore is painful. I'm not going to lie. But I'm not going to keep that from letting other people in anymore. Like Patty. Did you know she calls Cait and I *you girls*? It's so cute."

"Do you think he'll ever get over it? Alex, I mean."

"As in forgiving me? I…don't know. Part of me hopes he will because he's my brother. He's pretty much all the family I have. But another part of me wonders if our relationship would ever be worth the effort again."

"He *is* your brother."

"And what does that mean, really? When you say the firefighters you work with are like your brothers, that means you trust them to have your back. No matter what, you can trust them to be there for you. In my case, it's just a word that signifies we have the same biological parents."

"Are you okay with that?"

She shrugged one shoulder. "I don't really have a choice, since he won't talk to me."

"But if it *was* your choice?"

She didn't want to talk about Alex anymore. Talking about Alex made her think about Ben, and she definitely didn't want him in her head. He'd robbed her of enough time with Grant.

"Would you go back to Virginia?" he prodded when she didn't answer.

"No." That much, at least, she knew in her heart. She was never going to live in Virginia again. And it wasn't just because of Grant, though he was certainly a huge factor. She liked Boston. It was even starting to feel like home, though it would take years to explore all of it. "I chose Boston and it was one of the best decisions I've made in my life. I don't see myself leaving, whether Alex ever decides to talk to me again or not."

"I'm glad you want to stay," he said, squeezing her hand. "I want you to stay, too."

Chapter Fifteen

Right after they opened the doors wasn't a busy time for Kincaid's Pub, so Wren was able to get a table easily. She picked one close enough to the bar so Lydia would be able to stop by and chat easily, but not so close that Tommy and Fitz would be able to hear that chatting from their corner.

Cait showed up a few minutes later, slightly out of breath from a brisk walk in the cold air. "I had to park down the street because I have Gavin's truck while my car's in the shop and I need two spaces in a row to parallel park. I swear that thing is huge."

"You sound like a woman who deserves a drink," Lydia said, dropping a couple of menus on the table.

"You know, I think I'll have a glass of wine with my lunch," Cait said. "Do you drink red or white with cheeseburgers?"

"Let's play it safe and get a rosé," Wren suggested. She wasn't a huge fan of wine, but she didn't want one of Lydia's cocktails in the middle of the day and she didn't care for beer. Soda was an option, but what kind of friend would let Cait day drink alone?

When she'd gotten the text message from Cait suggesting lunch, she'd jumped at the chance. She didn't need to be at the market until four tonight, since she'd be staying a little later than usual to help polish the floors, so she had time.

Lydia brought their wine and took their orders, but other customers were filtering in, so she couldn't hang around.

"What's going on in your life?" Cait asked. "Anything new and interesting?"

"Did you hear Grant's taking me home to his parents for the weekend?"

She grinned. "I didn't hear that. Are you excited about it?"

"I'm not sure excited is the word I'd use. I'm happy that he wants me to go with him. But I don't know if his parents—especially his mom—will be quite so happy about it."

"I'm sure you've heard this before, but you worry too much. They liked you before and they'll still like you." She held up her hand. "And yes, there was that one time you broke their son's heart, but if he can forgive you, so can they. And, I mean, look at us. We're practically his family, too, and we're all glad to have you back. They will be, too."

Wren wished she could be as sure of that as Cait sounded. "I'll let you know how it goes. Possibly over a stronger drink than wine."

"Oh, we are so getting together after. We should do this more often. Every week might be hard to manage because neither of us have super set schedules, but every other week is doable."

"Definitely." Wren grabbed the edge of the table so she could shift her chair, but the twinge in her elbow made her wince. The chair could stay where it was.

"What's wrong with your arm?"

"Nothing." It wasn't a big deal, but Cait just gave her a hard look, eyebrow arched. "Wow, you take that whole EMT thing pretty seriously. I bet most people do what you tell them."

"Actually, you'd be surprised how many patients refuse to listen or even let us look at them. But you're easy. What happened to your arm?"

Lydia was on her way past with a basket of nachos, but she paused when she heard Cait's question. "I want to hear this. Talk fast."

"I'm not telling you."

"Oh, then I definitely want to hear it. But hold on. Don't tell until I get back." Lydia delivered the appetizer and took the table's lunch order in record time, and then she was back. "Okay, spill it."

"You know you're going to tell us," Cait said. "The longer you resist, the more awkward it feels, so just spill the details."

"Fine." Wren frowned and rubbed the sore spot. "Last night, Grant picked me up at work because he wanted to talk to me about going to New Hampshire this weekend and—"

Lydia held up her hand. "Wait, you're going home to the parents this weekend?"

"Yeah."

"That's a pretty big deal."

"I feel like the elbow story is a bigger deal," Cait said.

"Lydia!" Tommy's bellow echoed through the bar. People didn't go to Kincaid's looking for a quiet atmosphere.

"Just a second," his daughter bellowed back. "Okay, fine. Skip the parents and get to the elbow."

"He had to work this morning, so we were just going for a drive and—"

"Lydia, dammit!"

"Hold on!" She gave Wren a look.

"We had sex in his Jeep and my elbow is not only sore, but slightly Jeep-seat burned."

Both women laughed, and Lydia was still laughing when her father yelled a third time and she walked away.

"How on earth did you have sex in a Wrangler in the winter, with the top on?" Cait took a sip of her wine. "You know, I can't decide if that's a rhetorical question or not. On the one hand, I really don't need the finer details of Grant's sex life in my head, but on the other, I really want to know how it's physically possible."

"I can tell you it is physically possible, but it's a little uncomfortable and can lead to having to tell your friends how you got embarrassing injuries."

"Oh, speaking of sex." Cait pulled a paperback book out of the bag she'd slung over the back of the chair. "You need to read this one."

"I don't know anything about football."

"Look at the guy on the cover, Wren. The book lives up to that cover and, trust me, you don't need to know anything about football. Just read it."

"I definitely will." She slid the book to the side of the table, where it would be safe from the drinks. "As soon as I'm done with the one I'm reading."

"Not still the horror novel?"

"Yes. It's good, but it scares the crap out of me, so I can only read a little bit at a time."

Horror was where their reading tastes diverged. Cait had told her she used to read them, but nowadays she preferred books with happy endings. "Do yourself a favor and read this one in between scaring the crap out of yourself. I mean, there's no Jeep-seat burn or anything, but it's still pretty sexy."

Wren laughed. "Now I know how Grant is feeling when he says 'you're going to tell that story forever, aren't you' to Gavin."

"That's what friends are for."

When Lydia brought their meals, she had a few minutes to sit. She stole French fries from Wren's popcorn chicken platter and Cait's pickles while they talked about a movie they all wanted to see that was releasing the next month.

"Aidan said he'd go see it with me if I really wanted him to, but he sounded less excited than the time he told me he might need a root canal." Lydia shrugged. "I'd rather go with you guys."

Cait nodded. "What do you think the chances are of all of us going together?"

"Pretty slim," Lydia said. "We should get Olivia on board. If anybody can plan a trip to the movies with a bunch of women with crazy schedules, it's her."

"Lydia, am I paying you to sit on your ass and visit with your friends?"

She looked over at her dad. "Since I'm on the clock right now, yes. You are, in fact, paying me to sit on my ass and visit with my friends."

"You're even more of a smart-ass than your brother. This is why Ashley's my favorite, you know."

She just waved a hand in his direction and stole another fry. "I'll text Olivia and get her on this. We'll probably all have a detailed itinerary, complete with a list of the candy offerings the theater has, by the end of the week."

"I'm so glad Derek found her," Cait said. "Those kinds of logistics make my head hurt but she thrives on this stuff."

"So, Lydia, have you started thinking of baby names yet?"

When she groaned, Wren realized she'd managed to step on a possibly sore subject. "Apparently, my dad was a little disappointed his first grandchild was not named after him. Jackson *Kincaid* Walsh was not enough. So now, my brother and I are both on the hook. There are expectations, Wren."

"Maybe you'll have a girl," Cait said.

Lydia gave her a flat look. "He said, and I quote, 'Thomasina's a great name for a girl,' and I'm not even lying. He said we could call her Tommy even though she's a girl."

"Okay, that's…" Wren stopped talking because she didn't know what to say.

"Thomasina Joyce Hunt," Lydia said. "Joyce was my mom's name."

"Or Joyce Thomasina Hunt," Cait threw in.

"Oh, no. You've met him. He wants a Tommy."

"Jamie's due first," Wren pointed out. "Maybe she'll give him a namesake and you'll be off the hook."

"She said she'd cross her legs and hold her baby in because she doesn't want to deal with this."

Cait snorted. "As somebody who's delivered babies in surprising places, I can tell you that, from a medical standpoint, that's an empty threat. What does Aidan say? I mean, it's his baby, too."

Lydia rolled her eyes. "You know he adores my dad.

And he's also had some practice navigating the Kincaid family, so his response? Whatever makes me happy."

"That's sweet," Wren said.

"No, that's taking himself out of the line of fire." She sighed and took another fry. "Scott said maybe one of us should get a dog named Tommy because nobody can realistically expect you to name your child the same name as your dog."

"I've gotten to know your family a little," Wren said. "And, honestly, that's probably your best move."

They were all laughing when movement in the corner of Wren's eye caught her attention, and she turned her head in time to see a fellow diner stand too fast and bump her table. The empty glass fell off the edge and smashed onto the floor.

Immediately, Lydia was on her feet, making sure the woman hadn't cut herself. Then she put her hands on her hips. "You have to kiss Bobby Orr."

The woman must not have been a regular customer because she looked confused. "I have to what?"

"See that signed picture of Bobby Orr on the wall? When you break a glass, you have to kiss the picture or really bad things happen." Wren smiled when the woman's eyes widened. But Lydia only nodded. "I'm serious. Just kiss your fingertips and press them to the glass. It counts and, trust me, you don't actually want your mouth on that."

Once the ritual had been completed, everybody went back to what they were doing, and Lydia went back to work behind the bar.

"I love this place," Wren said.

"I do, too," Cait agreed. "But sometimes I wonder

what it must look like to people who just wander in here randomly, looking for a beer or a meal."

"There are probably people who only come here once." Wren shrugged. "Those aren't our people."

Cait laughed. "No, they're not."

These were Wren's people, she thought. Cait and Lydia and all the rest of them. Grant wasn't the only person she'd missed while she was gone, though she'd certainly missed him the most. And she recognized how blessed she was to have them let her back in.

"I'm going to hate myself," Cait said. "But you have to give me a *few* details of the Wrangler sex because I just can't picture it."

Wren laughed. "I'm not sure I want you picturing it."

"Not you two specifically. That would be weird. But in a general sense, considering he's fairly tall, I'm not grasping the physics of it. So spill." She paused with her wineglass halfway to her mouth. "But in very broad terms, of course. Obviously it involved your elbow and the seat fabric."

"I'm not drawing it on a napkin. Just so you know."

"Oh, it's *that* complicated?" Cait grinned. "I might need another glass of wine."

"The women are up to something again," Derek said, holding up his phone as if they could read the screen he was waving around. "Olivia needs me to reschedule a thing because there's apparently one night, and one night only, next month when all the women are available at the same time."

Grant raised his hands, palms out. "I don't even want to know. And I definitely don't want to know where they'll be."

"You say that now." Gavin rolled his eyes. "I'm just telling you now that I'm forbidden from using Cait's phone location to help any idiots—meaning you—crash girls' nights out in the future, so you'll have to find them on your own."

"You stopped being funny a long time ago, Gav." Grant turned his attention back to the television, though he was dying to know what the women were planning. If he kept his mouth shut, he knew he'd find out, though. The other guys would find out and talk about it. He just didn't want to be the one who asked.

"You're in a mood tonight," Chris said. "Wren shut you off?"

"Don't worry about me and Wren. We're good. I'm in a mood because there's nothing going on and the checklists are all done and there's nothing to do but sit and listen to you guys talk about nothing."

Wren *hadn't* shut him off, but he also hadn't seen her since the night they'd gotten busy in his Jeep after they'd decided that wasn't something they should try. They not only tried, but they succeeded. Her elbow got a little beat up and they snapped off the passenger-side visor, but they'd both agreed it was worth it.

He'd had to work the next day, and then she'd been the one who was busy. She had lunch with Cait on Wednesday, but then she was either at the salon, the market or sleeping after that. And she wasn't sleeping in his bed, where he could at least hold her while she slept.

But tomorrow morning he was going to pick her up and they'd head north. He'd have her mostly to himself for two days. No wise-cracking best friends. No bosses. No ex-boyfriends to worry about.

Just the two of them. And his parents, of course.

She still wouldn't be sleeping in his bed, but she'd be under the same roof, at least. In his childhood home, which wasn't just the place he'd grown up, but was the place that first popped into his head when he heard the word *home*. Hopefully that would change someday and wherever Wren was would be his true home.

"I think I'm going to hit the racks," he said, sick of the banter going on around him. "We're heading for New Hampshire tomorrow and I'm hoping we have a quiet night so we can leave first thing in the morning."

He shouldn't have said it out loud, he thought later, when the tone sounded in the wee hours and they all stumbled out of their bunks and into their gear.

They were the first on scene and it was a mess. Not only was there a house on fire, but a police officer was doing his best to separate two men who seemed intent on beating the crap out of each other on the sidewalk. One of the guys was in the kind of button-down pajamas Grant thought only catalog models wore and the other just had boxers on, so there was some serious dedication to hurting each other, considering the low temps.

"You just throw your damn cigarettes off your deck and you don't even look," pajama guy was yelling.

"Close your fucking recycling lid and they'll bounce off," boxer dude shouted back, and he didn't sound sober.

"Enough," Rick Gullotti shouted as he got out of the truck. "You two morons cut the shit and get out of our way or I'll hose you both down."

That got their attention long enough for a second police officer to join in the fun. Each officer took a combatant and went in opposite directions and the crews got to work.

The melted plastic that had presumably been the recycling bin in question had been against the ancient wood and ragged shingles of the garage wall. The garage was fully involved, but the guys hustled, wanting to keep it from destroying the house it was attached to.

The wind was picking up, too, so they also had to make sure the fire didn't spread to the other buildings packed together in the dense neighborhood, including the house the cigarette had come from.

It was grueling work, but they kept pushing and managed to get it under control. The occupants of the house would need a place to stay for a while, but it wasn't a total loss.

They were knocking down the last of it when a gas tank or something exploded and at the edge of what peripheral vision the SCBA mask allowed him, Grant saw a body get thrown backward. He'd ducked away from the blast, so it took him a few seconds to scramble to his feet, yelling into the radio.

It was Danny and for a moment Grant's fear was so strong he could taste it, like a metallic tang in his mouth. When Danny started pushing himself to his feet, Grant grabbed him by the coat and half dragged him toward the door. Scott appeared next to him, so they were able to get him out of the way as the other guys tried to deal with the aftermath.

"I can walk," Danny yelled as they crossed the yard, his feet sliding as he tried to dig his boots into the icy crust that was all that was left of the snow in the yard. "Dammit. Stop, right now."

They stopped. Finally able to get his feet under him,

Danny stood, though neither Grant nor Scott let go of his coat. He was weaving some, as if he'd had too much to drink, and Grant wasn't taking the chance he'd fall on his face.

With their LT down, Engine 59's crew pulled out and another crew went in. An ambulance was on standby, but Danny seemed to be okay by the time they got him to it. A little unsteady, but okay.

"It just knocked the wind out of me," Danny said. "I'm fine."

"Then it won't take long to check you out," the EMT said firmly.

Even before Gavin had hooked up with Cait, Grant knew there was no point in arguing with Boston EMS. The guy made quick work of it, though, and decided there was no reason for Danny to take a trip to the hospital.

"You just had the wind knocked out of you, like you said. Even though you didn't lose consciousness, you're not going back in, though. You're a spectator now."

They were all spectators while other crews finally knocked the fire down completely. Then they helped out with the overhaul until they were free to pack it up and head back to the station.

"You had to jinx it," Aidan said to Grant on the way back. "Saying out loud you hope it's quiet because you have plans is a sure way to end up in a shit show in the middle of the night."

"No shit." He leaned his head back, wondering if there would be any time at all for a power nap by the time they'd wrapped up things in the engine bays and cleaned up. Even if he didn't take a shower now, it probably wouldn't be worth hitting his bunk. He'd have to go home and sleep for at least a few hours, and *then* he could finally get Wren and get the hell out of the city for the weekend.

Chapter Sixteen

When they crossed the border into New Hampshire, Wren felt the anxiety creeping in. And when Grant pulled the Jeep off the highway and onto winding, tree-lined roads, the nerves had her shifting in her seat.

"Do you have to pee again?"

She gave him some serious side-eye. "No, I do not."

"You're squirming like a toddler over there and you drank all my soda. There's a gas station about a mile up, so I figured I'd ask."

"I didn't drink *all* your soda. I only had a little."

"But it was the last of it, so technically you drank it all."

"I had no idea car trips with you would be so much fun."

He laughed. "I'm not the one who has to pee every ten miles."

"You're exaggerating. And I'm nervous. When I'm nervous, I need things to do, but I'm trapped in the car, so I drank my soda. And some of your soda." She frowned. "The sugar didn't help the nerves."

"We're supposed to be coming here to relax. What are you nervous about?"

"This is going to be weird."

"Why? You've met my family a couple of times."

"But not like this."

His parents had driven down to Boston one day and they'd all had dinner together, about the time Wren had admitted to herself trying to keep a wall around herself hadn't worked and she was in love with Grant. Several times after that, they'd met his parents—along with Grant's brother, sister-in-law and their daughter—halfway between at different restaurants to visit for a couple of hours.

"What, because you haven't been to the house?"

She sighed, looking out her window at the passing scenery. "No. It doesn't matter where we see them. No matter what you say, your mother's not going to forgive me for what I did. And you won't know if she puts anything in my food unless you spend the whole time in the kitchen."

"Wait. You don't *actually* think my mom would do that, right? Like poison your food or make you sick or something?"

She laughed. "No. I'm aware it's just a funny way of saying she won't want me there, but will tolerate my presence for your sake."

"Okay, just checking."

"And we're already running late." She glanced at the clock again, and they were tipping past early afternoon.

"That's not your fault." He lifted a hand in a *what are you gonna do* gesture. "That would be the guy who decided to toss his cigarette butt off his deck into his neighbor's recycling at two in the morning."

"Maybe you *should* stop at that gas station."

"I already planned on it."

When they stopped, Wren took her time in the restroom while Grant topped off the Jeep's gas tank. After splashing cold water on her face, she tried to smooth down her hair. It was nerves, she knew. She'd looked absolutely fine when she glanced in the mirror before they left and all she'd done was sit in the Jeep. There was no way she looked as frumpy as her brain told her she did right now.

Just nerves. The only thing she could do was have faith in Grant. If his mother wasn't ready to accept Wren back in her son's life, he wouldn't bring her home with him.

Her stomach still got jumpy when he pulled off a back road onto a smaller back road, though. It was beautiful, with ice sparkling in the trees that separated the road from snow-blanketed fields, and Grant reached over and squeezed her thigh.

"I know you can't possibly have to pee again already," he said, "so you're worrying over there. Stop. It's going to be fine."

Even though it felt as if it was about ten degrees, not counting the breeze, Don and Jill Cutter were standing on the front porch of the big, white New Englander-style house when Grant killed the Jeep's engine.

"You ready?"

She gave him a nervous smile. "If I say no, what happens? Do we just sit in the Jeep for a while?"

"We can, but I'm not starting the engine again so you'll get cold pretty quick." He leaned across the center console and gave her a quick kiss, and it did help calm her a little. "Let's go inside where it's warm. And there's food."

He got out before she could respond and walked

around to open her door. The cold was more intense here and Grant was right. It certainly got her moving.

"It's good to see you again," Don said, holding out his hand as they reached the top step of the porch. She shook it while Grant hugged his mother.

"Wren." After looking at her for a long moment, Jill stepped forward and opened her arms. "I'm so glad you could come."

It wasn't the warmest hug she'd ever received, but it wasn't a stiff formality, either. No doubt it would be a while before they forgave her for what she'd done to their son, but she was welcome here, nonetheless.

"Let's get out of the cold," Don said, ushering them all into the house.

With Grant's hand at the small of her back, she got a brief tour of the downstairs. It was decorated in a classy, neutral style that was homey and welcoming, but not cluttered. It reminded her a lot of Grant's apartment, just more spacious.

She couldn't help pausing to look more closely at a grouping of family photos. There were several of Grant and his brother—they looked so much alike, and were both younger versions of their dad—at various ages. A few family photos, including a trip to Disney when the boys were young. And there was an old black-and-white photo of a woman posed with a man decked out in firefighting gear.

"My grandmother was a red phone operator," Don explained when she leaned in to see it better.

"Like a dispatcher?"

"Kind of. Before the town had a dispatch system, there was a group of women who answered emergency calls and then had to notify all the firefighters when there was a fire. I'm pretty sure it was my mom's stories about her that first made Grant want to be a firefighter."

"She did it just to spite me," Jill said. "That woman never did like me."

Wren was startled, but when Grant and his dad laughed and she saw Jill's smile, she realized this must be an old family joke.

"Mom would prefer I work as a test dummy in a bubble wrap factory," Grant said, and his mom rolled her eyes, but didn't deny it.

"I need to finish getting dinner ready," Jill said. "Why don't you take Wren and your bags upstairs and show her where she'll be staying. I made up the guest room for her."

Wren had to stifle a giggle as she followed Grant up the stairs. "I really wish you could remember what you said that night."

Grant showed Wren to the guest room, which was at the opposite end of the second floor from his room. Or rather, the room that *had* been his and was now the guest room that didn't have its own half bath. And they said chivalry was dead.

"So this is it," he said. He wasn't sure what else to say, since it was a bedroom. Double bed. Dresser. Nightstand. Quilt. It was pretty self-explanatory. "The bathroom's that door, and that one's the closet."

"I'm glad you told me which is which," she teased.

"Okay, I'm a little nervous," he confessed. "It's important to me that you're comfortable here."

"Relax." She wrapped her arms around his waist and pulled him close. "I think you're more wound up than I am right now."

"This helps." He kissed her, running his hands down her back to the curve of her ass.

She nipped at his bottom lip. "None of that. You know the rules."

"You're, uh…curing that problem I had, so we need to get back downstairs before I get in trouble."

"That wasn't much of a challenge." She laughed and let him go. "You go ahead. I'm going to use the bathroom and freshen up, and I'll be down in a few minutes."

Grant forced himself to walk out of the room because rising to the challenge didn't mean he was going to get busy with Wren under his mother's roof. He'd take the humiliation of that night to his grave.

He found his mom in the kitchen and a quick scan of the prep she was doing made him a very happy man. "Pork roast?"

"I haven't made it in a while, and you coming home seems like a good excuse for it. Where's Wren?"

"Freshening up. She'll be down in a few minutes."

She looked him over with her supermom emotional X-ray vision. "You look happier."

He tried not to read too much into the *happier* instead of just *happy.* "I am."

"I've been worried about you."

"You don't need to be." Not that she would stop. Grant could barely pick up a fork without his mom worrying he was going to hurt himself with it. She'd cried herself to sleep the night he told her he was going to be a firefighter.

"Don't you tell me I don't need to worry," she said in her sternest mom voice, punctuating her words by pointing the spatula at him. "I'm going to ask you a question and I know you might not answer it, but I'm going to ask it anyway."

This wasn't going to be good. "Go ahead and ask."

"Wren lost everything at the same time she crossed paths with you again, and I just…" She trailed off, frowning. "I'm not sure how to frame the question."

"Mom." She didn't have to. "The morning after the fire, I bought her breakfast. I took her shopping for a few essentials, and she paid for what she bought. She even insists on paying rent to Patty even though Patty fought her on it."

"I'm not trying to insult her, honey. But I worry about you."

"I know that." And he appreciated it. "Did she know I would take care of her if she needed it? Yes. But she didn't ask me to. She didn't expect it."

His mom nodded. "Good. Then I'll lay that concern to rest."

It was good timing, too, since he heard Wren's footsteps descending the wooden stairs and called out to her. "We're in the kitchen."

"That smells amazing," Wren said as she walked in, pointedly not looking at him.

He really hoped she didn't start laughing at him and force him to explain to his mother why she was so amused.

But she didn't. "What can I do to help?"

His mom looked around. "I'm finishing up the gravy, so if you want to mash those potatoes, we can eat soon. Grant, go visit with your father."

Dismissed, he gave Wren a reassuring smile and then went in search of his dad. He wasn't hard to find.

Every evening, before dinner, his father sat on the

front porch for a few minutes. It didn't matter that it was winter. It was a habit he'd had for as long as Grant could remember. He claimed it let him clear his head and put the work day behind him so he could enjoy dinner and the evening with his family.

But even though it was *his* time, he'd never minded if one or both of his sons joined him, so Grant sat in one of the wooden chairs and leaned his head back.

It was pretty, he thought, despite the low temperature. The lights from the house reflected on the snow and the trees that separated the property from the road were dusted with fresh powder. It was quiet and peaceful.

This had been the dream. All those times he'd mentally rehearsed asking Wren to be his wife, this was the dream he'd been asking her to share with him.

A house with a porch for sitting together at the end of a long day. If he stayed with Boston Fire and they had made their life there, the view would have been different, but there would still have been a porch swing and holding hands. Family. Friends. Food. Laughter.

"I guess your mother's probably fussed over you," his dad said after a few minutes.

"Yeah. She threatened me with the spatula when I told her not to worry about me."

"You should have seen her after you said you were bringing that woman home with you."

"That woman. Is that what Mom calls her?"

"When she's feeling generous." He turned his head so they could share a *you know how she gets* look. "She told me Wren's story. Sounds like she could have saved you both some heartache if she'd just told you what was going on."

Even though he'd obviously thought that himself, he was compelled to defend Wren. "She admits she reacted out of fear and didn't think it through."

"You're saying her instinct told her to run."

Grant's entire life, people had told him he was just like his dad and he was pretty damn proud of that. But it also meant they shared a similar thought process and he didn't like having his own thoughts said out loud to him. "I guess so."

"Even though she knew you loved her."

"Yeah, I thought I loved her. But I guess I didn't really know her well enough to truly love her, did I?" He shrugged one shoulder, a casual gesture that belied the emotions careening around in his head. "Because she didn't love *me* enough to share her story with me and I thought she did."

His dad made that *mmm...maybe* sound that drove him nuts. "That's how we see it. But I don't know what it feels like to be helpless while a man I'm afraid of beats my brother so badly he has to be hospitalized. I think if I watched that happen, I'd have a whole lot of fear of watching him beat somebody else I loved that badly."

"And her brother told her it was her fault and hasn't spoken to her since."

"Oh, that ain't right. Hard to trust people who say they've got your back once your own family doesn't."

Grant shook his head and sighed, watching his breath form an icy cloud. "I think I would have. But like you said, we don't know what it feels like to be in the situation she was in."

The big door opened, followed by the screen door opening just enough for Wren to see them. "Dinner's ready."

Considering their conversation, Grant was relieved when his dad gave her a warm smile. "We'll be right in. I hope you like roast pork, because my wife's is the best."

"I haven't had her roast pork yet, but I was the gravy taste tester, and it's delicious."

Once Wren had gone back inside and closed the door against the cold, neither of them moved right away.

"You just do what's right for you, son. If you're meant to be together, it'll be what's right for both of you."

Grant chuckled. "That's very cryptic of you."

"You guys didn't come with an instruction book. I have to make this stuff up on the fly."

"You wouldn't have read it, anyway."

"True." His dad stood and stretched his back. "But your mother would have and if I screwed up too badly, she'd slap me upside the head with it."

Grant laughed at the imagery, though his mother had never whacked him with a spatula or—as far as he knew—cuffed his father with a book. But she did like to wave things around when she got heated.

You just do what's right for you, son. If you're meant to be together, it'll be what's right for both of you. Cryptic though it might be, Grant turned his father's advice over in his mind, hoping he was right.

After dinner, they gathered in the family room and the guys put a game on the television, but kept the volume low. The conversation was friendly and there was a lot of laughter thanks to Jill spilling some funny stories from Grant's childhood. They asked Wren about her work and she talked about the salon and the market.

"You know," Jill said after a long pause, "I know I

asked you about your family, but I can't remember what you said. I feel awful."

"Please don't." Wren's cheeks felt hot and she was thankful when Grant reached over and squeezed her hand. "I know Grant told you about my brother and he was all the family I had left, so I probably distracted you somehow and changed the subject before you realized I didn't answer the question. I was good at that, and I'm sorry."

"You don't have to be sorry."

"Well, I am. But my dad left when I was very little and my mother died when I was in high school, so I don't have any family for you guys to meet."

To her credit, Jill didn't overdo the sympathy. She gave Wren a warm smile. "Then I'm very glad you found Grant because lord knows, he comes with a big circle of friends and family. He brought them all up to go four-wheeling one weekend a couple of years back and, I swear, I almost went and stayed at a hotel."

Wren laughed, relieved at the conversational redirection. "When I first met them, I didn't think I'd ever remember all their names. I was tempted to sneak pictures of them and write their names on them."

"You guys should come down and visit again soon," Grant said. "It's been a while."

"Your mother wants to see those big sailing ships when they come in the harbor," Don said. "See if you can find out when they're doing that and we'll figure something out."

That turned the conversation to other things to do while visiting Boston, and Wren and Jill talked about the things they both wanted to see. Neither of the guys had much interest in the museums, so Jill seemed thrilled when Wren offered to see them with her.

The visit was going a lot better than she'd dared hope, even though she knew Jill was still holding back a little, as if she was using company manners. When they'd met in the past, there had been a warmth there that wasn't quite as warm now.

It didn't take long before Don nodded off in his recliner which, judging by the affection in the glance and eyeroll Jill gave him, was a common occurrence. And a few minutes later, Wren heard Grant's snores join his dad's.

"When he sent me a text telling me you guys would be later in the day," his mom said softly, "he just said it had been a long night and he had to take a nap."

"It was a fire and Danny Walsh almost got hurt, and Grant said when things like that happen, it's hard to sleep when they get back."

Jill shook her head. "I did everything I could to talk that boy out of being a firefighter."

"I worry about him a lot," Wren confessed. "But it might be easier for me because I'm surrounded by the people he fights fires with and the people who worry about *them*, so it's just the way we live our lives, I guess. We worry, but we also know they're always as safe as they can be because they're a family, too. I can't really imagine him doing anything else."

"Me, either. It's hard to picture him wearing a suit and sitting behind a desk like his brother does, and they're both doing jobs that make them happy, which is I guess the best a mother could ask for." She chuckled, and neither man even stirred. "Even though their happiness doesn't keep me from worrying about them."

Wren turned her head to look at Grant, who had his arms crossed and would have looked like he was watching the game, if not for his closed eyes and the snoring. Don was in practically the same position in his chair, and she noted how much they looked alike, especially in profile.

As if he could sense her staring, Grant opened his eyes and turned his head to look at her. His expression softened and he gave her a sleepy smile. "I'm just resting my eyes."

"Like father, like son," Jill muttered, and Wren laughed.

She was aware of how carefully they skirted any discussion of the fire or the months she was away. As much as she enjoyed the evening, the avoidance felt like an elephant in the room to her and it was a relief when the signals were given that it was time to head to bed. And she wasn't surprised when Grant walked her to her room when it was time to turn in. He'd been on his best behavior in front of his mom, but he was going to want a kiss goodnight.

"You're going to be okay in here?" Grant asked. He'd waited while she went into the bathroom to get ready for bed, and now he was sitting on the edge of the bed next to her.

"It's a guest room, not a broom closet," she teased. "I'll be fine. I'm getting pretty good at being a houseguest, I guess."

"My parents get up early, so the coffee will probably be ready before you get up."

His parents had been nice to her, but she wasn't sure she wanted to be alone with his mom before she was fully caffeinated. "Will you text me when you wake up?"

"Are you going to pretend you're asleep until I go downstairs?"

His tone was teasing, but there was no judgment in it. The way he gave her space to pull back when she needed to was one of the reasons she'd fallen in love with him. "I might."

"I'll text you." He pulled the quilt up to her shoulders. "You're sure you're warm enough?"

"I'm sure."

When he leaned down and pressed his mouth to hers, she kept her arms under the quilt like a good girl. Even when his tongue flicked over her bottom lip. By the time he was done giving her a very thorough kiss goodnight, Wren was more than warm enough.

She chuckled when he had to clear his throat before he spoke. "I definitely have to go now. I'll see you in the morning."

"Sweet dreams," she responded, smiling when he groaned.

Chapter Seventeen

Wren had been afraid she wouldn't be able to sleep without the sounds of the city. It was quiet here, except for crickets and the very occasional sound of a vehicle passing by on the road. But there was something about snuggling into warm blankets in a slightly chilly room that made sleeping easy and she woke to her phone chiming.

I'm awake. Are you sitting on the edge of your bed, fully dressed, waiting for me?

She'd expected to be. Not yet.

I'm going down. I'll save you some coffee.

Because she didn't want to hang out with his parents in her pajamas, she took her bag into the bathroom and got dressed and brushed her teeth before going downstairs.

They were all in the kitchen, and his mom smiled when she saw her. "Good morning. How did you sleep?"

"I don't even remember the last time I slept so soundly. Thank you."

"I don't know how any of you sleep in that city. It's

like trying to sleep in the middle of an action movie. How do you like your eggs, Wren?"

"However everybody else is having them is fine." She took the coffee mug Grant handed her and smiled her thanks.

"I'll just scramble up a big batch, then."

"Is there anything I can do to help?"

"I've already got the toast keeping warm in the oven, so just sit and drink your coffee. It'll be ready in a few minutes."

"It's going to be warm today," Grant said. "I was thinking we could take the snowmobile out for a spin."

She gave him a look that made him laugh. She'd never been on a snowmobile and that word *snow* kept her from having any real desire to try it. "Define warm."

"It's supposed to hit twenty-five," his dad said. "Perfect weather for it."

Twenty-five degrees sounded like perfect weather for going back to bed. "I'm pretty sure I didn't pack any clothes for going whatever-miles-per-hour through twenty-five degree air, but I'm sure it would have been fun. So sad. Maybe next time."

"You can wear my gear, Wren," his mom said from the stove. "It'll be a little big on you, but not too bad."

Grant's smug grin made her want to kick him under the table. "Mom has good gear. You'll be plenty warm enough."

"You can take our two-up," his dad added. "Just had her tuned up and the belt changed and she's running great."

Wren had no idea what any of that meant, other than the Cutter family was unanimous in their desire to get her on a machine that offered no protection from the

below-freezing temperature. Maybe it was some kind
of twisted payback.

When Grant's foot nudged her ankle, she looked over
at him. "I really think you'll enjoy it."

The way he said it—and the sincerity in his expression—made it plain it wasn't a twisted revenge plot.
He knew her and he honestly believed she would have
a good time. And she knew him, so she knew if she
didn't like it, he'd turn around and find something else
for them to do.

"It seems like a good day to try something new, I
guess," she said.

And that's how, an hour after they finished eating,
Wren found herself swallowed up by outdoor gear. She
felt like a toddler who'd been bundled up to build snow-
men and she was thankful she'd gone to pee before
Grant started layering her up. First she was sent to put
borrowed wool base layers under her clothes, along with
wool socks because her cotton blend ones were a serious no-no. Then bibs, which reminded her of the snow
pants she'd worn as a kid, except heavier and a much
higher quality. They helped her put on the boots, which
were definitely too big for her, so more wool socks
were added. A lightweight coat liner was followed by
a wool hood with a long neck that tucked into it. Then
a heavy coat. Gloves. Finally, a helmet over the wool
hood, which Grant buckled for her.

If she had to pee again, she was in trouble.

"You look adorable," he said after tugging on the
helmet's buckle to make sure it was secure.

"I feel very…round."

"But adorably round."

He'd already pulled the snowmobile out of the garage, and she'd been thrilled to see it had an actual passenger seat with a back rest and little shields to help deflect the wind from her hands. She guessed that's what *two-up* meant. It sounded like a big, souped-up lawnmower, but he looked so happy, she didn't comment on it.

And unlike her, he managed to look pretty hot in his gear. It was black and hugged his body more, but she wasn't sure if it was because he had more fashionable snowmobile gear than his mother or because his actually fit him.

"You ready?"

Since she was becoming uncomfortably aware that gear meant to protect you at high speeds in cold weather was not meant for standing around in the yard and she was in danger of overheating, she nodded. Then she waddled over to the machine and very ungracefully climbed up to straddle the passenger seat.

"Hold on," his mom called, and Wren groaned. She didn't want to climb back off the damn thing with an audience, other than Grant, because it wasn't going to be pretty. "Once you get on, I want to get a picture. It's her first time."

Grant rolled his eyes, but Wren felt a warmth that had nothing to do with the many layers she was wearing. There was a certain acceptance implied by his mom wanting a picture of them together, and she was grateful for it.

Once his mom had checked the screen to make sure she liked the photo and given them a wave, Grant plugged a cord from her helmet into a port in the snowmobile and lowered her face shield for her.

"It's heated so it won't fog up," he explained. Then he climbed on in front of her and started the engine again.

Wren squealed when it lurched forward, but she hoped the shield on the helmet meant nobody could hear her.

He drove around the house and across the backyard—which was more like a back field—and through a break in the trees she hadn't even noticed was there. The trail was narrow and twisty through woods and she was afraid her fingers were going to ache from clutching the hand grips so hard.

But then they came out of the woods and he turned onto a trail so wide and smooth it was practically a road. He picked up speed and that made her nervous at first, but eventually she relaxed against the seat and watched the scenery.

Every once in a while, a sled would pass them going the opposite direction. And sometimes there were bumps and dips in the trail, but mostly it was like cruising along a back road made of snow. One of the most surprising things was how warm she was. Clearly the Cutter family didn't skimp on snowmobile gear.

After making turns at several intersections, Grant turned on a small trail that wasn't as twisty as the one that connected their yard to the big trail, but was close. She could tell by the engine sound and the way she leaned back against the seat that they were climbing a hill, though it was hard to tell visually since there were dense woods on both sides of them.

She had no idea how long they were on that trail before it broke into a clearing. There were tracks, so she knew others had been there, but it didn't have the hard-packed look the bigger trails had. When he pulled the snowmobile around sideways, she was able to see the view.

Looking out over the snowy trees and a picturesque small town—the kind that were always on postcards for sale at gas stations in New England—took her breath away.

He killed the engine and got off the sled. Then he unplugged her shield and helped her take her helmet and the hood off before she climbed down from the seat.

"You doing okay?" He took her hand as they walked toward the edge of the clearing.

"You were right. I'm enjoying it."

"Good. I was really hoping you would."

"It so pretty." She looked up at him. "You love it here."

"I do. It's good for me to reconnect with home every once in a while. And not just my family."

"What brought you to Boston? For somebody who loves this so much, it seems like a weird choice."

"The lure of the big city, I guess. Sometimes you don't fully appreciate where you're from until you've been somewhere else. And the challenge."

"I feel like you want to come back someday. Maybe when the challenges have been met?"

He shrugged. "It's all pretty and idyllic until you remember there's only one place in town that delivers and their pizza sucks. But you're right, I guess. I don't think that far ahead as a rule, but I think I had a fuzzy idea of retiring here someday. Way in the future."

"When the kids are grown?" she said lightly.

When he looked at her, his gaze was so intense, she shivered. "Kids, huh?"

They'd talked about kids the first time around. Not

in a specific *I want to have children with you* way, but enough to know they both wanted to be parents someday. "Yeah, kids. You'd be a great dad. And you'd teach them all sorts of things and bring them to visit their grandparents on the weekends. And they'd snowmobile and…do all the other stuff you guys do up here."

"Or maybe they'll curl up in a chair with a book like their mother."

He said it with so much affection, her eyes welled up a little. And not only the acceptance that reading books was as okay as romping around in the woods, but that she would be the mother of his children. Saying it out loud was a big thing to her. "I'm guessing a little of both."

"Go out and raise a little hell, and then go home and read by the fire?"

"Something like that."

"Don't cry out here. Your eyes will freeze shut when you blink."

Her gasp made him laugh and she punched him playfully in the stomach. "That is not funny."

"It kind of was." He put his arm around her shoulders and pulled her close. "You really need to get outside more."

"I don't hate this."

"Maybe we'll do it again."

"When it's warmer?"

He laughed so hard she got offended and stepped away. "I hate to break it to you, but this *is* warm for sledding. If it got any warmer, we'd be mudding. It's better if it's just a little colder, actually."

"That's easy to say when you're a guy who can pee on a tree."

* * *

Grant wasn't surprised his mom managed to pull him aside while Wren was packing up her bag for the journey home. She was his mother, so she was always going to have an opinion on Grant's life—even his love life—but she was too good a person to make comments in front of Wren or within her earshot.

"Grant, can you give me a hand with something in the garage before you go?"

It was a code he'd heard more than a few times in his life, no matter if she was talking to him, his brother or his dad. There was always something in the garage that needed tending to when she had something on her mind.

He just hoped he hadn't been totally wrong about the vibe in the house. He'd known his mom would act right because that's who she was, but he'd actually thought it had gone even better than that. His mom had been slightly cool at first, but he thought she'd warmed up to Wren by the time they went snowmobiling.

Just the idea of having to pick a side shook him up. He knew there were families with a lot of conflict when it came to in-laws, but he never wanted to be in a position to have to choose Wren or his mother. The idea hurt too much to even think about.

Just as he suspected, as soon as the door between the kitchen and the garage had closed behind them, she walked over and leaned against her car, folding her arms.

"I'm glad you brought Wren home this weekend," she said. "I was so worried about you after she left. You weren't yourself at all. And then, when you told me she was back, I had all different worries. And a lot of questions, of course."

"We're taking it slow, Mom. She didn't cast a spell on me that made me forget everything that happened." He shrugged. "You know how much she hurt me. But I think shutting her out when I found her again would have hurt me more than the risk of maybe being hurt again. I have to try."

"I can see why. Seeing you together this weekend makes me feel a lot better." She smiled. "Your dad and I were talking about it while you were out sledding, and we both think you suit each other. Even with what happened between you, she makes you happy."

"That means a lot to me."

"Hopefully what happened before was nothing but a bump in the road. Dad and I have been married a long time and you've seen it. While we've never separated like you two did, relationships are like driving the roads around here. Most of the times it's smooth, with some twists and turns. But sometimes it's bumpy and then, every once in a while, you hit a pothole that knocks the wheels out of alignment."

He chuckled, even though he knew it was a pretty accurate description of his parents' marriage. Luckily there hadn't been too many potholes, but they happened. "Right now I'm trying to remember we're cruising the back roads and not speeding on the highway, bypassing all the rest stops and scenery."

"I think rushing things would be a mistake," she agreed. "You don't want to get back to the place you were because that didn't work. Take your time, find your way to a new place, and when the past is in the rearview mirror, you'll know it's right."

Since that echoed what he'd told Gavin, he nodded. "That's what I'm hoping for."

"But this ex-boyfriend. He's still a problem?"

"I don't really know if he's a problem so much as the possibility of him being a problem is a problem." He laughed at himself. "Did that make sense?"

"How long are you going to let that possibility be a part of your relationship, though? Have you looked into him? I mean, what if you two are up here worrying about him, and he's wherever he is, starting a new life for himself?"

"I don't know, Mom. I know he's in Virginia and has to meet with a parole officer or whatever. But it's not really my place to dig deeper unless Wren wants to. He's not somebody we really want to talk about, but we can't not think about him, so… I don't know."

"Her past is a hard thing to move beyond, I'm sure. When there's a concrete problem, you can fix it. But fear is…it's personal and doesn't always make sense to other people." She shook her head. "It's going to take time and trust and patience to get past that, I think. In time, her fear will fade."

Talking to his parents always centered him, and he gave her a long hug. "Thank you for giving her another chance."

"As long as you're happy, honey." She sounded a little sniffly, but then she backed up and smiled. "And she loved snowmobiling, which is good. You guys will be coming back a lot more often in the winter. You should try to get more time off around Christmas so we can all go out riding together."

"Now who's on the interstate?" he teased. But if he was being honest with himself, he was already looking forward to it.

Christmas was nine months away, so if he and Wren

made this work, bringing her home would be a big deal. He'd brought a few girlfriends home with him in the past, but never for the holidays. Christmas was a *very* big deal to the Cutter family and he'd always known he wouldn't bring a girlfriend home in December unless she was going to be a part of his family.

That old hurt made its way under his skin as they went back to the kitchen. Not even an old hurt, really, but one that was starting to heal if he didn't pick at it.

Proposing to her at Christmas had been his plan from the time he decided she was the only one for him. Maybe on the front porch if it was warm enough. Or in front of the fireplace after his parents went to bed if it wasn't.

Wren was rinsing her coffee mug in the sink when he walked into the kitchen and the smile she gave him lit up her face and obliterated the faint sense of sadness that had gripped him.

He had new dreams now, and he wasn't going to let a broken dream from their past tarnish the future.

"Everything okay?" she asked, giving him a questioning look.

He walked over and wrapped his arms around her waist. She leaned back against him, setting the coffee mug upside down in the dish drainer, and he kissed the side of her neck.

"Everything is better than okay," he said.

"I almost wish we didn't have to leave yet. It's so quiet and peaceful here, and who cares if the only delivery place has crappy pizza when your mom can cook like that?"

"It means a lot to me that you like it here." He kissed her neck again, nipping with his teeth this time. "But it's still cold to sneak out to the barn, if you know what I mean."

By the time the bags were in the car and it was time to say goodbye, Grant had mixed feelings. On the one hand, being out of the city and showing Wren where he was from was as relaxing as he'd hoped. On the other, it was hell sleeping in separate rooms. Not that he really wanted to get busy under his mom's roof, but he liked holding her. He liked the sound of her soft breathing and waking up next to her.

After hugging both of his parents, he asked them to tell his brother he'd visit him and the family next time he was up. He hadn't wanted to overwhelm Wren the first time.

Then he watched each of them hug Wren. They'd developed an affection for her during their few meetings before, and there was no sign now of the distance they'd kept the day before.

"Text your sizes to Jill and she'll keep an eye out for gear that'll fit you," his dad told Wren as they walked out to the Jeep. "You'll need your own so we can ride together. And Grant, you help her find a good helmet that fits."

"I will," he said. "Keep that two-up in running shape for us, okay?"

"Absolutely. We'll see you soon, and drive safe."

Once they were on the road, he glanced over at Wren, who was thankfully sitting still in the passenger seat. No more nervous fidgeting. "Glad to be heading home?"

"Kind of." She smiled. "I wouldn't have minded staying a few more days, to be honest. Not only because I slept so amazingly well or had fun snowmobiling, but because it was nice reconnecting with them. I know that's important to you."

"They're your biggest fans again," he said, chuckling. "Except for me, of course. I was already your biggest fan, but not hating snowmobiling really elevated you to a whole new level."

She laughed. "You have interesting standards."

"I didn't like kissing you goodnight and then having to go sleep alone, though. That's not fun."

"I'm sure we can make up for the lost time."

He looked over and arched an eyebrow. "Can we start tonight?"

"I'm afraid if I say yes, you're going to rack up the speeding tickets on the way home."

"Between being a firefighter and my natural charm, I can probably talk my way out of a ticket." When she snorted, he chuckled. "Just being honest."

"Just get us back to Boston in one piece and then we'll see where that natural charm gets you."

Grant shifted in his seat and then decided it might be a good day to use the cruise control.

"I told you I wouldn't get a speeding ticket."

Wren rolled her eyes as Grant dropped their bags on the floor and locked the apartment door behind them. "Seriously, what are the chances you get stopped by a cop whose sister's dog was rescued from a tree by Engine 59 and Ladder 37?"

"I'd say the chances are pretty good since it just happened."

"Why was a dog even stuck in a tree? How does that happen?"

"He jumped off the roof of the porch and landed on the branch."

"What was he doing on the—" She stopped and held up her hand. "Never mind. I don't even want to know."

He took her coat and hung it in the closet with his and then lined their boots up on the mat, which made her smile. Grant wasn't really into being neat. He just subscribed to the theory of touching everything once. Mail didn't get tossed on the counter to sort later. He sorted it standing over the trash can. Junk got tossed and bills went into the bill stand. Coats and boots scattered around to be put away later didn't make any sense to him.

She had a tendency to touch things a lot more than once before they were finally put away, but one of the benefits of not owning much was that her room at Patty's didn't look cluttered. The things she had scattered around Grant's apartment probably drove him crazy because touching them once didn't do any good if they didn't have a place they belonged.

"I'm beat," he said, dropping onto the couch.

"It was a long day. Snowmobiling and then driving." She gave him a sideways look as she sat next to him. "I'm not sure which you drove faster. The snowmobile or the Jeep."

"The Jeep. Usually I'd say the sled, but I didn't want to scare you the first time out." He turned his head to grin at her. "Next time I'll take you on the lake and open it up a little."

"That sounds…" She wasn't sure. "Exciting and dangerous and scary and fun?"

"Exactly."

He leaned his head back and closed his eyes. Wren

looked at his profile, loving his face when he was totally relaxed. She loved his face all the time, of course, but she especially loved seeing him in moments other people rarely got to see.

She put her hand on his thigh, idly stroking the length of it through his jeans. He didn't open his eyes, but she saw the way the corner of his mouth quirked upward for a second. He wasn't *that* tired.

When she strayed a little farther north, brushing her hand over his zipper, he breathed in sharply. And when she popped the button on his jeans, he opened his eyes.

She gave him a saucy smile, or what she thought was saucy, anyway. It must have been close enough because he unzipped his jeans and lifted his ass off the couch enough to shove them and his boxer briefs down. She had to help get them over his knees before he could kick them away, and then she turned all of her attention to the really impressive erection he'd gotten going in the last minute.

Running the flat of her palm up the length of him, she felt it twitch against her hand before she ran her thumb over the tip. Then she got into a comfortable position and ran her tongue over the spot her thumb had grazed. Grant moaned and slid his fingers into her hair.

"No," she told him. "No touching me or I stop."

"Fuck." The word was harsh, almost guttural, but she didn't care. He liked to torment her. She could do the same. And he didn't like it, but he moved his hands.

As a reward, she covered him with her mouth and slowly drew him in. When she raised her head, she swirled her tongue over the tip before taking him in again. Again and again she worked him with her mouth, until she felt the weight of his hand on her head.

Wren stopped instantly, lifting her face to give him a stern look. He made a deep, frustrated sound, but took his hand away.

She rewarded him by running her tongue up the length of his erection and circling the tip before taking him deep against her throat in one thrust. He groaned and she curled her hand around him so her fingers followed her mouth, up and down his shaft.

She purposely let her hair fall, shielding her face from his view. It would be torturous for him, she knew. He liked to watch her mouth on his dick. His hand lifted and he clenched and unclenched his fingers, but he didn't touch her.

"Jesus, Wren. Please."

She smiled around his cock before lifting her head to look into his pleading eyes. "Please what?"

"Let me touch you. Your hair…" He cleared his throat. "I want to touch your hair."

Wren knew exactly what he wanted to do with her hair. "Yes, you can touch my hair."

The second her lips touched the tip of his erection again, he plunged his hands into her hair. He gathered it as if he was making a ponytail and then turned his wrist so it wrapped around his right hand. Gripping it hard, but not enough to make her wince, he slowed her as she took his length into her mouth.

Then he tugged again, pulling her head slowly back up. Over and over, her hair wound around his hand, he guided her mouth over him. And each time she took him in, he pushed just that little bit to give himself that rush of control. He knew her limits, and all she had to do was slap his leg and he'd release her.

When he wrapped his left hand around his dick and

gave it a long, slow stroke—using her hair to hold her mouth at the top—she knew he was close. She squeezed her thighs together, trying not to feel that rush of heat because this was about him, but it wasn't easy. Very few things turned her on like the sight of Grant stroking himself. He was so much rougher with it than she could bring herself to be.

He groaned as his dick slid through the tight grip of his hand, and he forced her head down. Her lips bumped the curl of his finger and thumb, and they moved in unison—her mouth and his hand—faster and harder until his hips jerked and he came in hot spurts against her throat.

She swallowed, feeling in his grip the effort it took not to push her head down and thrust harder until the orgasm passed.

Finally, he opened his hand and her hair slid free of his grasp, falling like a cloud around her face. Panting, he pulled her upright, yanking the throw blanket over his lap at the same time.

He kissed her hair, and then kissed it again, his hand running up and down her back. Wren curled against his side, a satisfied smile on her face. She loved being able to rock him so completely with just her mouth.

"That was…holy shit."

She chuckled. "I feel like *holy shit* is basically your sexual gold standard."

"You're not wrong. I would try to come up with something more elegant, but my brain's a little fuzzy right now."

"Good. Close your eyes and rest for a bit."

"Nope." He shook his head, but she could already feel the muscles in his body relaxing. "Give me a few minutes and then I'm going to take you to bed and pay you back for that."

"Take a nap," she said. "You'll want to be well-rested."

Chapter Eighteen

About forty minutes after Wren left for work the next morning, Grant couldn't take the thought of being cooped up in the apartment all day. He had some cleaning to do, since he'd been gone over the weekend and hadn't exactly been doing a great job of keeping up even before that. He'd had more important things on his mind than the expiration dates on things in the fridge.

After considering his options for the day, he picked up his phone and shot a text to Gavin.

Cait working today?

It was a few minutes before he got a response.

Yeah. What's up?

Bored. Wanna hit the gym?

If you want to work out instead of eating, something must be on your mind. Meet you there in an hour?

He hadn't come up with the gym idea for any reason other than wanting to work out, or so he thought.

Gavin was right, though. He usually went for restaurants over the gym, so maybe he did have some stuff to work through.

Sounds good.

An hour later, they met up in the locker room of their usual gym. It wasn't a pretty place, by any means, but it had the basic workout stuff, didn't have exorbitant fees and nobody was trying to sell them vegetable smoothies on their way out.

"I'm going to take a wild guess and say you want to hit the heavy bag today," Gavin said as they tied their sneakers and stowed their street clothes in lockers.

"I could go for that."

"How bad is it?"

Grant grinned at his best friend. "It's not bad. It's good. In fact, it's so good it's got me on edge because I don't know if I'm rushing things, and I need something physical to do while I sort it out."

"Yeah, you definitely need to hit the bag for that."

Luckily, nobody had beat them to it and after putting his gloves on, he squared up in front of it.

Gavin stood behind the bag to steady it. "Talk while you hit, dude."

He took a few shots at it first, warming up. The thoughts were such a jumble in his head, he wasn't sure he could get them out of his mouth in a way that made sense.

"I want Wren to move in with me," he said finally, because that seemed to be the loudest thought in his mind lately.

"Have you asked her?"

He punched the bag hard enough to feel it in his shoulder. "No."

Gavin let him hit the bag a few more times before he prompted him. "Is there a reason you haven't asked her, if that's what you want? I assume you're not sure if it's what *she* wants?"

"She can be hard to read," he admitted. "I know that's what she wants, but I'm not sure if she wants it now."

"It's not like it's a yes or no question and if she says no, that's it." Grant paused to give his friend a look, and Gavin rolled his eyes. "Okay, so living together was a messy issue for Cait and me, but it was a totally different situation. There's no reason you and Wren can't have a conversation about it."

"We had a great time up at my parents' house. Then we came home and went to bed and it was great. And then she got up this morning and left to, and I quote, *go home* so she could get ready for work. It sucked."

"It's not a mystery why you want her to move in with you." He grunted when Grant hit the bag a little harder than he had been. "The question is why you haven't brought it up yet. And it can't really be that you don't know if it's what she wants because you can't know unless you actually ask her. Something's holding you back."

"I don't know what it is." He dropped his arms to his side and shook them out. "I know we were going to take it slow and moving in with me already wouldn't be slow. It'd be pretty damn fast if we were actually dating for the first time. But we're not dating for the first time, and it's hard to separate the first time from this time."

"Obviously. I mean, yeah, you try not to think about

the five months she was gone and you want to start fresh, but the time you were together before she left still happened. You guys were together a long time. Like, what, almost a year?"

"Less than that, but a long time, yeah." He'd been building a friendship and then a romantic relationship with Wren for months before he'd told anybody, but once he'd let himself fall in love with her, he'd fallen fast and hard. "You can see why it's so fucked up."

"I don't think it matters how long it has or hasn't been. All that matters is what makes the two of you happy."

Grant raised his gloves again, but then he just rested them on the bag and looked at Gavin. "If she moves in with me—if we take that step and officially have a home together—it would hurt so much more if she took off again."

Gavin looked back at him for a long moment and then gave a sad shake of his head. "You're the one who told me she has no reason to do that again."

"And you're the one who pointed out she really didn't have a good reason to do it the first time."

"We've been friends a long time and I know two things about you without a doubt. One, you're rarely led astray when you follow your gut, but you overthink things to death. And two, you are absolutely and completely in love with Wren Everett."

"So you think I'm overthinking this?"

"I don't know. All I can do is make observations because I can't see the future. But I think if your gut instinct was that she might take off again, you wouldn't have gotten involved with her a second time at all, never mind be thinking about living with her."

"I feel like telling her I want her to move in with me is the right move," he said.

You just do what's right for you, son. If you're meant to be together, it'll be what's right for both of you. His dad's advice echoed in his mind.

"All I can say," Gavin said, "is that I don't think Wren intends to go anywhere. And if she did, her address isn't going to make a difference. You're already all in, dude. If she took off tomorrow, it wouldn't hurt any less because she lives with Patty."

Just the thought of it made his stomach hurt. The first time had hurt so badly he didn't think he could survive it, but he hadn't seen it coming. This time, he'd had to really open up to let her back in, so the betrayal would be even more painful.

"I don't think she'd do it," he said. He wanted to say he *knew* she wouldn't, but total denial of the possibility wasn't the right answer. "But you're right about the address, I guess."

"Have you tried dropping hints? Try to feel her out without actually putting it out there?"

"You mean besides lingering at her door and looking as pathetic and lonely as possible while I slowly walk back to my Jeep?" He laughed. "Not really."

"They can't read our minds. And while that's definitely a blessing about ninety-nine percent of the time, it does mean we have to communicate our feelings once in a while."

"I'm going to think about it a little bit longer. Make sure it's not an impulse triggered by being in New Hampshire with her—which I don't think it was—and then I'll probably bring it up."

"Of course you're going to think about it." Gavin

rolled his eyes. "Now, are you actually going to hit this bag some more or are we just going to stand here and talk all day?"

Wren was exhausted. The weekend in New Hampshire followed by working both jobs today because she'd taken the time off had wiped her out, but Grant showing up to drive her home had been a nice boost.

But then Gavin had called. He and Cait had been out doing some errands and then Aidan had called *him* because he needed somebody to shoot pool with and it turned into a bunch of them stopping into Kincaid's "just for a few minutes."

Nursing her one and only drink for the night—and even that might have her napping under a table, as tired as she was—she sat at a small table in the back with Cait and watched the guys argue over their game of pool. She wasn't even sure what they were arguing about, since she didn't know how to play, but it seemed heated in a good-natured way.

"So, is my mother driving you crazy yet?" When Wren laughed and shook her head, Cait smiled. "To be honest, I know I told you we'd all keep our eyes out for a decent, cheap apartment, but she loves having you there so much, it'll probably be almost as hard on her when you move out as it was when I did. And, really, you're probably going to move in with *him* anyway."

She'd leaned forward when she said the last bit and dropped her voice to barely more than a whisper, but Wren still glanced at Grant to see if he'd heard. He didn't seem to have, thankfully, so she whispered back. "Probably. At some point."

Then she sat up straight and took a sip of her beer.

"I actually really love living in Patty's house right now. She's like a second mom to me, and having a younger brother is fun. He tried to show me how to play his video game the other night and I was *awful* and he started yelling at me about some guy hiding behind a truck on the screen and then Patty was yelling at him to stop yelling at me." She laughed. "I feel like part of the family more than a friend renting the guest room."

"Because you *are* part of the family," Cait said, raising her glass to clink it against Wren's.

Warmth that had nothing to do with the alcohol spread through Wren and she was thankful she wasn't quite tired enough to hit the weepy stage. It felt incredible to be part of this family, and she knew it wasn't only because of Grant. She may have met Cait through him, but they were developing a friendship of their own that was probably one of the best Wren had ever had.

Grant rolled his eyes at the other two men and then walked over to their table. He pulled up a chair, which he sat on backward, and propped one arm on the back while the other draped across Wren's shoulders.

"Whatever you ladies are talking about has to be better than listening to those two."

"How do you feel about vegan food?" Cait asked.

"Okay, maybe not."

"No, seriously. I found this great restaurant that—"

"Nope."

"Grant," Wren said. "You might like it."

"I like steak." He shrugged. "And herbed potato croquettes, as it turns out."

Cait pulled up a picture on her phone and showed it to him. Wren laughed at his expression when he saw it, because he was clearly battling between liking what he saw and wanting to be stubborn.

"Okay, that looks good," he admitted reluctantly.

"Just because it's vegan, doesn't mean it's not good," Cait said.

"I'd like to try it," Wren added.

He made a low growling sound in his throat. "You guys could try lunch there. Or a girls' night. You all like going out together."

"It's more of a date night kind of place." Wren leaned closer and gave him a smile. "I like date nights with you."

His expression softened, and Wren felt a twinge of guilt for using his inability to resist her to get her hands on the seitan cutlets she'd seen on the website link Cait had sent her.

"Then we'll go," he said, his gaze locked with hers. "I guess I'll try anything once."

"Why don't you try telling this idiot how to play pool?" Aidan called over. "Or come take over for me so I can go visit my wife at the bar?"

"I'm good," Grant said.

"You'd rather sit on that chair than take over this game so I can go see my pregnant wife?" Aidan shook his head. "I thought you were a good guy, Cutter."

Grant laughed, but he stood up. "You're such an asshole. Hey, Wren, you want to learn to shoot pool?"

"Not really." She was probably too tired to hold the stick up, but when he gave her that *aw, come on* look, she set her drink down and stood. Apparently she couldn't resist him, either. "Just for a few minutes."

Cait stood, too. "I'll take over for Gavin, so you don't have him barking at you from across the table."

"I wouldn't bark at Wren," Gavin said, but he handed the cue to Cait. Then he winked at Wren. "You should know we just like the part where the women bend over the table."

They all laughed, and then Grant did his best to show her how to play the game. She was competitive, so she didn't like not being able to do it, but her hands were small and she had a lot of trouble controlling the cue once she decided to make her shot.

But she kept trying until both guys winced at a bad hit. Grant walked over and kissed her, using the distraction to take the pool cue out of her hand. "If we rip the felt, Tommy might throw us out."

She tried to stifle a yawn and failed. "Right now, being thrown out of here isn't much of a threat."

"We'll get out of here." He was about to put the cue stick back on the rack when Aiden reappeared with a soda and a basket of nachos.

"You lose already?"

Grant flipped him off. "We're heading out. Wren had a long day and we've all got to get up for work tomorrow."

"I'll let you know when we can get away for a double date night," Cait said.

Gavin groaned. "Tell me it's not the vegan place."

"I'll make it up to you," Cait told him, and Wren couldn't tell, but it looked like her hand might be on his ass.

"I'll try anything once, I guess."

"Good answer," Grant said. "No rush on scheduling that, though. We haven't been here, all four of us together, enough times yet."

Wren slid her arm around Grant's waist. "I can't wait to try those seitan cutlets, though."

His fingertips slid under the hem of her shirt, just enough to touch skin. "I guess we don't *have* to wait. Whenever."

She stood on her toes to reward him with a quick kiss. "I'll make it up to you."

After they'd said their goodbyes, they went over to the bar and Wren grabbed their coats while Grant waited for Lydia, who was probably out back, to show up at the register.

His mind was running through the possible ways Wren could make it up to him in bed, so he wasn't really paying attention to the far corner of the bar, where Tommy and Fitzy were holding court, until he heard him speak.

"You gonna stick around this time, girl, or what?"

Grant froze as Tommy's voice carried across the bar. The man was talking to Wren, but he may as well have been talking to everybody at Kincaid's. He'd brought her here for some company and a beer—which he was currently paying for—not to be interrogated by a guy who wouldn't know a functional relationship if it bit him in the ass.

But Wren just gave Tommy an easy smile. "I plan to."

Tommy gave her a long look, and Grant braced himself for the words that might come out of his mouth. If he got too disrespectful, he was going to have to say something, and that could get ugly. Grant didn't want ugly. Not only was he Tommy Kincaid—father and father-in-law to a lot of his friends—but they made good burgers. And when he wasn't insulting Grant's girlfriend, he genuinely liked the guy.

"I'm glad to hear it" was all Tommy said when he finally spoke. "You pretty up the place."

"Thanks, Dad," Lydia yelled from the hallway to the kitchen. "Oh hey, Grant. You calling it a night already?"

"Yeah, we've got plans." Plans to go to bed, judging by Wren's sleepy expression.

"Anything fun?"

"No, we made plans to be boring and not fun at all." When she paused in the act of handing him the slip to sign to give him a look, he chuckled. "Hey, I meant to ask you earlier, but I swear you never stand still. How's the baby?"

She laughed and put her hand over her stomach, which still looked pretty flat to Grant. "So far so good."

Then she knocked her knuckles on the wooden bar and winked.

Once they were outside, Grant took Wren's hand and they walked slowly down the block to where he'd parked.

"I'm sorry about Tommy," he said. "He can be an ass sometimes."

"He can. But I bet under that crusty shell, he's worried about you."

"Maybe. I mean, I know he cares about us all in his own way, but that doesn't give him the right to call you out like that. It was rude."

She laughed. "Sometimes I think he doesn't really know how loud he is."

"All the Kincaids are loud. When Jackson was born, he had a cry that was probably just a few decibels shy of shattering glass."

"It'll be fun, Lydia and Jamie having babies around the same time."

He laughed. "Yeah, you can say that because you won't be trying to fight fires with the sleep-deprived dads of those two babies."

After unlocking the Jeep, which he'd remote-started once they were in sight of it, he helped her in and went around to the driver's side. As he got in, he was struck by the sudden visual of trying to hoist a very pregnant Wren into the passenger seat.

That wouldn't really work. And her car was ancient. If—*when*—they had a baby, he wanted them so wrapped up in safety cages and airbags nothing could hurt them. They could trade hers in toward a newer family-friendly and very highly safety rated model.

"Grant?"

He shook away the thoughts and climbed into his seat. "Sorry."

"You looked a million miles away. What were you thinking about?"

Looking into her blue eyes, he almost said it. *I was imagining you very pregnant with our first child and shopping for a minivan.*

"Oh, nothing," he said out loud. "Talking about work made me think of something I need to do. That's all."

"You were smiling."

"With Aidan and Scott having babies, I was thinking—" At the last second, he chickened out again. "It might be fun to have a baby shower at the house for them when it's almost time. Just the guys."

She smiled. "That does sound fun. If you need any help planning it, just let me know. And…I'll call Olivia."

Laughing, he put on his seat belt. But then he realized they hadn't talked about what came next. "So, where to?"

She rolled her head against the seat to look at him. "I'm exhausted. And you have to work early and I have to do laundry in the morning, so I should probably go home."

Every time she said *home* and didn't mean his apartment felt like a fresh papercut to the heart, but he smiled and put the Jeep in gear. "I thought you were going to fall asleep at the table if I didn't get you out of there."

"I might have."

He reached out and took her hand as he steered one-handed through the narrow back streets to Patty's house. It didn't take long, but he was still surprised Wren didn't nod off on the way.

He'd hadn't overheard much of her conversation with Cait while Aidan and Gavin were arguing about some stupid rule they ended up searching for on their cell phones. But he'd heard a little bit.

I actually kind of love living in Patty's house right now.

He should leave it alone for now. Not for too long, but Wren had had a tough go when it came to family and if being with Cait's family was making her happy—maybe even healing some old wounds—he could wait. Did he like Wren leaving his place to go *home*? Or dropping her off like they were teenagers out on a date? Hell no. But he loved seeing her happy, relaxed and laughing about Patty making sure she ate well and bickering with Carter.

His resolve to leave it alone faltered, though, when he pulled into Patty's driveway. He left the engine running and walked around to help Wren climb down, and then walked her to the door.

"I'd invite you in, but I think Patty's still up and she'll want to chat and I'll never get to bed."

He smiled, brushing her hair back from her face. Then he leaned down and gave her a long, slow kiss that left him with an ache he knew would be with him until he saw her again.

"Get some sleep," he said softly.

"I'll talk to you tomorrow." She sighed. "And see you the day after. Be safe tomorrow."

"Always." He kissed her again, and then gave her a nudge toward the door. If he had his way, he'd stand on the step kissing her all night. Or at least until she got tired of kissing in the cold and agreed to go home with him.

"Goodnight," she said as she slipped inside.

Grant shoved his hands in his pockets as he walked back to the Jeep. *Nope, definitely not going to be able to wait much longer,* he admitted to himself. He wanted Wren with him, in *their* home, where she belonged.

Chapter Nineteen

"You're in a good mood this morning," Sadie said when she unlocked the salon door to let Wren in.

"I haven't even said anything yet."

"I could see your smile from across the street, and I bet you can see the bounce in your step if you look at your tracks in the snow."

Wren laughed and put her bag in the cubby with her name on it. Then she hit the button on the Keurig to brew herself a coffee to take to the desk.

She was definitely in a good mood this morning. On a whim—or rather because it had been in the back of her mind for months—she'd gone by the bookstore she'd worked at before getting that first phone call from Ben. They opened an hour before the salon, so she'd taken a deep breath and gone inside.

The owner had been surprised to see her, to say the least. Rhonda had been kind to her, and it meant a lot to Wren to finally apologize for disappearing and leaving her in the lurch. She told her everything because she deserved that much, and she left feeling a lot lighter, emotionally. And Rhonda had told her to come in any-time, which was good. She'd fallen in love with the bookstore as a customer, before she'd worked there, and she couldn't wait to go back and browse the shelves.

And in the days since they'd returned from New Hampshire, Wren had felt a shift in her relationship with Grant. She didn't want to jinx things by even thinking it, but she couldn't help wondering if they'd be having a serious conversation about their future soon. She got the feeling he *really* didn't like having to say goodbye to her and watch her go home, so he might ask her to move in with him soon.

As much as she loved living with Patty and Carter, she was pretty sure she'd say yes. She'd loved living with Grant more, and Patty and Carter weren't going anywhere. She knew she'd not only be welcome to stop in any time, but Patty would insist on it. Not that she was thinking about moving in with Grant, because she'd hate to jinx it.

"Maybe I should date a firefighter," Kelli said. "If they put that kind of smile on your face."

Wren nodded, then took a sip of her coffee. She'd been slowly letting bits of her private life come out as she got to know the women. They didn't know a lot, but they did know she had a firefighter boyfriend.

One who made her smile. A lot. Even more than bookstores did, which was no easy feat.

"I dated a firefighter once," Barb said. The nail tech was the quietest of the women in the salon and spoke even less than Wren did. "He did *not* make me smile like that."

They were all laughing when Sadie unlocked the front door, where the first two clients of the day were already waiting.

The first hour flew by because that's when the most

cancellations and requests for emergency appointments came in, from people who had to wait until they opened to call.

Answering the phones was her least favorite part of her job, but she still put a smile on her face when it rang because rumor had it you could hear a person's smile in their voice.

"Good morning," she said in a chipper voice, followed by the name of the salon and an upbeat "How can I help you today?"

"Wren?"

Her blood froze in her veins, and she couldn't move. It was only one word. It could be anybody, really. But how many times over the years she'd been with him had she heard Ben Mitchell say her name?

Most people would have said "hello?" again after a few seconds of silence, but he just waited. It felt deliberate. Creepy.

Forcing herself to calm down, she did her best to mimic the accents around her without going too far. The names in the appointment book blurred in front of her, but she focused on one. "No, this is Kristen. Can I help you?"

"Is Wren around?"

It was him. She kept breathing. She wouldn't let him hear her fear. "She quit yesterday. Just took off. Do you need an appointment?"

There was a clicking sound and then dead air. She'd been clutching the phone so hard, she had to force her fingers to unclench to drop it in its cradle.

"Kelli," she called out as the stylist walked by.

She detoured to the desk. "What's up?"

"Is there a way to find out what number just called

here? I didn't even look at the caller ID when I answered."

Kelli hit some buttons on the phone and then shook her head. "It was blocked. You okay?"

"I'm fine." She gave her a very tight smile that felt as fake as it probably looked. "Thanks. I forgot to get the woman's number when I made her appointment."

"You're sure? You don't look so hot."

She wasn't sure why she'd lied, since they knew about her ex and she'd have to tell them eventually, but she lied again. She just needed to process the fact this was actually happening.

Ben had found her. And she didn't know where he was.

"I'm sure," she lied again. "It's just hot in here."

"Let me get my client under the dryer and then you take a few minutes. I'll cover for you."

She nodded, her mind preoccupied with Ben.

It didn't mean he was in Boston. If all he had to go on was a Wren Everett working at a salon, it was far more likely he was sitting on his couch in Virginia, calling the salon's number until he got her on the phone. Maybe Grant could have the police in Virginia check on him again and make sure he was still there.

He didn't know about the market or Mr. and Mrs. Belostotsky. He didn't know she was living with Patty and Carter. There was no reason to believe he knew about Grant.

But it meant he hadn't forgotten her while he was in prison. It meant he'd thought about her enough so he'd typed her name into a search engine. And then he'd called the salon until she answered the phone. He hadn't moved on.

She'd have to tell Grant.

He would tell her not to worry. He'd probably give her the same reasonable explanation she'd given herself. But that's how Grant was wired. He didn't worry about problems until they were definitive problems. And he didn't want *her* to worry, so he'd downplay it.

It was dangerous to underestimate Ben.

Wren took a deep breath and let it out slowly. She'd let fear drive her once and it had been a disaster. She needed to stay calm and think about how to handle this.

And she definitely had to tell Grant.

Even a dusting of snow seemed to send cars careening into each other nowadays, so Grant wasn't surprised they'd just gone back online after the third MVA of the morning when the tone sounded.

Commercial kitchen fire. Possible cardiac arrest. Then the address was read off and they all froze for a second, trying to process what had sounded like the address for Kincaid's Pub.

"Dad."

One word from Scotty was all it took to get them moving again. As they rolled out, Grant listened to the LT's calm voice as he reminded them to stay focused and do their jobs. Left unsaid was the command to keep an eye on Scott. They all felt an emotional attachment to Tommy Kincaid and the pub, but Scotty was not only his son, but hotheaded as hell. There was a good chance if he got scared, he'd forget years of discipline and training and do something stupid.

The scene was chaos when they neared the bar. It looked as if the ambulance had barely beaten them there because the paramedic and EMT were hustling to where Lydia and Fitzy were bent over Tommy.

Grant allowed himself a brief moment of relief. At least they wouldn't have to stop Scotty from running into a fire to drag his dad out. He knew that possibility had been on the mind of every member of both crews.

He saw the cook come out the door, a kitchen fire extinguisher in one hand while he coughed into the crook of his other arm.

"Jesus," Scott said, over and over again, as they pulled to the curb.

As the siren died and they lurched to a stop, they saw Tommy lift his arm and slowly form his hand into a thumbs-up gesture and it was as though everybody in the truck exhaled as one.

It was enough reassurance so they piled out and got to work, letting EMS take care of Tommy. They charged the lines and made sure everybody was out and accounted for. There were no customers because they'd been prepping for the day, but hadn't actually opened yet.

The fire had been more than the cook could handle with the fire extinguisher, but they were able to knock it down quickly. And as soon as they did, they were back outside to check on Tommy.

When Grant got out there, they had just loaded the stretcher into the ambulance. Scott had dumped his gear on the ground and it was obvious he was going to climb in after it.

"We've got him," the paramedic said as the EMT walked around to the driver's door. "We're going to take care of him."

"I'm riding with you."

"Scotty, I'll ride with Dad." Lydia put her hand on her brother's arm as he shook his head. "You know he'd want you to stay and make sure his bar's okay. I want to be able to tell him you and Aidan are taking care of things here because as long as he knows you two are on the job, he won't stress about it and maybe I can keep him calm."

"Come on," Grant said. "Let's check on the bar. We can make sure the fire stays out and that nobody wrecks the place overhauling."

After Lydia climbed into the ambulance, the paramedic stuck his head out before closing the door. "He said to get Bobby Orr off the wall before you break him. I'm just going to assume he's talking about a picture. I hope."

The door slammed shut and the ambulance pulled away from the curb. Aidan hadn't managed more than a squeeze of his wife's hand before she got in with her dad, but he put his arm around Scott's shoulders.

"Everything's under control. Let's get Bobby Orr off the wall and we'll bring him back to the house with us. He can hang out with Engine 59 until this mess is cleaned up."

Since Aidan was going to keep an eye on Scott and take care of the picture, Grant and the others went back inside. The bar area itself wasn't too bad, but the kitchen and the storeroom were wrecked.

They poked and prodded everywhere, checking walls and the ceiling to make sure the fire wasn't hiding out, waiting to flare to life in some unexpected place. They always felt a little bad about doing additional damage to a property, but it was better than losing everything and maybe the neighbors', too, because they'd missed something. But this one hurt more, because it was theirs.

Location aside, it was pretty mindless work, so Grant wasn't really paying attention as he pulled bulk packages of paper products off the shelves to make sure none in the back were smoldering.

He caught the movement in the corner of his eye—*is that a pipe falling?*—and ducked his head, but it was too late. He felt his helmet shift and his head and shoulder exploded with pain.

Then everything went black.

"What the fuck, Cutter?" Hands grabbed his coat, rolling him to his back. *"Cutter!"*

He groaned, desperately wishing Rick Gullotti would stop yelling at him. Holy shit, his head hurt.

"LT, what's going—oh shit." That was Chris, who had a booming voice even when he wasn't yelling.

"Shh." He forced himself to open his eyes. If they knew he wasn't dead, maybe they'd stop shouting. "Quiet. Be quiet."

"What happened?"

"A pipe fell and hit me in the head."

When Rick looked around and then frowned at him, Grant looked at the ceiling. There was no piping run through the room that he could see.

"Maybe shelving. I don't know." Something had hit him in the head. Hard.

"Well, whatever it was, you earned yourself a trip to the ER. You need a medic?"

"No." He had no interest in an ambulance ride.

While Rick talked on the radio, Grant looked around as much as he could without moving his head, trying to figure out what had fallen on him. There was nothing.

"Cobb's going to take you in."

"Oh, lucky me." He pushed himself to a sitting position, very gingerly rolling his head from side to side. Nothing was too damaged. But when he put his hand to the spot on the side of his head, he winced. His helmet hadn't been secured and it must have slipped when he ducked, allowing the pipe or whatever it was to deal him a glancing blow.

They helped him to his feet and then Rick and Gavin supported him for the walk to Cobb's SUV. After loading him into the backseat, they decided to send Gavin along, too. They'd swing by and get his truck and then he'd meet them at the hospital so he could get Grant home when he was cleared.

By the time he'd been seen and poked and scanned, they'd gotten word Tommy would be okay. As heart attacks went, it could have been a lot worse, but he was going to have to clean up his dietary habits in a big way. And maybe develop some fitness habits. And lucky him, he had Lydia and Ashley to make sure he did.

"He'll be in better shape than us in six months," Gavin said, once he'd gotten the call from Aidan.

"If I don't have a concussion, why can't I go home?" Grant grumbled.

"You do have a concussion. It's just a mild one. And the nurse went to get you some meds. Just lay there and shut up."

"There was no piping. No shelving."

Gavin shook his head. "There was nothing on the floor, either. Nothing that resembled a pipe at all."

"Somebody hit me and took off?"

"I don't know, man. I hate to think that, but I don't know what else could have happened." He glanced at his phone, probably checking the time, and then shoved it in his pocket. "Maybe it was somebody taking advantage of the chaos to grab what he could get out of the cash register, but then he had to hide in the storage room when we went back in."

"That's pretty unlikely. There were a lot of people there."

"A lot of people not paying attention to the register. Or the tip jar under the counter."

Grant had to admit it was possible, but far from probable. "It doesn't feel like that to me."

"No, me either," Gavin said reluctantly. "Even if somebody did want to grab the cash, there was no reason to hit you because you weren't paying any more attention to it than anybody else."

"There was no reason to hit me at all. Unless it was personal." And if it was personal… "I don't want anybody outside the brass to know what happened."

Gavin gave him a look. "That's a mistake."

"I don't want Wren to find out." It would spook her and God only knew what she'd do.

"Remember that time you wanted to follow them to their girls' night out and I told you it was a bad idea and you said it wasn't and then it was?" He shook his head. "This is way worse."

"I'm fine. No harm done."

"Harm *was* done. And if there's even the slightest possibility this was related to her situation, not telling her is going to piss her off in a big way."

Grant couldn't take even imagining the look on Wren's face if he told her about this. "Do you tell Cait about every bump and bruise you get on the job?"

"Now you're just being an asshole." Gavin leaned

against the wall, crossing his arms. "If you won't listen to reason on that score, try this one. Right now, Wren's just out there living her life today, with no idea this guy might be nearby. Watching."

Grant's stomach rolled. "He never hit her. He was an asshole, but she said he never laid a hand on her. Just her brother."

"He never went to prison and then followed her five hundred or so miles, either."

"If he did. I don't want to scare her until I know what's actually going on."

"You mean you don't want her to take off again."

"She won't run." He was *almost* sure of it.

Chapter Twenty

Wren practically ran up the stairs to Grant's apartment. She'd been a wreck since he called to tell her he'd taken a knock to the head and he was okay, but he couldn't be alone overnight. His options were sleeping on Gavin's couch or Wren spending the night at his place.

"No offense to Cait's training, but if I have to have a private nurse, I'm choosing you over them every time," he'd said, not that he'd had to twist her arm.

There were worse phone calls to get, she knew, but this was the first time she'd ever gotten the call he'd been hurt on the job. And hearing his voice had helped, but she also knew Grant would do his best to downplay being injured so she wouldn't worry. She wasn't going to relax until she saw him with her own eyes.

She let herself in and called for him as she dropped her overnight bag inside the door. "Grant?"

"I'm right here on the couch. Nurse Gavin told me I wasn't allowed to get up until you got here."

The relief when she saw him was so intense, her knees felt weak. He looked okay. The pillows from his bed propped him up, and the throw blanket was over his legs. But other than the glass of water and package of crackers within reach on the coffee table, he looked as if he could have been hanging out, watching a movie.

"What happened?" She sat on the edge of the couch and rested her hand on his chest because she didn't know if he'd been hurt anywhere else, but she needed to touch him.

"Like I said, I took a knock to the head. It happens, but I'm okay." He covered her hand with his. "Maybe a mild concussion, if anything, but because it knocked me out, the doc wanted somebody to keep an eye on me overnight."

"It scared me when you called, so I might not even blink."

He chuckled, but only for a second because it obviously pained him. "I said keep an eye on me, not stare at me."

"Crackers and water? Are you sick?"

"I had a pretty intense headache and the stuff they gave me for it upset my stomach a little. Not a big deal."

It was a very big deal. "What aren't you telling me?"

What looked like guilt flashed across his face. "What do you mean?"

"If you were vomiting after a head injury, that's really bad. Everybody knows that."

He smiled and squeezed her hand. "Head injury is overstating it a bit, and I wasn't vomiting. I swear. The painkillers made me a little nauseated and the crackers helped."

"So how is this supposed to work? Do I wake you up every hour and make you tell me your middle name and what year it is?"

The quick bark of laugher made him scowl. "Ow. Don't make me laugh and, no, absolutely do not wake me up every hour to ask my middle name. You don't have to wake me up every hour at all."

"Are you lying?" It wouldn't surprise her at all if he ignored that paragraph on his discharge papers so he could sleep in peace. "I can text Cait and ask her what I should be doing for you."

"They just want somebody with me in case I need help. If I stand up and get dizzy or something. Mostly your job is to cuddle on the couch and watch a movie with me."

"Tough work. Maybe a nice, quiet romantic drama?"

"I didn't get hit *that* hard."

"What did you get hit with, anyway?" He hadn't actually said on the phone.

He looked at her for so long without speaking, she was afraid maybe he'd hit his head harder than he'd admitted. Then he gave her a tight, very un-Grant-like smile. "I don't actually know. Just one of those things, I guess."

Considering how dangerous his job was, she should be thankful he wasn't hurt worse, but it still turned her stomach to imagine how much worse that phone call could have been. "Sometimes I hate your job."

"Then we should stop talking about it and watch a movie. Preferably one with a car chase or a building imploding or something."

Once they'd settled on an action movie and she was stretched out next to him on the couch, Wren started to relax. Not too much, since she was precariously close to falling on the floor, but her mind relaxed and her anxiety eased.

About halfway through the movie, Grant nodded off. The arm he'd draped along her hip got heavy and he was snoring softly into her hair. At one point, he muttered something, but she couldn't make it out. He didn't normally talk in his sleep at all, so either something was really bothering him or it was the painkillers.

She was almost asleep herself when Ben's voice echoed through her mind. *Wren?*

She'd actually forgotten about him in her rush to get to Grant, and her concern about his injury had occupied her thoughts since then. But now that it was quiet and Grant was okay, her fear of Ben started creeping back in. Her skin tingled with it, but she focused on keeping her muscles relaxed and her breathing calm so she didn't wake Grant.

So he knew she worked at the salon. And he probably hadn't bought the fake name and accent, and the lie would make him angry. But she had no reason to believe he knew anything else about her current life and Boston was a very big city. If she left the job at the salon, he'd have nothing to go on.

When she felt herself tensing up again, she blew out a breath and tried to focus on the movie again. Tomorrow, she thought. She'd worry about Ben tomorrow.

For now, Grant was okay and she was at his side, and that was all that mattered.

Grant woke up with a throbbing head, a dry mouth and an armful of Wren. He didn't care about the headache or the thirst. But he liked waking up with her in his bed.

"You're awake," she whispered.

"Barely."

"I didn't want to wake you, but I can't lie. I've been awake for a while and I really, really have to pee."

He managed a smile, and then he pulled his arm off her and rolled onto his back so she could get up.

She wasn't gone long and he felt the dip of the bed when she returned. Reluctantly, he opened his eyes and blinked at the morning sun. He needed better curtains.

"Your head still hurts." It wasn't a question, but he nodded anyway. Gently. "I'll go get your pills."

"Not the prescription ones," he said. "Just a couple from the medicine cabinet. And some water, please."

"Are you sure those are strong enough? I can bring the crackers, too. I think you're allowed to get crumbs in the bed in cases like this."

"I think it's partly stiffness. I'll try the regular ones and if it's not better in a few hours, I'll take the prescription ones."

He usually didn't like having to depend on people for help, but he didn't mind Wren fussing over him. She even held the straw for him so he could drink his water.

A glance at the clock told him it was almost nine. "Do you have to work today?"

"Not at the salon." Her brows furrowed for a few seconds, but then her expression cleared. "I'm supposed to work at the market this afternoon, but I can call them. They're pretty easygoing and they'd understand if I tell them you got hurt."

"No, it's fine. I'll be okay by myself for a bit."

She laughed and set the water glass on the bedside table. "By this afternoon, you'll be sick of me hovering and be glad to have some alone time."

"Not a chance." He didn't think he'd ever get tired of her. He wanted Wren with him all the time and, if he was being honest with himself, nothing would make him happier than her moving in with him.

But he didn't tell her that because he'd lied to her and the guilt kept him from saying the words. Maybe it wasn't an outright lie, but he'd deliberately avoided telling her the truth of what had happened in the storage room yesterday and that was close enough.

He was going to tell her. He just wanted to wait until he was strong enough to support her through the emotional fallout. Right now, he wasn't sure he was strong enough to take a piss alone.

After giving the pills a few minutes to kick in, he made his way to the bathroom. Wren hovered as he walked across the bedroom, but he was able to make it on his own. He actually felt a little better as he moved around, though he wasn't going to overdo it. Especially after the walk to the couch kicked his ass.

"You should call your mom," Wren said when she set a plate of scrambled eggs and toast on his lap.

"She'd love you for saying that. I'll call her later, after you leave for work." It would have to be a video chat so his mom could see for herself that he was okay, and it wouldn't be a short call. He didn't want to use up the time he had with Wren talking to his parents.

Once they'd eaten, she cleaned up and joined him on the couch. He channel surfed for a while before landing on an old black-and-white western. He heard her groan when he set the remote control on the arm of the couch and chuckled.

"This is classic stuff," he said.

She didn't complain, probably because he was hurt, and he must have nodded off because his phone vibrating jerked him awake. He looked at the screen and saw a text message from Gavin.

Cobb wants a meeting this afternoon if you're up to it. Both of us, so I'll drive.

That wasn't normal, and alarm bells went off in his head. If Cobb was calling them both in, something was going on and if he had to bet, he'd put money on it being related to the imaginary pipe upside his head.

He typed in a response one-handed, because he didn't want to let go of Wren's hand with the other.

Yeah. Text me when you're on your way.

Will do.

"What's going on?" she asked.

"Cobb wants me to come in for a meeting." She looked concerned, so he gave her a wry smile. "Probably paperwork. They love to make us do paperwork."

"You can't drive, can you?"

"The doctor said I could drive when I was up to it."

"You don't look up to it." She sat up, looking concerned. "I can be a little late to work."

"Gavin has to go, anyway. He can swing by and get me." He laced his fingers through hers. "You must be sick of taking care of me by now."

"Nope. Besides, you can make it up to me when you're feeling better."

On any other day, the suggestive look she gave him would have resulted in both of them being naked as quickly as possible. But not today. And probably not tomorrow, either. "I'll take my time about it, too."

She leaned forward and kissed him, but she pulled back before it could get too heated. "I should probably leave soon. Since I'll be driving, I need to leave time to find a parking space. In that neighborhood, it can take a while and I need to stop at home first."

"Thank you for staying with me, even though it's a pain in the ass for you."

She looked at him for a long moment and all the playfulness faded from her expression. "I don't want to make this a big thing because I have to go and you're recuperating, but I never stopped loving you, Grant."

His pulse quickened at her words and he squeezed her hand.

"I know we're getting to know each other again and taking it slow," she continued, "but I loved you before and I loved you while I was gone and I still love you now. So, no, it's not a pain in the ass for me to be here with you."

When she started to get up, he refused to let go of her hand, keeping her there. While the weight of his omission was pressing hard on him, she loved him and he wasn't going to let her say the words and then run away.

"If you think telling me you still love me isn't a big thing, whether I got hit in the head or not, you're crazy. It's the *biggest* thing." He tugged her closer. "I've never stopped loving you, either."

He kissed her, long and slow. But when he pulled her closer and slipped his hand under her shirt so he could slide it up her back, she gently pushed him away.

"You are definitely not up to that. And I really should go."

"Are you going to come back?"

She hesitated. "I'll have to go home first. I'll probably shower and grab some clean clothes for tomorrow, and then I'll be back."

"You'll be tired, though," he said. "And you probably didn't sleep well last night because you were too busy staring at me, so I get it if you just want to go home and crash."

She laughed. "I did *not* stare at you all night. I might have checked on you a few times, but I did sleep. I'll text you when I get home and see if you need me to pick up anything on the way over."

For a moment he was tempted to change his mind—yes, he wanted her to call the market and tell them she needed the afternoon and evening off—but he had a meeting looming over him. And he might not like what they had to say, so it was probably best to have all the facts before he told Wren the truth about what had happened at Kincaid's. She wasn't going to be happy with him.

But he shoved that aside to worry about later and kissed her goodbye. "Be careful tonight, okay?"

She gave him a strange look. "I'm always careful. Are you okay?"

"Yeah." He had nothing, he reminded himself. Ben Mitchell was in Virginia, and whoever had hit him with the pipe could have been some punk who'd started the fire. There was no sense in scaring her. "I'll see you later tonight."

After giving him a bright smile and another kiss, Wren left and Grant sighed, hating the emptiness in his apartment when she wasn't in it. But he didn't have a lot of time before Gavin showed up, so he grabbed a glass of water and got comfortable to FaceTime his mom.

Chapter Twenty-One

Grant was ready to go by the time Gavin showed up. Maybe it was the adrenaline rush from hearing Wren saying she still loved him, but he felt pretty good. The headache was mostly gone and, though he wasn't going to run any marathons today, he knew he'd gotten off lucky.

"You look a hell of a lot better than you did yesterday," Gavin said when he'd let himself in to the apartment.

"The stiffness in my neck and shoulder eased up and the headache is mostly gone, though it comes and goes. The knot on my head still hurts like hell if I touch it, though."

"Then don't touch it."

Grant snorted. "Living with an EMT's really rubbing off on you."

After grabbing his wallet and keys, Grant reluctantly got in the shotgun seat of Gavin's truck—he always preferred to be the one driving—and they headed for the station. Traffic was a little dense and he hoped Wren hadn't had any trouble getting to work on time. She'd told him a few times that the couple she worked for were really sweet, but he knew it was important to her not to take advantage of their kindness.

"It's weird that they called us both in," Gavin said.

"I mean, I didn't see it happen or see anything out of the ordinary so I'm not sure what they think I can add to the conversation."

"Maybe they think I'll need you for moral support."

He drummed his fingers on the wheel while they waited out a red light. "Did you tell Wren what happened?"

Grant looked out his window. "I told her I got hit in the head. Which I did."

"I'm guessing she then asked *what* hit you in the head."

"Yeah, she did, and I changed the subject."

"That's going to bite you in the ass in a big way."

"I know." He did know. Since the moment he'd made the decision not to tell Wren the truth of what had happened—as much as they knew, anyway—it had been a lead ball in the pit of his stomach.

When they finally walked into Cobb's office, only three minutes late, Grant's gaze went straight to Walsh and Gullotti, sitting on the battered leather love seat and looking grim. Having both LTs in the meeting didn't bode well.

"Have a seat," Cobb said, nodding toward the two metal chairs. "How you feeling today?"

"Better, sir. I got lucky."

"Good." He shuffled some papers around, which they all knew was his way of buying time to gather his thoughts, and then pushed them to the side and folded his hands. "They determined the fire at Kincaid's Pub was arson."

"Okay." There was more. And he could tell by the body language, it was going to be bad.

"Based on the method, accelerant and location, it looks like whoever set the fire wanted a response, but wasn't looking to hurt anybody or cause substantial damage to the property. If Tommy's heart hadn't gone on the fritz, the fire probably wouldn't have been a big deal."

The pieces started falling into place. "It was just a way to get the fire department there."

"To get *us* there," Danny said. "Specifically. This was our call to answer, in our own backyard. It was our family and there's no doubt we'd be the first on scene."

The chief nodded. "And when you factor in the situation with Wren and that several of the other guys had already walked through the storage room without incident, it's not unreasonable to think this was a deliberate attack on you, Cutter."

Grant sat back in the chair, trying to sort through his thoughts before he voiced any of them. These guys were like family and had his back, but they were also his superiors. He was not going to lose his shit in this room.

"After talking to Walsh, I took the liberty of making some phone calls," Cobb continued, "and the local PD can't put eyes on Ben Mitchell. He missed his meeting with his parole officer, too."

The anger came first. The guy had attacked him. He'd risked lives and property to hurt Grant. He'd come for Wren and he was going to pay for it.

There was fear because the asshole hadn't given up and moved on. And he was willing to hurt people to get to Wren.

And then there was a rush of something Grant couldn't really name. Ben Mitchell was here. He'd come for Grant, which meant he was in Boston and he'd shown his hand. Grant knew he was here and he'd be watching.

He could end this and Wren would be safe.

"Nope." Danny shook his head slowly without breaking eye contact with Grant. "The shit going through your head right now? That's not gonna happen."

"I haven't even said anything yet."

"You don't need to. It's written all over your face, and I'm telling you, it's not going to happen. You'll let the people whose job it is to handle this shit handle it."

"You're out on medical leave, effectively immediately," Cobb said. "It'll be on the news tonight and tomorrow morning that there was a fire at a beloved local bar and a firefighter who was injured will be out on medical leave until he recovers. In a break from the usual department protocol, you'll be named, but I'll need you to okay that."

"I'm okay with that." If it kept the bastard from starting another fire to get to him, he'd go along with it. He had no reason to put citizens and firefighters at risk if he couldn't get to Grant that way. "I understand."

"You won't be using your unexpected vacation time to play vigilante." Cobb gave him a hard look. "Like Walsh said, you're going to let law enforcement handle this so you don't make it any worse. What you're going to do is lie low and keep yourself and Wren safe."

When he didn't say anything, Danny spoke. "You might want to consider taking her and going home to New Hampshire for a few days."

"Law enforcement's looking for this guy and they're looking hard because he fucked with us," Cobb assured him. "Hopefully it won't take long to find him and then he's going away again. You wouldn't have to be gone more than a few days, if all goes well."

They were probably right. Taking Wren and getting out of the city would get her out of harm's way.

Maybe.

He thought of what Mitchell had done to Wren's brother. He'd gone to prison for it, and yet here he was. He'd set a fire to get to Grant, and then he'd dealt him a blow that might have killed him if not for his equipment.

Mitchell had found her in Boston. He knew about Grant. He knew about Kincaid's Pub. He knew a hell of a lot more than he should about Wren's life. And Grant's. He'd been watching.

Grant thought about his parents. His mom. He knew what they'd say. They'd tell him to get his ass home and bring Wren with him, and his dad would dust off the old shotgun from his duck hunting days.

He couldn't do it. As much as he loved Wren, he couldn't risk bringing Mitchell to his mother's doorstep.

Exhaling slowly, he closed his eyes. If he thought his presence threatened his mom, he wouldn't hesitate to leave. To go anywhere else, as long as it kept her safe. And if being with Grant endangered Wren, he'd run if that's what it took to keep anybody from hurting her.

Because sometimes, no matter how hard you fought, you didn't win.

Wren. She'd told him she'd run to keep him safe, but it hadn't made any sense to him because he hadn't experienced her fear. He didn't get it. But now he knew what the man was capable of and the reality of Grant's presence endangering his mother while his absence kept her safe, and the knowledge he was going to make that decision for her because she'd care more about him than herself gave him an inkling of what Wren had been feeling the day she told him they were done.

He opened his eyes. He wasn't going to hide, either,

because God only knew who Mitchell might go after next to flush out him and Wren.

"You," Cobb said, pointing a finger at Gavin. "Keep him on a short leash."

"I'll try, Chief. He doesn't always listen worth a damn, as you know."

Cobb didn't smile. "That's it for now. Stay out of trouble. I can't stress that enough, Cutter. Right now you've got the high ground, legally speaking. Don't jeopardize that trying to be a hero."

"I'm sorry about all of this, Chief."

"This doesn't reflect on you, son. The only person responsible for any of this is Ben Mitchell, and I'm already looking forward to being present to offer testimony at his arraignment."

Once they were back in Gavin's truck, Grant rested his head against the seat and closed his eyes. "I can't put my parents in this."

"I didn't think you would. You should call them, though. Tell them everything just so they know, especially since you've brought her there. I don't know how the hell he's getting information, but he's smart, I guess. Smarter than we gave him credit for."

"I'll call them in a little while. It's going to be a shitty phone call and I need more ibuprofen first." He opened his eyes as the truck started to move. "I have to tell Wren."

"Yeah. And you know we've all got your back, but Patty needs to know what's going on, too. Cait'll be worried about her mom and I need to be able to tell her you've taken her into consideration."

"No, I have to tell Wren *now*." His head was starting to throb in earnest, but he did his best to stay focused.

"If he knew starting a fire at Tommy's would get me there, then he knows everything about her and he might know she's at the market right now. Take me home so I can get my Jeep."

"You look like you're about to pass out. You're not driving anywhere."

"I don't want to call her and panic her without somebody there to be with her on her way home."

"We'll get somebody." Gavin used voice commands to initiate a call to Cait. "We don't need to panic, but Cait will make sure her mom and Wren are both okay until we figure this out."

When Cait answered and Gavin started explaining, Grant rested his head against the seat and closed his eyes. The pain was bad, but the fear for Wren was worse. He tried to remind himself that the man had never physically hurt her when they were together. That he hurt other people to manipulate her.

But, as Gavin had said before, that was before Mitchell did time behind bars. And he'd come to Boston to find her. That was an escalation and that meant all bets were off.

It wasn't until he made up his mind to call her—she had to know Mitchell was in Boston—that he realized he'd left his phone at home. *Fucking concussion.*

Taking a deep breath, he tried to calm himself to ease the pounding in his head and waited for Gavin to get off his freaking phone so he could use it.

"Does Wren Everett work here?"

Wren froze as a flush of fear spread over her body like a wildfire. It wasn't a voice on the phone this time and it felt as if a vise was tightening around her chest, keeping her from breathing.

She couldn't be seen from the aisle she was in, but there was no way to get to the back office—or down past the walk-in to the back door—without being seen by whoever was at the front of the store, near the cash register.

If you get scared, call me. If you think something's wrong, call 9-1-1 and then call me.

"Can I help you find something, sir?" Mr. Belostotsky sounded friendly enough, but she noticed he didn't answer the question. And he was greatly overexaggerating his accent, perhaps to make the other speaker think he couldn't understand him.

"I'm supposed to find Wren Everett and this is the address I was given, but my LT couldn't remember the name of the market."

She pulled her cell phone out of her pocket as she moved, wincing at the beep when she hit the button for the nine. But then she paused before hitting the one.

That wasn't Ben's voice.

My LT.

That's what Grant called Danny and Rick, she thought, gathering the courage to peek out from behind the shelving. If she was seen and had to run, she could probably make the back door before he could catch her.

A man with dark salt-and-pepper hair was frowning as he lifted his phone to his ear. "Hey, Jamie. I'm here but I'm not sure if I've got the right place."

He was wearing a Boston Fire sweatshirt and talking to Jamie. Most importantly, he wasn't Ben.

Keeping her finger over the button on her phone because it made her feel better, Wren stepped into view. "I'm Wren."

"Never mind, I've got her." The man hung up and smiled at her. "I'm Steve and I work with Jamie Kincaid. I guess somebody with 59's looking for you and I live around the corner, so I was closest."

When her phone buzzed in her hand, Wren dropped it, choking off a startled scream.

"You okay?" Steve asked.

No, she was definitely not okay. She looked down and saw Cait's number on the screen of her phone, which luckily didn't look cracked. After glancing at Steve to make sure he hadn't moved any closer, she bent and picked it up. "Cait? What's going on?"

"You sound scared. Are you okay? Somebody from the fire department should show up any second, but I'll call the police if you need them."

"No, I don't think so. Steve is here, and his sweatshirt is from the fire department. He said he works with Jamie."

"Yup, I know Steve. Nice guy. He's going to give you a ride to my mom's house, okay?"

"No, it is *not* okay," she said, fear making her loud. "What is going on? Did something happen to Grant?"

"Grant's okay."

"Then why didn't he call me? I want to talk to Grant."

"He left his phone at home and then he was vomiting in Gavin's truck and—"

"Wait, he was throwing up? Is his concussion worse?" A sobbing sound choked off her words and she could feel herself losing control.

"Wren, stop. Grant is okay." Cait's voice was firm. "He went in for a meeting and overdid it and the headache made him sick. But he's no worse than he was before. And I don't know exactly what's going on yet. They were on their way to my mom's and I'm waiting for somebody to come and relieve me. And Steve's going to bring you home, or he can stay with you on the bus and we'll give him a ride back to his car later. Whatever you're comfortable with. All I know is Grant and Gavin don't want any of us alone."

Ben.

The back of Wren's neck prickled. They knew something. And she couldn't think of any other reason why Grant would send a stranger to pick her up at work. He was afraid for her and he couldn't get to her himself, so he'd sent another firefighter.

"Wren?"

"I'm here."

"Just let Steve bring you home and the guys will tell us everything, okay? It was more important to get somebody to you than to get all the details. But everything will be okay."

"I'll let you drive if it helps you feel safer," Steve said, holding up a set of keys.

She shook her head and, after assuring Cait she was okay and would be home soon, hung up the phone. "I don't think I'm up to driving."

After explaining to Mr. and Mrs. Belostotsky there was an emergency, she got her coat and followed Steve out to a small SUV. He held the door for her, and she was aware of the way he looked around while she climbed in, as if watching for somebody.

She thought maybe Cait knew more than she was telling her, and when Steve climbed in, she looked at him. "Did they tell you what's going on?"

He shrugged as he pulled onto the street. "I know your boyfriend's on a crew with my LT's husband, they want you home and I'm supposed to keep my eyes open for anybody who looks like a problem."

"I'm sorry you have to do this," she said quietly, not sure what else to say.

"Don't worry about it." He flashed a quick grin. "Never hurts to have guys owe me a favor. You look a little shook, so go ahead and find a radio station you like and just try to relax, okay?"

That was easier said than done, since there was no doubt in Wren's mind at this point that Ben was somehow the trigger that had them sending a stranger to get her home safe.

The panic was like acid reflux, rising in her throat and trying to choke her, but she listened to the radio and concentrated on her breathing. She was okay. Grant was okay.

But when Steve pulled up in front of Patty's house, she could feel herself getting emotional again. "Thank you so much. I can't... Do you want money for gas? I can—"

He held up his hand. "Don't worry about it. Like I said, someday I might need a favor and I'll know who to reach out to."

Gavin walked out to the street as she climbed out of the car, and his smile looked forced. "Hey, Wren. Sorry for the drama, but Steve was the fastest way to get eyes on you."

"Why do you need eyes on me? What does that even mean?" In her gut, she knew the answer, but she wanted to hear it. "Where is Grant?"

"He's inside. And yes, he's fine."

"Cait said he threw up," she said as they walked up the sidewalk.

"Yeah, in my truck, the jerk. He got his blood pressure up enough to make the headache so bad he threw up from the pain. But he's better now."

Gavin opened the door for her and she didn't stop until she saw Grant in the living room. He looked pale, but he stood as she walked in and she went straight into his arms. Stroking her hair with one hand, he held her tightly with his other arm until she mostly stopped shaking.

"What's happening?" she whispered.

"I'm sorry I didn't call you myself. I forgot my damn phone and by the time Gavin was done with his, I was sick and then you were with Steve and there was no sense in doing this over the phone."

"Doing what? Cait said you were sick." She pulled back and cupped his cheek in her hand, as if she could feel a fever.

He turned his head to kiss her palm. "It was the pain, but I took a couple of painkillers and Patty gave me some crackers, so I'm feeling better. I promise. Let's go in the kitchen and we can all talk."

After threading his fingers through hers, he led her to where the others were waiting. Patty and Carter. Gavin and Cait. They'd been talking in low voices, but a hush fell over them and they all looked at Grant, waiting.

"Okay, so Gav and I had a meeting with Cobb today. There's a possibility—hell, I guess a probability, actually—that the fire was personal. That it was deliberately set to get to me." He paused and Wren's stomach lurched as she realized what he was saying. And when he turned his head to look at her, she knew it was about to get worse. "The cops down in Virginia can't locate Ben Mitchell. He blew off a meeting with his parole officer. He's gone and nobody knows where he is."

But Wren knew where he was. She could feel it in her gut, and it made her sick. He was in Boston. He'd come for her. And just like before, he'd hurt somebody she loved.

"He called me at the salon again yesterday," she managed to say. "I was going to tell you, Grant, but then you got hurt and… I should have called you. I should have called you as soon as he hung up."

"Did he say anything?" Gavin asked.

"Just my name. And then I told him my name was Kristen and that Wren quit and he hung up, but I don't think he believed me. I should have called you right that second and maybe you would have been careful. Maybe he wouldn't have hurt you."

Grant squeezed her hand. "Even if you'd called me, I wouldn't have been looking for him at a scene. Especially since it was the bar and we were all worked up about it, plus Tommy having a heart attack. It wouldn't have changed anything that happened."

"I knew he'd hurt you. That's why I left the first time." She could hear the rising panic in her voice, but she couldn't do anything to control it. Ben had hurt Grant just like he'd hurt Alex, and he wouldn't hesitate to hurt anybody else in this room.

"Wren, you need to stop," he said quietly. "We'll figure this out."

"I can't stay here anymore." It was the only coherent thought she had. "I have to go."

"You need to slow down and take a deep breath,"

Patty told her. "You're not going anywhere until we've talked about this."

"There's nothing to talk about." She jerked her hand free and left the kitchen. "I have to go before he hurts you, too."

Grant followed Wren up the stairs because he knew she wasn't thinking clearly. She was being driven by blind fear, and as soon as she got in that room, she was probably going to start packing her stuff. Or maybe she'd just leave it. She'd take her keys, her purse and her phone and go.

He wasn't going to let her do that. Not again.

Once they were in her room, though, she stopped and just stood there. He closed the door softly behind them and walked around her until he could see her face. Tears were streaming down her cheeks.

"Wren, you're safe. Everybody's safe right now and you need to take a few minutes and then we'll figure out what to do next."

"He hurt Tommy. He hurt *you*, so don't try to tell me he won't hurt Patty or Carter or anybody else." She looked as if she was struggling to breathe and he knew he needed to calm her down somehow. "What if he knows we went to New Hampshire, Grant? Your parents…"

"I called Dad already. I told him everything and he'll tell Mom and my brother. It's very unlikely Mitchell will leave Boston as long as we're here, but they'll be vigilant, just in case."

"I didn't want this." She could barely get the words out, and it was starting to scare him. "*This* is what I didn't want to happen. This is why I ran."

"This is not your fault. None of this is your fault and you are not alone. Do you understand me?" When she didn't answer, he tipped her chin up so she looked at him. "You're not alone. You're not going to *be* alone because you're not going to run. We'll get through this together."

"I'm so scared, Grant."

He wrapped his arms around her and buried his face in her hair. "I'm not going to let him hurt you. Or anybody else."

She stilled for a moment, and then she spoke. And when she did, her voice was clear. "You can't stop him."

Her certainty chilled him. "The police are looking for him. We're all going to be watching for him now that we know he might not be in Virginia."

"If he'd caught you alone, you might have ended up like Alex."

"No, I wouldn't, because I'm not that easy to take in a fair fight. He sucker-punched me, basically, but he won't get the drop on me again." She was trembling, but at least her breathing had slowed. "Why don't you grab some things and come home with me tonight?"

"What about Patty and Carter?"

"The police will be patrolling this area and her neighbors are nosy as hell. This isn't an easy neighborhood to be sneaky in. And to be honest, he's a coward, Wren. He couldn't even confront me face-to-face. And he didn't go *in* the salon. He just kept calling."

"But Alex…"

"I'm going to take a wild guess here. Alex has your build and isn't really a tough guy?"

"No, he's not, but—"

"I think he wants to control you and I think he

wanted to hurt me because I replaced him, but I don't think he's going to go after other people." He kissed the top of her head. "Why don't you pack up some things? We'll go to my place, lock the door and get some rest. You belong with me, anyway."

"No." She pulled away from him. "No, that's not how I want my things to end up at your place, Grant."

"What are you talking about?"

"I don't want to just bring my things to your apartment because I need a place to stay and then just not leave. That's not how I want this to happen."

"Wren, now is not the time for this."

"It *is* the time because I spend half my time at your apartment anyway. What do you think's going to happen if I bring my things there with me? I don't want to live with you because you thought it was a good way to make me feel safe. I want it to be because it's what *we* want."

"I had your ring picked out," he said in a quiet voice. He was tired of pretending this newly dating thing was ever going to work. They had a history and it wasn't going away.

The color drained from her already pale face. "What?"

"I had your ring picked out and I was only a paycheck or two away from having enough saved to buy it when you told me we were done." He had to stop and clear his throat. "We're not a new couple, Wren. We're not just getting to know each other. I was going to ask you to be my wife."

She pressed her fingertips to her mouth as tears ran down her cheeks.

"I'm sorry that hurts you," he continued. "It hurt me,

too. And it hurts me when you stand here and make it sound like you spending the night at my place is some kind of shortcut, because I was at that place. I was ready. But if it makes you feel better, just shove a pair of clean underwear in your pocket and grab your toothbrush. Leave the rest here."

"I don't know what to do," she said, her voice so small he had to strain to hear it. He was surprised he could hear anything, really, with the way his heart was thumping in his chest.

"You're not going to be alone tonight, Wren. The people who care about you—because I'm only one of them—are not going to let you do that to yourself. You can stay here, you can stay with Gavin and Cait, or you can come home with me."

Her indecision was painfully clear in the way she chewed at her lip and clenched her fists.

"I *want* you with me," he said softly. "You don't have to bring your stuff if it's too much right now. I just want to know you're okay. But it's up to you."

"I want to be with you."

"Good." He smiled and smoothed her hair back. "Get whatever you need and then we'll go. But you're going to have to drive."

Chapter Twenty-Two

Wren woke with a start, her heart racing and her hairline damp with sweat. It was dark and Grant was snoring softly next to her. He shifted a little when she sat upright, but he didn't wake up.

She was surprised she'd even fallen asleep. Long after Grant had drifted off, she'd lain awake and tried in vain not to think about Ben out there somewhere, looking for her.

He could be standing out front right now, watching their window. Waiting.

She thought about Tommy Kincaid, having a heart attack while trying to put out a fire Ben had started just to get to Grant. She worried about the women at the salon. The thought of Mr. and Mrs. Belostotsky being in danger made her stomach hurt. Patty. Carter. Anybody connected to her.

Grant.

An image of Ben swinging a pipe and hitting Grant from behind in the storage room played through her mind constantly, like a horror movie she couldn't turn off.

Grant kept assuring her they were safe. Gavin, Cait and Patty all seemed willing to accept the risks having her in their lives brought. But they didn't know. To them, he seemed to be no more than an ex-boyfriend who was still hung up on her and had some control issues.

They hadn't stood, helpless, and watched what he did to her brother. The beating he'd given Alex had been brutal and Ben hadn't cared about the consequences. He hadn't cared that the neighbors were calling 9-1-1. He hadn't cared about her screaming and then sobbing so hard she vomited.

Ben had wanted to make a point about what happened to people who tried to come between him and Wren.

Grant was between Ben and Wren. And all the people in her life who knew where she was but probably wouldn't tell him if he knocked on their doors were between them.

When her stomach rolled, she got out of bed and hurried to the bathroom, but nothing came up. Sinking to the floor, she leaned her head against the door of the linen closet and closed her eyes. But no matter how hard she squeezed them shut, she couldn't stop the tears.

She had no idea how long she sat there, feeling nothing but fear and uncertainty. Until her body started to ache from the cold tile and her head hurt from trying to cry silently.

Forcing herself to her feet, she soaked a washcloth in cold water and pressed it to her face. It helped a little, shocking her into focus.

Then she took a deep breath and crept back through the bedroom. Grant was facing her side of the bed, his arm flung across her empty place as if he'd reached for her in his sleep. She loved him so much her heart ached with it, and she watched him for a few minutes, trying to settle her mind.

"Grant." He didn't even stir, so she crawled onto the mattress and squeezed his hand. "Grant?"

He mumbled something and tried to roll onto his back, but she had his hand. When she didn't let go, he opened his eyes and blinked a few times at her. "Wren? What's wrong?"

"I'm scared."

He sat up, frowning. "Did something happen?"

"No." The tears started again, and it took her a few seconds to get any words out past the lump in her throat. "I'm just really, really scared."

Wren expected him to tell her everything would be okay, pull her down to her pillow and tell her to go back to sleep. Instead he got out of bed and yanked on the sleep pants he hadn't bothered putting on earlier. After turning on the bedroom light, which made them both blink, he started to pick her up. But a small sound escaped his lips and he took her hand instead, leading her into the living room.

He hit the light switch as they went through the doorway, flooding his apartment in light. And then after settling her on the couch with the throw blanket around her shoulders, he went and turned on the kitchen lighting and got her a glass of water.

Her Grant, she thought, chasing the shadows away.

After she swallowed some of the water, he set the glass on the coffee table and sat next to her, taking her hand in his. "Talk to me, honey."

"I just… I'm just scared for everybody. Scared for you." He knew what she was afraid of, so she tried instead to explain why she was having a meltdown in the middle of the night. "I had a horrible nightmare and then I woke up and he was in my head and I started thinking about all the people he can use to get to me."

"I can keep you safe. We can keep Patty and everybody else safe, too. The police are looking for him. Hell, the fire department's looking for him. His picture's been circulated everywhere." He squeezed her hand. "You saw yesterday how we all take care of each other when somebody needs help. Just keep trusting us."

"But what if he actually hurts somebody in *your* life. How are you all going to look at me if he hurts Patty? Or Cait? Or any of them." Her heart ached just thinking about it. "If he puts one of you or your family in the hospital, do you think that's not going to change everything?"

"That's not how you do family, Wren. Your brother's an asshole, plain and simple, but the people—the family—you have in your life now won't turn away from you."

"No. He's not an asshole, though. Alex warned me over and over again that Ben was no good and I didn't listen. He tried to help me and I rejected it and he kept trying to help me. And he almost got killed for it. Alex almost *died*, Grant. Because of me. Because I was stupid and trusted the wrong man."

"The only person responsible for Alex being assaulted is Ben. It's not your fault." He blew out a breath and ran a hand over his hair. "Yeah, Alex had the right to be pissed. He could even tell you he told you so. But even if he did blame you, he should have worked through it because you're his sister and cutting you out of his life is the one thing he can't do."

"Not everybody has a family like yours. And not

everybody has this…brotherhood that you have, where everybody's family and has each other's backs no matter what."

"You have it. You have *me*. You have this family. We have your back no matter what and we're all here and ready to prove it to you if that's what you need. You're not alone."

"Maybe I don't know how to do this," she said in a small, quiet voice.

"Do what?"

"This. I don't know to be in a relationship with you. How to believe that no matter what, you're going to still love me at the end of every day."

"Where is this even coming from? I told you I love you."

"I've had five men in my life tell me they loved me. My father loved us but he and my mother weren't good together, so he took off and left all of us. Then there was a stepfather who loved us for a few years before he decided he loved his secretary more than he loved my mother. Ben told me he loved me. And Alex. Alex loved me until the day he told me he didn't want me in his life anymore because of what Ben did. And then you told me you loved me."

"I'm not them. And the only way you're going to believe that, no matter what, I'm still going to love you at the end of every day is to let me *be here* at the end of every day. To let me wake up next to you every morning."

"I won't want to wake up to the look on your face if he comes after you again and really hurts you."

"If he comes after me again, I'll be ready. And relieved since showing his hand will get him nothing but a beating and a long time behind bars." He pushed back the strands of hair sticking to her wet cheeks, tucking them behind her ear. "We're okay, Wren. Do you believe I love you?"

"Yes," she whispered, because she did. If she dug down beyond her fear, she knew this man loved her with every fiber of his being.

"And I know you love me. So we're going to believe in each other and we're going to get through this together, and everything else life decides to throw our way. Together."

"Together." She squeezed his hand and nodded.

Grant could still see the shadow of fear in her eyes, and even though the most important thing to him was that she'd gotten spooked and hadn't run—that she'd come to him instead—he wished he could make those shadows disappear.

"Look," he said, making up his mind. He was going to do what was best for Wren's peace of mind, no matter what it took. "If you need to run to feel like you're protecting people you care about—to really feel safe— then we'll run together. We can go away until they catch this guy."

Her eyes widened. "And go where?"

"Anywhere. Florida. Alaska. Arkansas. I don't have a passport, so we can't leave the country, but I'll go with you. I love you. I'm going to keep saying that, because it's true."

"You said running's not the answer."

"I don't think it is, but if you do and it's what you need to feel safe, we'll talk about it." He grinned. "And you can't go alone. Even if you won't let me in your car,

I'll just follow you in my Jeep. We've already established I have boundary issues when it comes to you."

As he intended, she smiled through her tears at the reminder of him making an ass out of himself at their girls' night out. "I wouldn't go without you. But if you're sure everybody's being careful, then we won't go at all. I love you and I trust you and I just want to be here with you."

Then she was moving toward him and he pulled her into his arms. He kissed her, trying to chase the last vestiges of her nightmares away, and then he just held her close. Her arms squeezed him so tightly he could barely breathe, but he didn't care.

"Have I mentioned how much I love you?" he asked, because he was going to say it all the time now. He never wanted Wren to doubt how he felt about her.

"I won't ever get tired of hearing that, because I love you, too." She tilted her head back and smiled up at him. "And I don't really want to go to Arkansas. I'm sure it's a perfectly nice state to visit, but I'd rather just go back to bed with you."

"I can talk in a Southern accent if you want," he said as he got up and went to turn off the lights, trying to mimic the accents he'd seen on TV. "So you can pretend."

She laughed, the joyful sound echoing through his apartment. "That was awful. Don't ever do that again without letting me get my phone to record it first."

Once they were back in bed, in the dark, Grant stared at the ceiling while Wren slowly drifted off to sleep. He was thankful he'd calmed her fear enough to let her rest, but now he was wide awake.

More than anything, he wanted to get out of bed and

go kick over every rock in Boston until he found the one Ben Mitchell was hiding under and make damn sure the asshole would never bother Wren or anybody else Grant cared about ever again.

He wasn't helpless. Even in his weakened state, he could keep Wren safe if her ex came after her. But sitting and waiting made him feel powerless and he didn't want this situation dragging on like a black cloud hovering over their lives.

As if sensing his tension in her sleep, Wren stirred, frowning and shifting away from him. Grant forced himself to relax and kissed her hair. Ben Mitchell's day would come, and Grant would do the smart, responsible thing and focus on Wren instead of trying to bait the guy out of hiding.

All that mattered was the woman in his arms. She loved him and she'd trusted him enough to come to him with her fear so they could work through it together. There may be a wolf at the door, but he wasn't getting in tonight. And no matter what, he would never come between them again.

For two days, Wren and Grant hung out in his apartment, eating takeout and watching movies. She wasn't ready to make any big decisions about her employment yet, so she called in still-sick to the salon and told the market she was okay, but the emergency was ongoing. The lie made her feel guilty, but she wasn't ready to face the world just yet.

And since Grant was out on medical leave until they ran Mitchell to ground, they were taking lazy to a whole new level. He was feeling a lot better, and starting to get antsy about being confined. And on day three, she admitted to herself she was getting bored.

She did her best not to think about Ben but sometimes, when it was quiet or Grant was sleeping, she couldn't help it. It was hard, trusting in the system to take care of him, but she trusted Grant. When the fear started taking hold, she told him—even if she had to wake him up—and when he held her and told her they were safe, she allowed herself to believe him.

But something would have to change soon. They both needed to get back to work and start living the normal life they were going to build together. Yesterday had been hard on Grant because his crew worked without him. And tomorrow would be worse, because St. Patrick's Day was an all-hands-on-deck kind of day for the city, and he'd be sitting it out.

"I think we watched this movie yesterday," Wren said, frowning at the television. They were curled up on the couch because it was raining and cold and there was nothing out in the world they needed that badly. "I *know* we did. The jousting and the dancing and rock music."

"But it's a great movie. It's this, talk shows or reruns of cop shows."

"It really is a good movie."

But when he started saying the dialogue along with the characters, she elbowed him in the ribs. "Stop that. It's annoying, and just how many times have you seen this movie, anyway?"

"As often as I can." He nuzzled her neck. "Let's dance, you and I."

"I don't think that's what he means when he says that."

"I'm going off-script." He pulled her closer and

nipped at her earlobe. "I'd probably be censored on TV, though."

"I think your phone is vibrating."

"I think so, too, though it was weird there for a second." After she shifted away from him, he fished it out of his pocket and frowned at the screen. "It's Danny. Why the hell is he using FaceTime?"

"Maybe you should answer it and find out."

He did. "Hey, LT. What's up?"

"I hate this thing."

"Maybe hold it a little further from your face. And get one of those pore strips for your nose."

"Maybe you should go f— Oh hey, Wren. Nice to see you."

"Literally," she said, smiling.

"Why the video?" Grant asked, cutting to the chase.

"It seemed like the easiest way to talk to you and Wren at the same time. In retrospect, speakerphone would have worked. Anyway, they found Mitchell."

The words, dropped so casually like that, shook Wren to her core. She sucked in a breath, her body cold all of a sudden, and was barely aware of Grant's free hand closing around hers.

"They arrested him at a gas station about an hour ago. Cuffed and stuffed, and he didn't want to go, so he got taken to the pavement pretty hard."

"They're sure it's him?" Grant asked, squeezing her hand.

"They're sure. Cobb confirmed it before he called me. Mitchell violated parole in Virginia, plus he's got the new charges here. Arson. Assault. Resisting. Anything else they can tack on to it. But the bottom line is that Ben Mitchell is going away for a long time."

It's over. Wren trembled, squeezing Grant's hand back so hard she was surprised she didn't break his fingers. She heard Grant asking more questions and then thanking Danny, but she couldn't pull her thoughts together enough to speak.

It was really over.

Grant tossed his phone on the table and then hauled Wren into his arms. "You're shaking."

"It's relief, I think," she said, finally able to string words together. "He's been a shadow in my life for so long and now he'll be gone."

"I told you to have faith in the system. And faith in us." He kissed her forehead. "I'm glad you listened."

She laughed and slapped his hand. "Did you seriously just *I told you so* in this moment?"

"According to the married guys on the crew, I need to celebrate the times I'm right because there won't be many." He shrugged. "Just practicing."

After straddling his lap, she held his face between her hands and kissed him. "Thank you for sticking with me. I know this hasn't been easy."

"You're worth it." He ran his hands over her hips. "*We're* worth it."

She rested her hands on his shoulders and sighed. "I don't even know what to feel right now."

"Relief. Joy." His nudged his hips up. "Maybe a little horny."

"I'm definitely relieved. But I'm going to need a minute on the rest." She considered. "Maybe half a minute."

"So the coast is clear now," he said, and she could tell he was getting at something, but she couldn't tell what.

"Yes. Finally."

"It was important to you that you not end up living

here because you were here for your safety and just didn't leave." He paused and cleared his throat. "So now that the coast is clear, there's no reason you couldn't go back to Patty's if that's what you want to do."

"And you bring this up while I'm straddling your lap?"

He grinned. "Besides being naturally charming, I'm also pretty clever. Especially when it comes to getting what I want."

That he was. Looking down into his dark eyes—crinkled as he smiled at her—she wasn't sure she could resist him if she wanted to. But she didn't want to. "I can go back to Patty's for a night so you can officially ask me if you want, but I'd rather not. I just want to be here with you. Is that what you really want?"

"I want you in my bed. Forever," he said in a voice that was almost a growl against her lips. Then he shifted her body so he could stand with her in his arms.

"What about your head. Should you be carrying—"

"My head is fine. It's my dick that aches right now." He shrugged. "Plus, sex releases endorphins, which are your body's natural painkillers."

"Then we should go to bed," she said, giving him that slightly naughty half smile she knew drove him nuts. "For science."

It was probably the fastest they ever got naked, but Grant being Grant, he tried to slow things down the second they hit the bed.

"I like to take my time with these things, you know." He tickled her with a soft, butterfly kiss to the middle of her stomach.

"I know you do. But I just want you, Grant. There's

been so much and so many emotions and I just want to *feel* you."

Rather than teasing her any more, he moved up the bed so his face was next to hers. "I love you."

She smiled and wrapped her arms around him. "I love you, too. But I'm still not going to let you tease me today."

"I'll have the rest of my life to torment you, so you tell me what you want."

Instead of telling him anything, she pushed him onto his back. Then she grabbed a condom package from the nightstand and handed it to him. While he opened it, she stroked his erection, loving the contradiction of silky soft and hardness. She was tempted to go down and take that hardness into her mouth, but she hadn't let him go down on her, so she didn't.

Once he'd rolled on the condom, she straddled his thighs and leaned down to kiss him thoroughly. He cupped her cheek in his hand, his thumb running tenderly over her skin as they kissed, and his tenderness warmed her heart.

Then she straightened and reached down to guide him into her. They held eye contact as she slowly lowered herself, then lifted before lowering more, until he filled her completely. She was still, savoring the feeling, and he reached up to cup her breasts.

"Have I told you how beautiful you are?" he asked in a husky voice.

"Not tonight."

"You are so fucking beautiful, Wren."

Tears sprang to her eyes, and she shook her head. "Do *not* make my cry right now."

Because she was busy trying to blink away her blurry

vision, his fingers brushing her clit made her gasp. He stroked softly as her hips started to rock.

"I bet I can make you do something else instead," he said, that cocky grin back on his face.

She swiveled her hips while squeezing and he sucked in a breath. She could be cocky, too, even if she couldn't pull off the grin like he did. With his thumb on her clit—brushing, pressing, stroking—she knew it wouldn't be long before she came, and she leaned forward to brace her hands on his chest.

Before she could react, Gavin rolled until he was on top and when she opened her mouth to protest, he drove into her. She gasped and clutched his shoulders.

"Come for me, Wren."

Hearing the tremor in his voice, she realized he was on the edge. Her teasing, take-it-slow lover needed her as much as she had needed him, but he wouldn't give in until she let go.

She slid her hand between them and stroked her clit while he thrust into her harder and deeper until all the stress and emotional upheaval of the last two days were blown away by the force of her orgasm. She said his name as she came, and his body shuddered as he let himself find release.

When he lowered his body onto her gently, she stroked his back and kissed his forehead. They were quiet as their breathing slowed, and then he kissed the top of her breast before getting up to dispose of the condom.

Even though they'd have to get up and forage for food soon, Grant got back into bed and Wren moved closer, as always. He stared at her for a long moment, twirling strands of her hair around his finger.

"You and me," he said softly. "Always."

She lifted her head to plant a hard kiss on his mouth. "You and me."

Epilogue

Summer

Kincaid's Pub was definitely pushing max capacity. It was a private event, but when the invitation was open to firefighters and the event was the grand reopening of a firefighters' bar, everybody showed up.

Wren moved easily through the crowd, a frosted mug of beer in each hand. People spoke to her as she passed and she responded, but kept moving. She had drinks to deliver.

As usual the guys from Engine 59 and Ladder 37 were holding court in the pool table alcove. She didn't know all of them because there were different crews for different days, but she knew most of them.

The mugs were for Chris and Rick, who were engaged in a fairly heated game of pool. She set them down and, when she saw Grant sitting in the corner with Aidan and Scott, decided to take a short break.

He grinned when he saw her and patted his knee. There were no free chairs, so she sat sideways on his lap and waited for him to finish his conversation.

Though she'd been helping with the preparations for tonight for a while, this was her first official shift at the bar. She'd be part-time, learning the ropes and filling in as necessary as Lydia's baby bump grew. Her primary job would still be at the bookstore.

When a very tearful Mrs. Belostotsky had told her they'd decided to sell the market and retire to someplace warmer, Wren had hugged her and wished them well. On her way home, she stopped at the bookstore because it was comforting to browse, and Rhonda had offered her her old job back. The women at the salon had graciously accepted her notice and had pizza delivered on her last day for a lunch break party.

As Grant's arm snaked around her hips, holding her close, Wren smiled. Life was so very good.

"This story's never going to end," he murmured. "Let's go outside and get some fresh air."

"Just for a few minutes," she said, standing. "I'm supposed to be working."

"You get a break."

She laughed. "Yeah, when I've been here longer than an hour."

But he took her hand and led her through the crowd to the door. It had been a hot and humid day and even though the sun had gone down, the city was steamy.

"Can you believe Tommy won't give me a family discount?" he asked as they walked hand in hand down the sidewalk to a small bench.

"I can't believe you asked him."

"Hey, the only thing better than a cold beer is a cheap cold beer."

She laughed. "I don't think he even gives Scotty and Aidan a discount, and they're actually his family."

Putting his arm around her shoulders, he shifted his

body sideways so he was looking at her. "You look beautiful tonight. And happy."

She smiled. "It's funny you should say that. When I was sitting on your lap, I was thinking about how happy I am right now. I have everything. You. All these friends. The bookstore. I think I'm going to love working here. And I'm going to say *you* twice because you are definitely the best part."

He caught his lip between his teeth, looking at her so thoughtfully that she got a little nervous about what he might be thinking. "I love you. Completely."

She hadn't been expecting that. "I love you, too."

He sat up straight and scrubbed his palms over this denim-clad thighs a couple of times, and then he reached into his pocket. "I've been waiting, trying to figure out a perfect time or place to give you this."

It was a small velvet box and Wren's breath caught in her throat. Then he opened it and she exhaled in a long, shaky sigh. It was an emerald-cut diamond, with two smaller, square diamonds on either side. It was simple and yet stunning at the same time and she pressed her hand to her chest.

"It seems like proposals are supposed to be an event," he continued. "But sitting here with you and you telling me how happy you are and that I'm the best part of it is… Well, this is the happiest moment of my life, so it seems like the right time to ask you to be my wife."

She nodded, trying to talk, but just making a squeaky sound.

"I love you, Wren. Will you marry me?"

"Yes." The word practically burst out of her mouth.

He slid the ring over her finger and it fit perfectly. She admired it, watching it sparkle in the lights around them. Then she threw her arms around his neck and put everything she felt into kissing him until neither of them could breathe.

"So I guess I didn't blow the proposal?" he asked, and he was teasing, but she could see the relief on his face.

"This is so perfect." And she meant it. Fancy, staged proposals weren't really her style. But this was.

He smiled. "People always say you just know when the time is right and I always wondered what that meant. Is it like a physical shock? A voice in your head? And then one day we responded to a CO call and it turned out to be a false alarm, but it was the jeweler. The one who made the ring I'd finally picked out for you before."

Wren felt a pang of sadness, but it was fleeting. They'd both reached a place where that time could be mentioned in passing without it reopening the old wounds.

"And it was still there, which blew my mind. I mean, how could the most beautiful ring I'd ever seen not have sold in all those months?" He chuckled, sounding a little embarrassed at the emotion in his voice. "And I knew. It was waiting for you, because it was *your* ring. And now it's on your finger, where it's supposed to be."

Tears shimmered in her eyes, making the diamond sparkle even more brilliantly. "Please tell me you didn't sell your new wheels."

"No, although I would have in a heartbeat. I'd already started saving up again because no matter what, I was going to ask you to be my wife." He ran his thumb over the stone. "Remember a couple months ago when all of us guys went to Maine to help a guy rebuild a hunting cabin that had taken some damage during an ice storm?"

"Yes, I remember you talking about Cobb and the other guys trying to cover you all wanting a shift off at the same time like it was the world's most annoying puzzle. And I obviously remember you being gone for four days because I missed you."

"It was the jeweler's family cabin. The money I had stashed away and the work on the cabin combined paid for the ring, and I got to keep my wheels." He nudged her. "Admit it, they're really nice wheels."

She nodded, but she couldn't speak because her throat was all closed up from the swelling of emotion. That was family, she thought. The guys inside who'd all given up time off to go to another state and spend four days working to help Grant get this ring. The administration, trying to make it work. The firefighters who'd covered their shifts.

They were *her* family now, too, she realized. They came with the guy.

"You okay?"

She threw her arms around his neck so she could bury her face in his neck. "I love you. I love them. I swear, I'm so full of love and happiness right now, I might cry happy tears all night."

"Hey!" Tommy's voice boomed from the door of the bar. "Stop making out with my staff, Cutter, or you're going to pay a pain-in-the-ass tax on every beer you buy."

"I'm coming," Wren called, pulling away from Grant and mopping at her face.

"As a sign of my maturity as a soon-to-be-married

guy," Grant said, "I'm not going to make the obvious joke here."

She rolled her eyes at him and stood. Then she took his hands and pulled him to his feet. "One more kiss, future husband of mine."

"Gladly, almost wife." And he gave her a kiss that curled her toes.

The next hour passed in a blur of congratulations and toasts and beer. The women gushed over her ring and, on the clock or no, Wren took the time to hug every one of the guys who'd gone to Maine to help Grant work off the balance of her ring.

Olivia actually got teary eyed over it. "It's so beautiful, Wren. You have no idea how happy I am to see it on your finger. Derek told me the story of the ring when he was explaining why Amber and I would have to work out the kids' schedules minus one adult while he was away for a few days, and I've been *dying* for him to finally ask you so I could see it."

"Before he found that one," Derek said, "he actually had us guys looking at pictures of rings at a freaking Red Sox game, of all places. Trust me, we were *all* happy when he finally found the perfect one."

"On to the most important question," Ashley said. "When does the wedding planning start?"

"Oh!" Olivia grinned. "I love planning weddings."

Jess laughed and tucked her arm around Rick's waist. "You love planning everything."

"Good point."

"I'll need you, Olivia, because it'll have to be a big wedding." Wren looked around her new family. "There is no way I'm picking and choosing, so I'm going to have a *lot* of bridesmaids."

Amidst the laughter, Wren caught Cait's eye. And when Cait scrunched up her shoulders, grinning, to show how excited she was, Wren knew she wouldn't even have to ask. Cait would be her maid of honor.

Chris Eriksson pushed his way into the group surrounding them. "Fitzy just told me it's time to bring it out and we should all head out front."

Grant laced his fingers through hers and kissed her again. A lifetime of kissing this man was all she'd ever need, she thought as they followed the others out to the bar.

Tommy Kincaid stood in front of the framed photo of Bobby Orr. His daughters were on either side of him as Scotty and Aidan tightened the final screws securing it once again in its place of honor on the wall.

The last couple of years had seen a lot of upheaval, which must explain why he was so emotional tonight. Every man and woman in the bar tonight was somebody he considered family, and he felt their wins and losses.

It had started with Danny and Ashley separating, which brought Lydia home to help out at the bar. His relationship with his daughters had been a mess. Then Lydia had started seeing Aidan, which had put Aidan at odds with Scotty. For a while, Tommy had despaired that he'd let his wife down so badly, he could never make it right and that, even in heaven, she was heartbroken.

But Kincaids were nothing if not stubborn, though, and they'd all worked it out. This past Thanksgiving had been perfect. Danny and Ashley, with little Jackson. Lydia and Aidan. Scotty and Jamie. And this coming Thanksgiving, he'd have a brand-new grandchild to hold.

Tommy had watched with pride, from his barstool, as the guys of Engine 59 and Ladder 37 had had their lives turned upside down and come out the other side better for it. And tonight, watching Grant and Wren basking in love and congratulations brought it almost full circle.

Scotty and Aidan putting Bobby Orr back on the wall where he belonged, marking the true reopening of his pub, with Lydia and Ashley at his side was the closing of the circle. It was symbolic in a way he couldn't explain in words. He just felt it in his heart.

He hadn't always done right by his wife, and he hadn't really known the truth of it until after he'd lost her. But at least if he was lucky enough to see her again on the other side, he could tell her their children were happy and loved. That was all Joyce had ever really wanted for them.

As his son and son-in-law stepped back from Bobby Orr's picture with game show hostess flourishes, emotion tightened Tommy's throat and he wasn't sure he could speak.

Instead, he touched the tips of his fingers to his mouth for a long moment and then pressed them against the glass.

* * * * *

Author's Note

The processes and organizational structures of large city fire departments and emergency services are incredibly complex, and I took minor creative liberties in order to maintain readability.

To first responders everywhere, thank you.

Acknowledgments

Thank you to my editor, Angela James, and to every member of the Carina Press team. Your support for and work on the Boston Fire series meant the world to me. And a huge thank-you to all the readers whose enthusiasm for the men and women of Boston Fire made it a pleasure to write.

Dear Reader,

They say you always remember your first and it's true, the first book that Shannon Stacey and I worked on together here at Harlequin still holds a very fond place in my heart. *Exclusively Yours* became not only an instant reader favorite, but it launched Shannon's much-beloved Kowalski series. If this is your first time getting a look at the Kowalskis, welcome and enjoy the ride (four-wheeler optional). If you're revisiting an old favorite, like I am, please join me in reminiscing about that time that Joe and Keri...well, never mind, I don't want to spoil it for anyone. But it's probably time for a reread!

Please enjoy this extended excerpt from *Exclusively Yours* by Shannon Stacey, available in print, audio and eBook.

Angela James
Editorial Director, Carina Press
Editor and lifelong fangirl of the Kowalski series

When Keri Daniels' editor finds out she has previous carnal knowledge of reclusive bestselling author Joe Kowalski, she gives Keri a choice: get an interview or get a new job.

Joe's never forgotten the first girl to break his heart, so he's intrigued to hear Keri's back in town—and looking for him. Despite his intense need for privacy, he'll grant Keri an interview if it means a chance to finish what they started in high school.

He proposes an outrageous plan—for every day she survives with his family on their annual camping and four-wheeling trip, Keri can ask one question. Keri agrees; she's worked too hard to walk away from her career.

But the chemistry between them is still as potent as the bug spray, Joe's sister is out to avenge his broken heart and Keri hasn't ridden an ATV since she was ten. Who knew a little blackmail, a whole lot of family and some sizzling romantic interludes could make Keri reconsider the old dream of *Keri & Joe 2gether 4ever*.

Chapter One

"You got busy in the backseat of a '78 Ford Granada with Joseph Kowalski—only the most reclusive best-selling author since J. D. Salinger—and you don't think to tell me about it?"

Keri Daniels sucked the last dregs of her too-fruity smoothie through her straw and shrugged at her boss. "Would *you* want anybody to know?"

"That I had sex with Joseph Kowalski?"

"No, that you had sex in the backseat of a '78 Granada." Keri had no idea how Tina Deschanel had gotten the dirt on her high school indiscretions, but she knew she was in trouble.

An exceptionally well-paid reporter for a glossy, weekly entertainment magazine did not withhold carnal knowledge of a celebrity on the editor-in-chief's most wanted list. And having kept that juicy little detail to herself wouldn't get her any closer to parking her butt in an editorial chair.

Tina slipped a photograph from her purse and slid it across the table. Keri didn't look down. She was mentally compiling a short list of the people who knew she'd fogged up the windows of one of the ugliest cars in the history of fossil fuels. Her friends. The cop who'd knocked on the fogged-up window with a flashlight at a really inopportune moment. Her parents, since the cop was in a bad mood that night. The approximately six hundred kids attending her high school that year and anybody *they* told. Maybe short list wasn't the right term.

"It was 1989," Keri pointed out, because her boss clearly expected her to say something. "Not exactly a current event. And you ambushed me with this shopping spree."

Actually, their table in the outdoor café was surrounded by enough bags to stagger a pack mule on steroids, but now Keri knew she'd merely been offered the retail therapy *before* the bad news. It shouldn't have surprised her. Tina Deschanel was a shark, and any friendly gesture should have been seen as a prelude to getting bitten in the ass.

"Ambushed?" Tina repeated, loudly enough to distract a pair of Hollywood starlets engaging in some serious public displays of affection in a blatant attempt to attract the cheap tabloid paparazzi. A rabid horde that might include Keri in the near future if she didn't handle this correctly.

"How do you think I felt?" Tina went on. "I reached out to a woman who mentioned on her blog she'd gone to high school with Joseph Kowalski. Once there was money on the table, I made her cough up some evidence, and she sent me a few photos. She was even kind enough to caption them for me."

Keri recognized a cue when it was shoved down her throat. With one perfectly manicured nail she hooked the 8x10 blowup and pulled it closer.

A girl smiled at her from the photo. She wore a pink,

fuzzy sweater, faded second-skin jeans and pink high heels. Raccoon eyeliner made her dark brown eyes darker, frosty pink coated her lips and her hair was as big as Wisconsin.

Keri smiled back at her, remembering those curling iron and aerosol days. If the EPA had shut down their cheerleading squad back then, global warming might have been a total nonissue today.

Then she looked at the boy. He was leaning against the hideous brown car, his arms wrapped around young Keri's waist. Joe's blue eyes were as dark as the school sweatshirt he wore, and his grin managed to be both innocent and naughty at the same time. And those damn dimples—she'd been a sucker for them. His honey-brown hair was hidden by a Red Sox cap, but she didn't need to see it to remember how the strands felt sliding through her fingers.

She never failed to be amazed by how much she still missed him sometimes.

But who had they been smiling at? For the life of her, Keri couldn't remember who was standing behind the camera. She tore her gaze away from the happy couple and read the caption typed across the bottom.

Joe Kowalski and his girlfriend, Keri Daniels, a few hours before a cop busted them making out on a back road and called their parents. Rumor had it when Joe dropped her off, Mr. Daniels chased him all the way home with a golf club.

Keri snorted. "Dad only chased him to the end of the block. Even a '78 Granada could outrun a middle-aged fat guy with a five iron."

"I fail to see the humor in this."

"You didn't see my old man chasing taillights down

the middle of the street in his bathrobe. It wasn't very funny at the time, though."

"Focus, Keri," Tina snapped. "Do you or do you not walk by the bulletin board in the bull pen every day?"

"I do."

"And have you not seen the sheet marked '*Spotlight Magazine*'s Most Wanted' every day?"

"I have."

"And did you happen to notice Joseph Kowalski has been number three for several years?" Keri nodded, and Tina leaned across the table. "*You* are going to get me an exclusive feature interview with the man."

"Or...?"

Tina sat back and folded her arms across her chest. "Don't take it to that point, Keri. Look, the man's eleventh bestseller is going to be *the* summer blockbuster film of the decade. More A-listers lined up to read for that movie than line up on the red carpet for the Oscars. And he's a total mystery man."

"I don't get why you're so dedicated to chasing him down. He's just an author."

"Joseph Kowalski isn't just an author. He played the media like a fiddle and became a celebrity. The splashy NY parties with that gorgeous redhead—Lauren Huckins, that was it—on his arm. Then Lauren slaps him with a multimillion dollar emotional distress suit, he pays her off with a sealed agreement and then he disappears from the map? There's a story there, and I want it. Our readers will eat him up, and *Spotlight* is going to serve him to them because you have access to him nobody else does."

"Had. I *had* access to him." Keri sighed and flipped the photo back across the table even though she would rather have kept it to moon over later. "Eighteen years ago."

"You were his high school sweetheart. Nostalgia, darling! And rumor has it he's still single."

Keri *knew* he was still single because the Danielses and Kowalskis still lived in the same small New Hampshire town, though Mr. and Mrs. Kowalski lived in a much nicer house now. Very *much* nicer, according to Keri's mother.

"You've risen fast in this field," Tina continued, "because you have sharp instincts and a way with people, to say nothing of the fact I trusted you. But this…"

The words trailed away, but Keri heard her boss loud and clear. She was going to get this exclusive or her career with *Spotlight* was over and she could start fresh at the bottom of another magazine's totem pole. And since her career was pretty much the sum total of her life, it wasn't exactly a threat without teeth.

But seeing Joe again? The idea both intrigued her and scared the crap out of her at the same time. "He's not going to open up his insanely private life to the magazine because he and I wore out a set of shocks in high school, Tina. It was fun, but it wasn't *that* good."

Now she was flat-out lying. Joe Kowalski had set the gold standard in Keri's sex life. An ugly car, a Whitesnake tape, cheap wine and Joe still topped her personal "Ten Ways to a Better Orgasm" list.

Tina ran her tongue over her front teeth, and Keri had known her long enough to know her boss was about to deliver the kill shot.

"I've already reassigned your other stories," she said. It was an act of interference entirely inappropriate for Tina to do to someone of Keri's status at the magazine.

"That's unacceptable, Tina. You're overstepping your—"

"I can't overstep boundaries I don't have, Daniels. It's my magazine, and your promotion to editorial depends on your getting an interview with Kowalski, plain and simple." Then she reached into her purse and passed another sheet to her. "Here's your flight information."

The reclusive, mega-bestselling author in question was trying to decide between regular beef jerky or teriyaki-flavored when he heard Keri Daniels was back in town.

Joe Kowalski nodded at the cashier who'd actually left a customer half-rung up in an attempt to be the first to deliver the news. It wasn't the first time Keri had been back. If she'd gone eighteen years without a visit home to her parents, Janie Daniels would have flown out to L.A. and dragged her daughter home by an earlobe.

It was, however, the first time Keri had come looking for him that he knew of.

"She's been asking around for your phone number," the cashier added on, watching him like a half-starved piranha. "Of course nobody will give it to her, because we know how you feel about your privacy."

And because nobody had it, but he didn't feel a need to point that out. But he was surprised it had taken Keri as long as this to get around to looking him up, considering just how many years Tina Deschanel had been stalking his agent.

"Maybe she's on the class reunion committee," Joe told the cashier, and her face fell. Committees didn't make for hot gossip.

Members of the media had been hounding his agent

for years, but only Tina Deschanel, who took tenacious to a whole new level, was Keri Daniels's boss. Joe had been watching Keri's career from the beginning, waiting for her to sell him out, but she never had. Until now, maybe.

While he wasn't a recluse of Salinger-esque stature, Joe liked his privacy. The New England dislike of outsiders butting into their lives, combined with his own fiscal generosity—in the form of a ballpark, playgrounds, library donations or whatever else they needed—kept the locals from spilling his business. By the time he struck it big, classmates who'd moved away didn't remember enough about him to provide interesting fodder.

Nobody knew the details of the lawsuit settlement except the lawyers, his family and Lauren—who would be financially devastated should she choose to break her silence. And, as unlikely as it seemed, he and Keri had never been linked together in the media reports his publicist monitored. He managed to keep his private life pretty much just that, despite the hype surrounding the movie.

"You're not old enough for a class reunion," Tiffany said, batting her way-too-young eyelashes at him.

A half-dozen of each, he decided, tossing bags of beef jerky into his cart. He had a lot more list than cart space left and he kicked himself for not making Terry come along. She could have pushed a second cart *and* run interference on nosy cashiers. She was good in the role, probably from years of experience.

As if on cue, the loudspeaker crackled. "Um… Tiffany, can you come back to register one, please? I have to pick up my kids in ten minutes."

The girl rolled her eyes and started back toward the front of the town's tiny market, but not before calling over her shoulder, "She's staying with her parents, but I guess you already know where they live."

Yeah, he guessed he did, too. The only question was what he was going to do about it. He and his entire family were preparing to leave town for two weeks, and it would be a shame if he missed out on whatever game Keri was playing.

Assuming it was even true. Not that she was in town, but that she wanted to give him a call. In his experience, if there wasn't enough dirt to keep a small town grapevine bearing fruit, people would just add a heaping pile of manufactured fertilizer.

Joe gave a row of pepperoni sticks the thousand-yard stare. If Keri Daniels *was* looking for his phone number, it had to mean somebody had spilled the beans. The rabid pit bull of a woman she worked for had discovered her star reporter had once been the girl of Deschanel's favorite prey's dreams. If that was the case, he and Keri were heading for a reunion and *this* time Keri could do the begging, just like he had before she'd run off to California.

Two hours later, after he'd unloaded his groceries at his own place, he faced his twin sister across the expanse of their mother's kitchen. Teresa Kowalski Porter was *not* a happy woman.

"You are one dumb son of a bitch."

Whereas he liked to play with words—savor them—Terry just spat them out as they popped into her head.

"I thought you were a moron for putting up with her shit then," she said. "But now you're going back for a second helping?"

"I'm ninety-nine percent sure her boss sent her out here in order to use our history to manipulate me into giving the magazine an interview."

"Keri Daniels never needed any help when it came to manipulating people. And I don't even want to think about that other one percent on an empty stomach."

The entire Kowalski family had once held some resentment toward Keri, but Terry's had festered. Not only because his sister knew how to hold a grudge—although she certainly did—but because Keri had hurt her even before she'd gotten around to hurting Joe.

Terry and Keri had been best friends since kindergarten, despite how corny their names sounded when said together. The trouble started during their freshman year when Mr. Daniels got a big promotion. Between the new style Daddy's money bought and a developing body that just wouldn't quit, Keri had soon started circling with a new group of friends. By the beginning of sophomore year, Keri had left Terry in her social dust, and she hadn't been forgiven. Joe's relationship with Keri had been the only thing to ever come between him and his twin.

And that's why he'd come to Terry first. "Aren't you even a little curious about how she turned out?"

"No." She pulled a soda from the fridge and popped the top without offering him one—never a good sign. "She broke your heart and now, almost twenty years later, she wants to capitalize on that and sell you out to further her career. That tells me all I need to know about how she turned out, thanks."

Joe kicked out a chair and sat at the kitchen table. "It's just dinner, Terry. Dinner with somebody who used to mean a lot to both of us."

"Why are you even talking to me about this, Joseph? I could give a shit less about Keri Daniels. If you want to have dinner with her, then do it. You're an adult."

"I need you to cover for me with the family."

Terry laughed, then grabbed a list from the fridge to double check against the army of plastic bins at her feet. "Okay, *almost* an adult."

"You know Mom's going to be all over my ass about being ready to go day after tomorrow even though I'm the first one packed every year. If I fall off her radar for even a few hours, she'll have a fit."

"You really are a dumbass. Mom knows she's in town. Tell her you're going to dinner with the bitch who ripped your heart out of your chest and stomped on it. Do you think three jars of peanut butter are enough?"

"We're only going for two weeks. And I don't want the whole damn town to know I'm going to see her."

"Eight adults and five kids… I guess three will be enough."

"Terry." He waited until she looked up from her list. "Seven adults."

"What? Oh. Yeah." She laughed at herself, but the pain was written all over her face. "Who's the dumbass now, huh?"

"He is," Joe said, not for the first time. "Did you call that divorce lawyer my agent recommended yet?"

"I'm putting it off until the trip is over." She held up a hand to ward off the argument she knew was coming. "I never thought I'd say this, but I'd rather talk about Keri Daniels."

"Fine. If she agrees to dinner, I'm going to tell everybody I've got a meeting in Boston tomorrow night. Will you back me up?"

"Why didn't you just tell *me* that, too?" she asked, clearly exasperated now.

"I thought about it. But I kept seeing Keri a secret from you once, sis, and it hurt you when you found out. I didn't want to do it again."

She sighed and Joe tasted victory. "Okay, I'll back you up, but I still think you're a moron. How many jars of pickles did we go through last year?"

"You want me to do *what*?"

Joe stretched out on the battered leather couch in his office and tried not to laugh at the tone of horrified shock in his agent's voice. "Dinner date. Reporter from *Spotlight Magazine*. You heard right."

"Did that Deschanel bitch kidnap one of the kids? Threaten your mother? I know people, Joe. I can take care of this for you."

"It's Keri. Keri Daniels."

A loaded pause. "That's great. Sure I want to do that for you, Joe, because with a big movie premiere coming up and a deadline approaching, I absolutely want your head fucked up over your high school sweetheart. And exposing yourself professionally to somebody you've exposed yourself to personally? Great idea."

"Dan. Take a breath."

"Oh, I'm taking so many breaths I'm hyperventilating. I need to put a fucking bag over my mouth. Or maybe put a bag over your head because your brains are leaking out."

"I'm pretty sure Tina Deschanel found out Keri and I dated in high school and I doubt Keri wants to do this any more than I do."

"Then don't do it. Please, for the love of my fifteen percent, don't do it."

"I'm just going to have dinner with her and then she can go back to California and tell her boss she tried."

"Then why don't *you* call her?"

Good question. One he didn't particularly care to share the pathetic answer to with Dan.

After all these years, he didn't want to be reunited with Keri by telephone. He wanted to see her face at the same time he heard her voice. Okay, if he was being honest, he wanted to know if he could see the Keri he'd loved in her.

Worst-case scenario, whatever business she felt she had with him could be conducted over the phone and he wouldn't get to see her at all. It was just curiosity— for old times' sake—but he wanted to see her again.

"I'm famous," he said lightly. "I pay people to make my phone calls for me."

"Bullshit. And speaking of paying people, why are you dumping this on me? Jackie's in charge of publicity and press."

"Her head would explode."

The silence on the other end lasted so long Joe thought his agent might have hung up on him. But no such luck. "Joe, we've been together a long time and, speaking as a guy who's had your back for almost a decade and a half, I think this is even a worse idea personally than it is professionally."

"I know, but I'm going to do it anyway."

Keri swallowed another mouthful of non-designer water and resisted glancing at her watch again. Maybe she'd been spoiled by a generous expense account, but meeting in a cheap chain restaurant in the city was too high a price to pay for privacy, in her opinion.

And what was with Joe having his agent contact her to set up the dinner? He couldn't pick up the phone and call her himself? Maybe his over-inflated ego interfered with telephone use, so he had to use his agent as though she were a total stranger. As if she didn't know he had a birthmark shaped like an amoeba on his right ass cheek.

Unfortunately, her opinions didn't seem to matter. Tina had made it very clear that if Joseph Kowalski held up a hoop, Keri was to jump through it, wearing a pom-pom hat and barking like a dog if that's what it took to make the author happy.

It really burned her ass to be in this predicament, and just thinking about her boss made her temples throb. The temptation to walk out was incredibly strong but, while she knew she could walk into any magazine editor's office and come out with a job, it would set her back years in her quest to climb to the top of the masthead.

It was only an interview, after all.

There hadn't been a new press or book jacket photo of Joe since his sixth book. That picture had pretty much looked like him, albeit without the grin and dimples. It was one of those serious and contemplative author photos and she'd hated it. But by now, especially considering the coin he was pulling down, he was probably a self-indulgent, fat, bald man with a hunched back from too much time over the keyboard.

She, on the other hand, thought she'd aged well. Nothing about her was as firm as it had been in high school, but she was still slim enough to pull off the pricey little black dress she'd chosen for tonight. Her hair, now sleek and smooth to her shoulders, was still naturally blonde, though she would admit to some subtle highlighting.

"Hey, babe," a voice above her said, and just like that the sophisticated woman was gone. She was eighteen again, with big dreams, bigger hair and an itch only Joe Kowalski could scratch.

She could almost taste the Boone's Farm as she turned, braced for an old, fat Joe and finding…just Joe.

He'd aged even better than she had, the bastard. His face had matured and he had a trace of what men were allowed to call character lines, but he still had that slightly naughtier version of the boy-next-door look. Of course, he wasn't *quite* as lean as he used to be, but it probably wasn't noticeable to anybody who hadn't spent a significant amount of senior year running her hands over his naked body.

All in all, he resembled the boy who'd charmed her out of her pants a lot more than he did the stodgy author she'd hoped to charm into an interview.

"Hi, Joe." She'd stored up a mental cache of opening lines ranging from cute to funny to serious, and every single one seemed to have been deleted. "Thank you for coming."

He slid onto the bench seat across the booth from her. "Time's been pretty damn good to you, if you don't mind my saying so."

No, she didn't mind at all. "You, too. Interesting choice of restaurant, by the way. An eccentricity of the rich and reclusive author?"

He flashed those dimples at her and Keri stifled a groan. Why couldn't he have been fat and bald except for unattractive tufts of hair sprouting from his ears?

"I just like the all-you-can-eat salad bar," he said. "So tell me, is Tina hiding under the table? Waiting to pounce on me in the men's room?"

Keri laughed, partly because it was such a relief to have the topic out in the open. "No, she refuses to leave the city. Says her lungs can't process unpolluted air."

His smoky-blue eyes were serious even though his dimples were showing. "Terry's been expecting you to sell me out for your own advantage since I first made the *NYT* list."

Hearing his sister's name made her wince, and knowing she still held such a low opinion of Keri just made her sad. During the very rare moments she allowed herself to dwell on regrets, she really only had two. And they were both named Kowalski.

"I'm being professionally blackmailed," she admitted. "If I don't get an exclusive interview for *Spotlight* from you, I'm out of a job."

"I figured as much. Who spilled the beans?"

Keri pulled the 8x10 from her bag and handed it to him. "I don't know. Do you remember who took that?"

"Alex did, remember? The night we…well, the caption's pretty thorough."

She remembered now. Alex had been a friend of Joe's, but they'd all traveled in the same circle. "But Tina said the blogger who claimed to go to school with you was a woman."

"His name's Alexis now. You wouldn't believe how much he paid for his breasts."

Keri laughed, but Joe was still looking at the photo. Judging by the way the corners of his lips twitched into a small smile and how he tilted his head, Keri figured Tina had been right about the nostalgia angle.

The waitress approached their table, order pad in hand.

Joe still hadn't looked up. "Remember the night you started drinking your screwdrivers without the orange juice and did a striptease on Alex's pool table?"

"I bet the jokes about Alex's pool table having a nice rack went on forever," the waitress said, and *then* Joe looked up.

"You bet they did," he said easily, but he was blushing.

"There must be a whole new slew of jokes about Alex's rack now," Keri said, making Joe laugh.

The waitress tapped her pen on the tab. "So do you guys know what you want?"

And then he did it, just as he always had whenever he'd been asked that question—he looked straight at Keri with blatant hunger in his eyes and said, "Yes, ma'am, I do."

The shiver passed all the way from her perfectly styled hair to her Ferragamo pumps. Then she watched in silent amusement while he ordered for them both— her regular high school favorite of a medium-well bacon cheeseburger with extra pickles, fries and a side of cole-slaw. There was no mention of salad, all-you-can-eat or otherwise.

When the waitress left, she gave him a scolding look. "That's more calories than I've consumed in the last two years, Joe."

He waved away her half-hearted objection. "Let's get down to business."

Keri didn't want to. She was too busy enjoying that sizzle of anticipation she'd always felt when Joe looked at her. Apparently those blue eyes hadn't lost their potency over the last two decades.

Joe leaned back against the booth and crossed his arms. It was probably supposed to look intimidating, but all the gesture really did was draw attention to how tan and incredibly well-defined his biceps were against his white T-shirt. Typing definitely wasn't the only workout his arms got.

"Let's see if I can synopsize our situation," he said. "I never give interviews. You want an interview. No, strike that. You *need* an interview, because the rabid jackal you work for has made it clear your job is on the line. Am I close?"

The sizzle receded to a tingle. "You're in the ballpark."

"I'm not just in the ballpark, babe. I'm Josh Beckett on the mound at Fenway. If I don't give you what you need, you're hiding behind palm trees waiting for drunk pop stars to pop out of their Wonderbras."

And that pretty much killed the last of the lingering tingle. "Payback's a bitch and all that, right, Joe?"

The dimples flashed. "Isn't it?"

Keri just shrugged. She wasn't about to start putting deals on the table or making promises. After years of dealing with celebrities, she usually knew how to handle herself. But this was Joe Kowalski. He'd seen her naked and she'd broken his heart. That changed the rules.

"I'm leaving town tomorrow," he said. "I'll be gone two weeks."

The tingle flared up again, but this time it was a lot more panic and a lot less anticipation. "There's always the telephone or fax or email."

"Not where I'm going."

She laughed. "Would that be Antarctica or a grass hut in the Amazon Basin?"

"I'm not even leaving the state."

Joe had sucked at cards in high school—he had no poker face—but she couldn't read him now. The instincts that had skyrocketed her to the top of the *Spotlight* food chain were giving her nothing, except the feeling he was setting her up for something she might want no part of.

The waitress brought their food, buying Keri a few more minutes to think. One thing Joe had never had was a mean streak—if there was no chance in hell of the interview happening, he wouldn't have agreed to meet her for dinner. He'd never had it in him to humiliate somebody for the sake of his own enjoyment.

Granted, the kind of checks he had to be cashing changed a person, but she'd already seen enough of him—and heard enough from her mother—to know Joe was still Joe. Just with more expensive toys.

That didn't mean he wasn't going to have her jumping through hoops, of course. Probably an entire flaming series of them.

She bit into the bacon cheeseburger and the long-forgotten flavor exploded on her tongue. She closed her eyes and moaned, chewing slowly to fully savor the experience.

"How long has it been since you've had one of those?" Joe asked, and she opened her eyes to find him watching her.

Keri swallowed, already anticipating the next bite. "Years. Too many years."

He laughed at her, and they enjoyed some idle chit-chat while they ate. She brought up the movie and he talked about it in a generic sense, but she noted how careful he was not to say anything even remotely interview worthy.

There would be no tricking the man into revealing something that would get Tina off her back.

"You know," she said, still holding half her cheeseburger, "I *really* want to enjoy this meal more, and I can't with this hanging over my head. What's it going to take?"

"I gave it some thought before I came, and I think you should come with me."

"Where?"

"To where I'm going."

Keri set the cheeseburger on the plate. "For two weeks?"

The length of time hardly mattered, since she couldn't return to California without the interview anyway. But she'd like an idea of what she was signing up for.

"Whether you're there for two weeks or not is up to you. For each full day you stick it out with the Kowalskis, you get to ask me one question."

Keri, unlike Joe, did have a poker face and she made sure it was in place while she turned his words over in her head. "When you say the Kowalskis, you mean..."

"The entire family." The dimples were about as pronounced as she'd ever seen them. "Every one of them."

Her first thought was *oh shit*. Her second, to wonder if *People* was hiring.

Joe reached into the back pocket of his jeans and pulled out a folded sheet of spiral notebook paper. "Here's a list of things you'll need. I jotted it down in the parking lot."

Keri unfolded the paper and read the list twice, trying to get a sense of what she was in for.

BRING: Bug spray; jeans; T-shirts; several sweatshirts, at least one with a hood; one flannel shirt (mandatory); pajamas (optional); underwear (also optional); bathing suit (preferably skimpy); more bug spray; sneakers; waterproof boots; good socks; sunscreen; two rolls of quarters.

DO NOT BRING: cell phone; Blackberry; laptop; camera, either still or video; alarm clock; voice recorder; any other kind of electronic anything.

She had no clue what it meant, other than Joe wanting her half-naked and unable to text for help.

Chapter Two

The first day of the annual family vacation was always hell for Terry Kowalski Porter. Her twelve days of fun and relaxation were bookended by two days of wanting to throw herself under a speeding RV.

The convoy of Kowalskis usually managed to make it up the interstate and across Route 3 in a somewhat organized fashion, but as soon as they entered the campground they scattered, leaving Terry to run her ass off helping everybody get settled in.

First, her parents, because their forty-foot luxury liner on wheels brought all campground activity to a screeching halt until it was docked. Leo Kowalski refused to let anybody else drive the baby his son had bought him, so Terry's main purpose was keeping her impatient brothers on a tight leash while Dad executed a precision eighty-point turn to back it in to their site.

Then came landing pads, leveling and sewer pipes. Water hoses and electrical connections. They had the routine pretty much down by this point, but heaven forbid Leo and Mary Kowalski not have drama.

"That seem level to you, Mary?" One thing about their parents, they were *loud*.

"I'm inside, Leo! How would I know?"

"Are you listing to the left?"

Next came her middle brother Mike and his family, who needed three adjoining sites for their sprawl. The first site held their RV—a much smaller one than their parents'—in which Mike, Lisa and their two youngest boys slept. The site also held a multi-burnered barbecue grill-slash-cooking center so massive it took all three brothers plus the oldest of Mike's sons to lift it out of the trailer.

The second site held the pop-up camper they pulled behind the RV and in which their two older boys slept. It was also here Lisa erected the complex and extensive network of clothesline strung from tree to tree until it was large enough to contain their family's wet clothes.

The third site would contain a large screenhouse and a series of tarps which served to guarantee that, no matter how hard it rained, Lisa would not be confined in her RV with her four rambunctious boys.

The youngest of the Kowalski siblings, Kevin, was the easiest to get set up. Since his divorce, he required only a small tent, a hibachi and the largest cooler money could buy. He claimed to be a camping purist, but Terry knew he didn't see any point in going whole-hog when his parents were four sites over in a half-million-dollar home away from home.

Joe always rented one of the campground's cabins so he could bring his laptop and have relative comfort and privacy to write, and normally Terry would help him unload his SUV. But she didn't happen to be speaking to her twin brother just now, so she sent her nephews in her place.

The havoc the four boys would wreak on his cabin

would be just the beginning of the payback Joe Kowalski would suffer.

The minute she'd heard her brother's voice on the other end of the line telling her they might need another jar of peanut butter after all, Terry knew what the dumb son of a bitch had gone and done.

As if the Kowalski family *vacation* wasn't hectic enough, he'd thrown Keri Daniels into the mix. Even worse, the rest of the family threw in behind Joe. Their parents were thrilled. Mike and Lisa couldn't spare the energy to care one way or the other, and Kevin? Terry knew Kevin well enough to know he was going to weasel his way into Keri's pants if he could, or at least use her to needle his big brother if he couldn't.

Of course, none of *them* had a twelve-year-old daughter who hated camping, hated being disconnected from IM for more than a single hour and—most of all—hated the fact her parents were separated. And of course she couldn't understand why her Uncle Joe's ex-girlfriend was invited, but not her dad, who technically wasn't even an ex yet.

The same twelve-year-old daughter who was at that very moment sitting in a lounge chair, sipping Coke in front of their still closed RV. Terry's brothers had helped her get it backed in and they'd leveled it and done the sewer and water hook-ups before she shooed them away. She and Steph had to get used to doing things for themselves now that there was no man around the house.

Unfortunately, getting her daughter to do anything at all was a challenge in itself. "Stephanie, I asked you to at least get it plugged in and open the windows."

"Dad always does that part."

"Dad's not here. And you always helped him, so I know you know how to do it."

Eye roll. "Why couldn't I stay with him?"

Terry took a deep breath, reminding herself for the umpteenth time it was about who had Internet access for the next two weeks and not which parent Stephanie loved most. "Because his apartment isn't big enough and you're too old to share his damn futon with him."

"When is Uncle Joe's old girlfriend supposed to get here?"

"I don't know, Steph. Let's just get set up so we can—"

"I think that's her."

Terry turned, then muttered a word she tried, as a rule, not to say in front of her daughter.

Of course that was her. God forbid Keri Daniels should ever gain a pound or twenty or have visible roots, dammit. No, she was still thin, still gorgeous, and—unlike Terry's—none of her body parts appeared to be migrating south.

Keri was staring in horror at the trailers littering the common area, waiting for the campers and trucks that had hauled them to be situated before they were unloaded. On the trailers sat twelve four-wheelers of various sizes and colors, one of them brand-spanking-new.

Keri turned, making eye contact with Terry for the first time in decades. "What the hell are those?"

"They're four-wheelers. My dad took us riding when we were ten, or did you forget that, too?"

Keri's crimson lips pursed in disgust. "Oh, for heaven's sake. Joe must have more money than God. You people couldn't take a cruise or something?"

"Us people like four-wheeling. Besides, nothing brings a family together like a post-ride tick check."

"Tick check?" Terry had the satisfaction of seeing her best friend-turned-nemesis turn pale under her expertly applied blush. "*Tick check?* I can't do this."

"Steph, let your uncle know Keri Daniels has arrived."

"Uncle Joe, you're girlfriend's here!" the girl bellowed in the direction of the cabins.

"If I wanted it screamed across the campground, Stephanie Porter, I could have done it myself."

But in reality, she didn't feel like yelling. She felt a lot more like rolling on the grass laughing her ass off.

Miss Perfect looked like she'd just taken a flying leap into a steaming pile of cow manure, and Terry had to think the next two weeks might not be so bad after all. Payback was indeed a bitch.

When Keri saw Joe walking toward her, his hands in his pockets and his dimples visible from the moon, she couldn't even articulate all the things she wanted to say to him.

She settled for, "You are *not* checking me for ticks, Joseph Kowalski."

"Damn, babe, don't go squashing all my hopes on the first day." It was Keri who felt like an idiot, but Joe who was grinning like one. "I see you found Terry."

"I'm not riding one of those." She pointed at the trailers of ATVs.

"See that shiny new red one? That's yours, babe. And don't tell me you forgot the rules already."

As if she could. The Rules had been hand-delivered to her parents' house before she'd even gotten out of bed that morning.

(1) Only "official" answers to "official" questions may be published in Spotlight.

(2) Any mention of where we go, what we do, or any other family member but me will result in the best legal team money can buy raining all over you and your magazine like a Georgia thunderstorm.

(3) For every full day you spend with the Kowalski family, you can ask one question.

(4) For each answer I give, I get to ask you one question. Failure to answer forfeits your next question.

(5) Disclosure of any information other than the official interview questions and answers to Tina Deschanel, especially the attached MapQuest directions to your destination, will result in a horror show you don't want any part of. Trust me.

(6) Refusal to participate in any Kowalski family activity will result in no interview. (Unless it involves Kevin and nudity, which, with him, may or may not include sex.)

Keri didn't intend to get naked with *any* of the Kowalskis. No tick checks. No sex. No skinny dipping. Her swimsuit was a one-piece. And pajamas were *not* optional.

That last thought stuck in her head and she looked at the row of campers and tents with a rising sense of alarm. "Where will I be sleeping?"

Joe was still grinning, though Terry had wandered

away to help the girl who must be her daughter hook up their camper. "Cabin, around the corner."

"A cabin?" That didn't sound too bad. "You mean like with walls and a door and a bed?"

"And electrical outlets, even."

Keri snorted. "Those will come in handy for all those electronic devices you made me leave at home."

"Pull your car around and maybe we can get you settled in before the rest of the family finds out you're here. They all walked down to the store to visit the campground owners and buy wood for campfires."

Keri drove her compact rental up the narrow dirt lane and pulled in at the first cabin, parking in the shadow of Joe's massive SUV. The cabin was small, but looked sound enough, and it even had a nice little porch.

At Joe's gesture, she opened the door and stepped inside. It seemed even smaller on the inside, but it had ceiling fans and a gas fireplace, and a dinette set. Along the back were a double bed and a set of bunk beds. A cheery braided rug covered the hardwood floor.

And Joe's stuff was strewn across every surface but the bottom bunk. "What is this?"

"Our cabin. You get stuck with the bunk bed because I'm the famous author."

"You're the famous *freakin' insane* author if you think I'm sharing a cabin with you."

"The others are booked for the coming weekend. You can go home if you want, of course. I'm sure your boss would understand."

"Or you can sleep in my tent."

Keri whirled around at the sound of a second male voice. The man was incredibly tall, incredibly built, and… "Oh my God, Kevin? What the hell have they been feeding you?"

"Virgins and Budweiser, three times a day. You look great, Keri. It's been a long time."

She tried to remember how much younger Kevin was than her, Joe and Terry. Six years? Something like that. He'd been gangly and acne-prone the last time she'd seen him. He certainly wasn't anymore.

"*You* barely fit in your tent," Joe told him before Keri could think up a response, "never mind a woman, too."

"She could sleep on top of me."

"Get out," Joe said while Keri laughed. "Go grab Keri's bags out of the car before you go, though."

Kevin sighed and cast a mournful glance at Keri. "The curse of being the only Kowalski son with any muscles."

He disappeared and Keri took a moment to try to calm herself. It didn't work. Even after almost twenty years in California, she still hadn't found her center, chi, Zen or whatever the hell it was she was supposed to find.

On the one hand she had living with Joe Kowalski for fourteen days. On the other, she had a career in the toilet and her living in some sublet fleabag apartment.

Then it occurred to her to wonder if pajamas were optional for Joe, too, and she had to find the switch for the ceiling fans and flip them on. It was awfully hot all of a sudden. And she wasn't sure whether a pajama-free Joe went in the pro or the con column, which *really* played hell on her Zen.

Kevin returned, setting her bags inside the door. "I intercepted the mob and turned them back. I'd say you've got fifteen minutes max before they come looking again."

Then he was gone. Keri took another useless deep breath and tried to brace herself for the minutes/days/weeks ahead. It wasn't working.

"This is so unprofessional of you," she accused Joe, who was making a big show of plumping his pillow and testing his comfortable-looking mattress.

"Right, because expecting me to expose my private life to the masses because we had sex twenty years ago is the epitome of professionalism."

Keri walked over to test her own mattress. It was what it looked like—a slab of foam on a sheet of plywood laid over 2x4 supports. Lovely. "I wouldn't do this if I had a choice, but my career means everything to me."

"No, babe, your career *is* everything to you. And we're going to remind you success doesn't equal by-lines and bottom lines."

He wasn't smiling, so she wondered if he actually believed the tripe he was spewing. "So you're doing this for my own good? To save the shallow princess from her gleaming ivory tower?"

Now the dimples made an appearance. "As the good and pure-hearted prince the shallow princess stomped all over on her way up the ivory steps, I just want to see you get mud in your hair."

"So it's all just a grand scheme to humiliate me." She stood, intent on getting to her car. "You probably never intended to answer my damn questions at all."

Keri didn't get far before Joe spun her around so she ended up, as luck would have it, with her back against the footboards of the bunk bed. When he tucked one leg between hers and rested a hand on either side of her head, her traitorous body immediately recognized *the locker position* and relaxed. She even had to curl her hands into fists to keep from tucking her fingers into the front pockets of his jeans.

They'd spent every spare moment at school in just this position—her resting her back against her locker with Joe leaning over her. Inevitably a teacher would come along and bark at them. "Daniels and Kowalski, I want to see daylight between you two!"

There wasn't much daylight between them right now. And there weren't any teachers coming, either, though odds were good his family would at some point. What she didn't know is if they'd be horrified or encourage him.

"I didn't bring you here to humiliate you, babe."

Keri wished he'd quit calling her that, but she couldn't make him stop without drawing attention to the fact it bothered her. "Then why am I here? You could have flat out said no, or you could have scheduled the interview for two weeks out."

"But then I wouldn't get to spend the time with you."

How had she not drowned in those eyes back in high school? It was hard to focus on the words coming out of his mouth when he looked at her like that. "It's been almost twenty years, Joe."

"Exactly. You weren't just my girlfriend, you know. You were my best friend, and I want to catch up. Oprah would say I need closure."

"Like you watch Oprah." Keri's fingers were practically itching now to tuck themselves into his front pockets, so she shoved them into her own.

"My niece does, and I'm sure if I asked her, she'd tell you that's what Oprah would say."

"I think it's about ten percent closure and ninety percent payback."

Joe grinned. "Seventy-thirty."

"Thirty-seventy."

He leaned in closer, and Keri had no room to back up. A billion thoughts seemed to fly through her head, but only two stuck. Was he going to kiss her? And why, after all these years and a few significant—albeit doomed—relationships, did she care?

It had to be nostalgia. They said a girl never forgot her first, after all. She'd had more than one dream set in the backseat of a 1978 Granada. But this was too much.

A brief flash lit up the cabin, and Joe swore so softly only somebody practically pressed up against him would hear it.

"Say cheese!"

"That would be Bobby," Joe told her before stepping away—much to her surprising dismay. Had he really meant to kiss her? "He used his allowance to buy a package of disposable cameras for the trip."

"I thought we couldn't have cameras."

"No, babe, *you* can't have a camera. *We* have cameras—disposable, film, digital, video, digital video, you name it. Hell, there's a good chance Ma's still got her old 110 in the bottom of her purse."

Keri looked at the little boy giving her a grin that would probably be as potent as his uncle's when he got older. "Hi, Bobby. Aren't I supposed to say cheese *before* you take the picture?"

"When I do it that way, people hide their faces, so I like it to be a surprise."

She smiled, but she was wondering how surprised Bobby's mother would be to find a picture of Joe pinning her against the bunk bed come up in her son's vacation pictures.

"Grammy sent me to tell you to stop hiding and get the machines unloaded so the trailers can go in the parking area. And she said Miss Keri better go say hello right now or Uncle Kevin gets her s'mores."

Joe walked around the trailers, loosening tie-down straps while keeping an eye on Keri as she was given the quick, but probably not easy, tour of the Kowalski family tree. Considering her line of work and the fact their mothers remained friends, he was pretty sure she'd already been given a rundown on who was who, but they still made for a daunting group.

Keri knew his parents and siblings, of course, but Mike and Kevin had changed a lot in the last eighteen years. Mike's wife, Lisa, had moved up from Massachusetts right after Joe graduated, so Keri didn't know her at all. And their four boys—Joey (fifteen), Danny (twelve), Brian (nine) and Bobby (six)—never stood still long enough to pin a face to a name. Terry's girl, Stephanie, was hovering on the brink of teenage attitude. Throwing in Kevin, with his frat boy charm, and Terry, with her decades-long grudge, made for an interesting mix.

And speaking of interesting, Joe couldn't believe Keri thought his sole aim in inviting her along was to humiliate her. So maybe *inviting* wasn't quite the right word for what he'd done, but he hadn't realized until she'd thrown that accusation at him they weren't on the same page. Hell, they weren't even in the same chapter.

Maybe he'd totally misread the vibe he'd gotten in

the restaurant. He could have sworn she'd also felt the flicker that lingered from the burning inferno that used to be their chemistry, and when she agreed to the ridiculous offer he'd expected her to turn down flat, he thought she was as interested in fanning that little flame as he was. Instead she'd taken what was a half joke, half refusal gone wrong and blown it into a revenge plot of Shakespearean proportions.

And Joe was left looking and feeling like an asshole. There was no way to explain to her the proposal he'd come up with in the car on the drive to the restaurant had been nothing more than a chickenshit way of refusing the interview without outright saying no. He'd started thinking it might be fun when she gave him the same look that turned his head in high school, and he *really* got on board when she closed her eyes and moaned after taking a bite of the cheeseburger. When she agreed to the stupid plan, he assumed she was on board, too, and the cool and calm demeanor was a bid for not looking too eager.

Now he knew it was merely stoicism in the face of anticipated emotional torture, and that royally sucked. If he backed down now he'd have no control over what she printed, plus he'd have to explain why he hadn't made it through day one, which couldn't be done without making a massive fool of himself.

"If you're going to stand around and stare at your exgirlfriend all day, get out of the way first."

Mike's voice dragged Joe back to what he was doing—which was, apparently, standing there with a tie-down strap in his hand, mooning over Keri Daniels.

He tossed the strap to the older of his younger brothers and straddled the first machine. "Got the keys?"

Mike held up a handful, then tossed him the correct one. "You know Terry won't let anybody back out of the driveway until every key is accounted for. She'd staple them to our foreheads if she could find a staple gun strong enough to penetrate our thick skulls."

Joe fired up the ATV, backed it down the ramps and pulled it off to one side. After giving the look of death to Mike's four boys, who were watching him like turkey vultures, he climbed back onto the trailer.

"Lisa likes her," Mike said, since he was taking his own turn at watching the family drama unfold.

"Key. How can you tell?"

"Body language. We've been married sixteen years, Joe. I can tell when she needs to take a piss at this point."

"But you can't tell how she feels about unballing your dirty socks?"

Mike took a swipe at him, but Joe hit the throttle and laughed as he unloaded Joey's machine. He glanced over at the campsites to see his namesake practically jumping up and down, so he gave him another look of death for good measure before climbing up the ramp again. Through the corner of his eye he saw Keri holding an armful of riding gear, looking utterly baffled.

"She wants to get pregnant."

Joe's head snapped around. *Pregnant?* "What the hell are you talking about?"

"Lisa wants another kid."

"Oh." That made a little more sense than what he'd initially thought, but not much. "You guys are barely surviving the four boys you have, and Lisa is actually planning to throw a party when Bobby starts first grade in the fall. Are you sure?"

Mike nodded and tossed Joe the key to Danny's ATV. "She said it straight out. Said it might be a girl this time."

"Or it could be a boy. And it ain't like twins are unheard of in the Kowalski family. Think about it, Mike. Six boys. We'd have to hire people to drive all your campers and machines here."

Mike laughed, but Joe could see the tension in him. Though two years younger, he often seemed like the oldest now, and Joe wasn't the only one to notice it lately.

"You know what you need? Let's get these suckers unloaded and go for a brothers-only ride."

"The boys will have a fit," Mike said, but his face lit up just thinking about it.

The Kowalskis rode their ATVs at a wide variety of speeds. When the little kids were on their own machines and Grammy was along, half-dead pack mules made better time. When the two youngest boys rode with their parents and Grammy was napping, the entire crew could be a little more adventurous. Sometimes *all* the children were left with Leo and Mary, allowing Joe, Kevin, Terry—and last year her husband, Evan—Mike and Lisa to go bombing through the trail system.

But the brothers-only rides, those were special, with a high pucker factor. Just Joe, Mike and Kevin—testosterone, mud, rocks and a combined twenty-one hundred cc's of four-wheel-drive power. It was almost as good as sex, although the attrition rate was generally higher.

Mike cast a glance at his wife, scoping out her mood. "Lisa'd be pissed if the boys are underfoot while she's trying to get everything set up. Remember '04 when she made me sleep in the screenhouse?"

Joe called out his sister-in-law's name and beckoned her over. "We feel a need for speed."

Lisa was a short, fragile-looking brunette with a tall, not-so-fragile attitude. "You are *not* going riding with all this work left to do."

Joe flashed his winningest grin, but she'd been a Kowalski wife for sixteen years and was raising four of her own. She'd built up an immunity. "Forget it."

"Keri and I will take the boys into town for pizza in a few days." She wasn't immune to bribes involving freedom. "You and Mike can sneak off and ride up to that hidden grassy spot you guys like so much. It puts color in your cheeks."

As always, the promise of sex free of juvenile interruption made her cave like a wet napkin. "One hour. And you guys pull lifeguard duty for the first trip to the pool."

"Three hours, two lifeguard duties, and we'll keep the boys out for ice cream, too."

"Two hours, all of the above, plus s'mores duty tonight."

"Done."

After Lisa walked away, Joe grinned at his brother. "Piece of cake."

"Never works for me."

"That's because you're her husband. She likes me better because she doesn't have to wash my underwear. Plus I'm better lookin'."

Mike laughed. "You keep telling yourself that while I'm getting laid out in the woods, my friend."

"You just like it out there because the mosquito bites make your dick look bigger."

Joe ducked Mike's swing and launched Danny's machine down the ramp. Keri was watching him, and he thumbed the throttle a little, making the engine rev. She tossed her hair back when she laughed, just like she had in high school, and Joe pondered his chances of a little trip to the grass clearing of his own.

Thoughts of Keri, a bed of grass and a bottle of Deep Woods OFF! lotion got all jumbled in his head until he had to douse himself with a mental cold shower. Heading out for a brothers-only ride with a hard-on that wouldn't quit was a recipe for masculine disaster.

Chapter Three

Keri wasn't sure how just yet, but Joe was going to pay for abandoning her. While he and his brothers went off on their brothers-only ride—whatever the hell *that* meant—she was left to fend for herself with the Kowalski clan.

Flash. "Say cheese!"

"Cheese." Keri smiled at the clothesline she was trying to knot around a tree.

By her count, it was the eleventh boring picture of her Bobby had taken since Joe's departure. "Don't use up your camera on the first day."

"You're pretty."

"Thank you."

"Aunt Terry said you probably had work done, like Daddy did on his truck at the body shop."

She glanced at Terry, who seemed *very* interested in the knot she was tying across the site. "Nope. No work done."

"She said you were probably plastic and Uncle Kevin said he'd give you a feel and let her know and then Uncle Joe punched him in the shoulder and said the only thing he'd feel is his A-S-S getting kicked if he tried."

"Robert Joseph Kowalski!" Lisa descended on the

boy and started shooing him away. "Put the camera away and hit the playground, short fry."

Terry was still intent on her knot, which was kicking her ass if the redness in her face was any indication. Lisa gave Keri a sheepish grin, then went back to her own knot tying.

Keri probably would have minded the plastic comment a lot more if she wasn't feeling all warm and fuzzy about Joe's hitting Kevin for offering to feel her up. He'd been possessive like that in school—without crossing over the line into controlling—and she'd felt like a treasured princess. While she didn't feel exactly regal right now, standing on a cooler breaking fingernails in the name of clothesline, it was kind of sweet. Not sweet enough to get his butt out of the sling, but enough to give her a little tingle.

Terry, the overachieving show-off, was done with her share of clothesline hanging, so she popped open a soda and sat on another cooler. "The guys will be back any minute, Lisa. Got your quarters ready?"

Lisa blushed and Keri was dying to be let in on the inside joke but she couldn't bring herself to ask Terry what she meant. They'd managed to avoid direct communication for two hours now, and she figured careful planning and pure stubbornness could extend the streak to two weeks.

Then again, she didn't want to spend fourteen days with two decades of tension weighing on her, and they weren't in junior high anymore. Plus, she had two rolls of unexplained quarters in her bag. So she took a deep breath and looked right at Terry. "What are the quarters for?"

"The bathhouse showers." For a second Keri thought

those terse three words were all she was going to get, but then Terry took a deep breath of her own and seemed to relax. "When the guys ride like that they get...wound up. All that testosterone and grunting, I guess. Anyway, Mike always drags Lisa off to the bathhouse as soon as he gets back."

"Tick check," Lisa muttered, but she was damn near as red as Terry had been a few minutes before.

"So...who checks Kevin and Joe for ticks in the shower?" Keri asked. *Finally* her knot seemed secure. She tugged on it and, when it didn't pull loose for the umpteenth time, jumped off her cooler.

Terry shrugged, but her dimples—which were never quite as pronounced as Joe's—made a brief appearance. "I guess they have to take matters into their own hands, so to speak."

Keri went from warm and fuzzy to hot and bothered just like that. Back when she and Joe were doing everything but *it*, he'd shown her how he took matters into his own hands, so to speak, and that wasn't an image a girl forgot.

Only now the image morphed into an older Joe, naked and soapy and...

Holy crap, it was hot again all of a sudden. If she'd known being around Joe would be like suffering from menopause, she might have rethought her career path. Or at least packed some herbal tea or something.

"Don't you even think about it, Keri Daniels."

Keri could almost see the fork in the road of maturity rising before her. She could take the high road and assure Terry her interest in Joe was strictly professional, or she could take the low road, which she had no doubt was the path Terry would be traveling on for the next two weeks.

"Oh, I'm thinking about it, Teresa Kowalski."

"Her last name is Porter," a voice called from a camper, and all three women jumped. While it was impossible to overlook the four boys playing some demented cross between football and basketball on the playground, Keri had forgotten about Steph. Oops. Hopefully she was a little more discreet than her younger cousin.

Terry was glaring at Keri, no doubt trying to warn her away from Joe without saying the words out loud. Fat chance of that, since they'd be sharing a cabin every night, with his pajama status still to be determined.

"I should fire up the grill and throw on some dogs," Lisa said with the air of somebody desperately trying to smooth over a rocky patch in a conversation.

"No sense in that until after the guys get back," Terry pointed out. "Especially since Mike will have some excuse for needing your help in the bathhouse."

"Gross!" Stephanie yelled. "FYI, I'm putting my headphones on now."

Lisa waited a few seconds, then grinned at Terry. "Don't even use that tone with me. You and Evan spent more time in the bathhouse than anybody."

Terry's smile slipped a little and even Keri could tell Lisa was giving herself a mental slap upside the head. Her mom had given Keri the details she knew over a hurried breakfast that morning, but there weren't many.

Evan Porter had left his wife three months before, moving into a tiny studio apartment over the Laundromat. Nobody seemed to know why, but there'd been no hint of another woman. Or another man, for that matter.

"Don't the RVs have bathrooms?" she asked, feeling some pressure to fill the conversational pothole.

Both women laughed, but it was Lisa who said, "I'll take your lifeguard duty at the pool for three days if you can have sex with a Kowalski man in that shower without knocking the camper right off its levelers."

"I'll hide your bug spray if you even try to have sex with my brother in the RV—or anywhere else for that matter," Terry said, and the way Lisa gasped made Keri think it was a dire threat indeed. "Go ahead, Keri, laugh at me. But once the sun starts going down you'd duct tape your own thighs closed for a bottle of Deep Woods OFF!. Trust me."

"Since she'd be the only woman for ten miles not reeking of DEET, she'd have guys trying to gnaw their way through the duct tape within minutes," Lisa countered.

Keri was blessedly saved from having to comment on that interesting visual by the restrained rumble of approaching ATVs. There was an obey-or-die speed limit in the campground, but as soon as the three Kowalski brothers rounded into view—putting sedately along—Keri could see they'd done some serious hell-raising somewhere. Men and machines both were covered in dirt and mud, and about the only clean thing she could see were three grins' worth of white teeth.

Joe expected her to subject herself to *that*?

Their arrival brought the boys swarming back from the playground, while Stephanie, Leo and Mary emerged from campers.

"Finally, I get to have some lunch," Leo yelled.

Though it had been far too long since she'd last seen him, Keri's adoration of Leo Kowalski was total and unabashed. He was a deceptively short and wiry man, but she knew he could probably bench press one of those four-wheelers if he got stubborn about it. He'd worn his hair in a gray crew cut for as long as she could remember, and he was the source of the pretty blue eyes. Mary, who had become the quintessential Grammy, gave the kids their dimples.

Many years before, Keri had been terrified of Leo Kowalski. Her own father was a quiet sort—other than the five-iron incident—and Leo was like a firecracker of energy with a built-in megaphone. She didn't know what to make of the man who very loudly threatened his children with such dire consequences as having their asses kicked up around their ears and trips behind the woodshed. Of course, neither Keri nor the Kowalski kids knew what a woodshed was and he'd never laid a hand on them in anger, but that didn't make the promises any less foreboding. She'd discovered after only a few visits it was Mary and her wooden spoon a kid really had to watch out for.

But what Keri liked most about Leo and Mary right then was the fact they'd greeted her as if it had been eighteen hours, not years, since they'd seen her. No melodrama, resentments, admonishments or exuberance. They were just…normal.

Unlike the rest of them. Joe, Mike and Kevin were shouting over each other to tell the family about their ride. There were words like off-camber, high-sided and roost being thrown around that could have been German for all she knew, but the gist of it was they'd ridden to the edge of breaking their idiot necks, but had come home in one piece.

Now they were filthy, starving and—judging by the

smoking way Joe kept looking at her over his nephews' heads—as wound up, so to speak, as the women said they'd be.

Sure enough, Mike was beckoning to Lisa. "Hold off on lunch for a few minutes so I can shower this mud off. You should come check me for ticks, too."

"Lucky bastards," Kevin muttered before heading to his tent for a change of clothes.

Keri wasn't sure what was up with the plural bastards until she saw Joe moving toward her. Other than a raccoon mask of white where his goggles had rested and his hair, every inch of Joe looked as though he'd taken a mud bath and skipped the rinse.

"Don't you even think about touching me," she warned.

"I think there's a tick on my back, so you should come to the bathhouse and check me over."

She could tell by his expression the only thing keeping him from claiming the tick was in his pants was the presence of the kids. "Nice try, Kowalski. As filthy as you are, a tick couldn't find your skin with MapQuest and a GPS."

He sighed. "I guess I'll have to make do on my own."

Again with the freakin' hot flashes. She watched him jump on his four-wheeler and head for the cabin, trying like hell to kill the visual of Joe making do on his own.

When he passed by a few minutes later with a duffel bag tossed on the ATV's front rack, she was still trying. She watched him turn up toward the bathhouse, seriously reconsidering her refusal. There couldn't be an interview if she let Joseph Kowalski die of some tick-borne disease, could there?

Then came the realization everybody else was watching her watch Joe, followed closely by the thought he was heading to the bathhouse not because the cabin's shower was too small, but because it didn't have one. Or a toilet. What if she had to go pee in the middle of the night?

Flash. "Say cheese!"

Keri watched Terry slip nine-year-old Brian a dollar and shook her head. Ten bucks he'd be the first one to get melted marshmallow in her hair if she didn't keep an eye on him.

It was s'mores time and she watched Leo and all the women place their chairs well outside of the campfire perimeter because the guys had apparently promised Lisa they'd help the kids tonight. Even though Keri had breasts, she was exempt because of her status as Joe's flaming hoop-jumping lapdog.

But she was ready for this. During an assignment at a summer camp for underprivileged kids founded by an A-lister early in her career, Keri had mastered the art of the perfect s'more.

The key was in the organization and careful preparation. First, a square graham cracker had to be set on the picnic table with a smaller square of chocolate centered on top of it. Another graham cracker set next to it. Only then should the marshmallow be toasted to a perfect golden brown. Set it on top of the chocolate, along one edge of the cracker, put the other cracker on top, exert slight pressure and then drag the stick out in the direction of the opposite edge, thereby spreading the gooey marshmallow along the chocolate. Count to ten, then eat. A perfect s'more.

"Everybody got a stick?" Kevin asked.

In case the chorus of cheers wasn't enough, the

five kids offered visual proof in the form of a flurry of wildly waving sticks. Keri flinched when Danny's threatened to take off the tip of her nose.

Kevin ripped open the bag of marshmallows and Bobby squealed with delight. Before Keri could point out it was time for neither sticks nor marshmallows yet the kids had presented their sticks like Musketeer swords and their uncle shoved a marshmallow on the end of each one.

She could only watch in horror as, after throwing elbows for position, the kids converged on the fire. Joe, Mike and Kevin circled constantly, adjusting stick heights and pointing out when one needed to be turned. Bobby's burst into flames and only Mike's reflexes kept him from jerking the stick and winging the flaming marshmallow into the air.

Suddenly sticks pointed at her from every direction, marshmallows varying from light beige to charcoal black drooping from the ends.

"You're not ready!" Stephanie shrieked, just as Bobby's overcooked glop let go of the stick and dropped onto the toe of Keri's sneaker.

"I need a cracker!"

"Where's the chocolate?"

"Uncle Joe, she doesn't even know how to make a s'more!"

Keri scrambled, dispensing crackers and chocolate as fast as she could while Bobby's burnt marshmallow bonded with her shoelaces. By the time Brian was shoving his in his mouth, Joey was roasting his second marshmallow.

Thirty minutes later, when Lisa finally called a halt to the sugar consumption, Keri was exhausted, sticky and feeling slightly nauseated by the s'mores each of the kids had made special just for her. She'd tried accidentally dropping Stephanie's on the ground and kicking it under the picnic table, but the girl had seen her and, not wanting her to be sad, promptly made her another.

And Brian, the little twerp, had definitely earned his dollar. He was responsible for the marshmallow gluing Keri's hair to her left ear, the smear of chocolate down the leg of her jeans and the graham cracker crumbs he'd managed to dump down her back while giving her a *thank you* hug.

As soon as the last mouthful was gulped down, the kids disappeared to the playground, leaving the grown-ups to deal with the fall-out. Keri was about to drop into a chair, but Joe grabbed her by the elbow and held her up.

"You've got marshmallow on your ass," he said, and she could tell by the damn dimples it was killing him not to laugh in her face.

"That was the most demented display of s'mores making I've ever seen," she hissed, resisting the urge to kick him in the shin.

"You've got chocolate on your lip."

Before she could react his finger was there, the tip dipping into the hollow of her mouth and then gliding across her lower lip. She shivered, unable to look away as Joe brought that finger to his mouth and sucked the chocolate off the end.

The faint suction sound made her insides quiver and she had a hell of a time swallowing. He was sure taking his time about it, and a glimpse of tongue flicking away the last of the chocolate spiked her body temperature.

A moan almost escaped her throat and Keri dug her

fingernails into her palms. What was wrong with her? Her body was acting as though she hadn't had sex in…

How long had it been? Months? Years, even? No, it couldn't have been years since she'd had sex. That would be sad. The last time had been Scott, colleague with benefits until he'd moved to New York. That had been…thirty-one months ago.

She hadn't had sex in thirty-one months.

"Get a room," Kevin told them as he shoved Joe out of his way. He picked up an empty Hershey's bar wrapper and walked away.

The trance broken, Keri turned her back on her tormentor and busied herself gathering the graham crackers strewn across the picnic table. Thank goodness for Kevin, or who knew what her traitorous body might have coerced her into doing.

Clearly she needed to avoid being alone with Joe. Sure, that was problematic with them sharing a cabin and sleeping only a few feet from each other. But she could make sure his family was always around during the day and then feign sleep as soon they retired to the cabin at night.

Being alone with Joe Kowalski was going to get her in trouble. Only this time giving in to his charm could get her in trouble with Tina, who was a lot scarier than her dad, even without a five-iron.

Way too many long and torturous hours later, Joe finally found himself alone with Keri.

Unfortunately, she was wearing pajamas that buttoned clear up to her eyebrows and was tossing and turning like a princess in a pea-riddled bunk. Every once in a while she'd emit one of those female sighs that said she was annoyed and he wasn't going to get any sleep until he acknowledged it.

Not that he'd been anticipating a good night's sleep anyway. Arranging to have Keri Daniels spend the night in a bed only six feet from his own wasn't one of his brighter ideas. Arranging to have her sleep six feet away for *thirteen* nights was just downright moronic.

Keri sighed again. They were getting louder, and he knew why.

"The more you think about it," Joe said, "the more you'll have to go."

She picked up her head and punched her pillow into a ball. "I didn't have anything to drink for hours."

"I noticed, but now you're thinking about it and you aren't thinking quietly."

"Fine." He heard her throw back her covers and then stumble toward the door.

"The flashlight's on the floor to the right of the door."

There were some fumbling noises, and the flashlight clicked on. She managed to shine it in his eyes twice while slipping her shoes on and heading out the door.

She was gone all of twenty seconds.

"Oh my God," Keri yelped, slamming the door behind her. "There are eyes out there."

Yup, sleep really was just a pipe dream tonight. "Furry woodland creatures, babe."

"I think it was a raccoon." It was hard not to laugh at her when she twisted the deadbolt.

"Look on the bright side—if the raccoon's hanging out at our site, the skunks and bears are probably visiting somebody else."

"How can you find this funny?"

"I'm not the one who's gotta take a leak."

Four D cells' worth of light burned into his retinas
when Keri turned the flashlight on him. "I can't sleep
until I've gone to the bathhouse, Kowalski. And if I
don't sleep, you don't sleep."

That much was obvious, so Joe swung his legs over
the edge and stood. Unlike Keri, he wasn't wearing
pajamas that buttoned to his eyebrows and he laughed
when the flashlight beam ran down over his black boxer
briefs before whipping back to the door. He pulled on
his sweatpants and shoved his bare feet into his sneakers. After a brief hesitation, he pulled a shirt over his
head. While his bare chest was still buff enough to attract the females, up here they'd all be of the buzzing,
biting variety.

"Let's go," he said, and he wasn't surprised when she
made him go out the door first. Without relinquishing
the flashlight, of course.

There were a couple of low fires burning in the
campground as they made their way to the bathhouse,
but all was mostly quiet. The Kowalskis always arrived on a Monday so they could be all set up and get
a few rides in before the place filled up. Joe reached
over and took the flashlight out of Keri's hand so he
could turn it off.

"I can't see," she protested.

"Just be still a second and let your eyes adjust."

"If I stand in one place too long the bugs will hang
an all-you-can-eat buffet sign on me."

He chuckled softly and started walking again. "You
used to love being outside with me at night."

"I used to strip on pool tables to Guns N' Roses, too,"
Keri said, "but times change. People change."

Joe would have liked to deny he'd changed all that

much, but it probably wouldn't have been true. He'd been a gung-ho boy who'd made good on his dreams, only to end up jaded and still looking for…something. But even though Keri had changed a lot more than him, just being with her made him remember being young.

"It doesn't get dark like this at home," Keri whispered, and he was reminded how far her home was from his.

"Bright lights in the big city," he muttered, thankful their arrival at the bathhouse derailed any further discussion about Los Angeles.

Keri was in there a few minutes, then emerged with a sheepish smile. "Thank you. I think I can sleep now."

"Or we could go make out on the see-saw," he said, just to make her laugh.

It worked. "Terry said she'd hide my bug spray until I duct tape my thighs together if I try making out with you."

Keri stumbled on a rock and Joe instinctively took her hand to steady her. After she regained her balance, he just sort of kept it. "How did that happen to come up in conversation?"

She turned her head and he could see the gleam of her teeth when she smiled. "It was right after Lisa offered three days of lifeguard duty if you and I can have sex in her RV's shower without knocking it off its levelers."

Joe stopped, still holding her hand. "Why the hell was anybody talking about us having sex? Not that it's a bad thing, but…why?"

"Mostly to annoy Terry." But she looked away when she said it.

"Three days, huh?"

She tried to pull away, but he yanked her back, so she poked a finger at his chest instead. "Forget it, Kowalski. Sitting by the pool happens to be one of my more finely honed skills."

"You've never been poolside with my nephews."

So he wasn't the only one in the campground mentally combining the words *Joe*, *Keri* and *sex*. Interesting.

Then he spotted his sister. Across the dark playground, Terry sat in one of the swings, drawing in the dirt with the toes of her sneakers.

"Hey, I'm going to talk to Terry for a sec. Take the flashlight and go on ahead."

He could see the urge to protest cross Keri's face, but then she looked across the playground, too. "Fine, but if I get mauled by a bear, you're going to feel like an asshole in the morning."

Joe waited until the flashlight beam—moving at a very fast clip—rounded the corner toward the cabins, then made his way to the swing set. He took the one next to her, careful to hold it still. Damn things made him carsick for some reason.

"I thought it would be easier away from the house," Terry said without looking up from her dirt scribbles. "But I can't sleep without his snoring and the quiet here only makes it worse."

"Everybody will understand if you pack it up and head home, you know."

She snorted. "And leave you all here to fend for yourselves?"

The old conversational high-wire—how to remind her they were all reasonably competent adults without minimizing the work she put into the family. "A temporary diet of hot dogs and marshmallows won't kill anybody."

When she didn't even crack a smile, Joe started mentally combining the words *Evan, head* and *baseball bat.* His soon-to-be-ex brother-in-law was a good guy he'd always considered a friend, but Joe was in big brother mode—even if he was only nine minutes older.

"I thought he'd come running right back," Terry said. "But he didn't, and now… He said he was leaving because there had to be more—something *better*—and now he lives alone in a basic closet over a freakin' Laundromat."

"I know it seems like forever, but it's only been three months. You guys can still work it out if you both want it."

"Why should I try, when he could flush thirteen years down the toilet because I wouldn't have a quickie on the kitchen table?"

That was a part of the story Joe hadn't yet heard. "No offense, but I don't think that fancy brass and glass set of yours would stand up to it."

"That's what I told him, and that I'm not serving up Corn Flakes on his ass prints. He was gone forty minutes later."

"A guy doesn't walk out on his family because he ain't getting lucky on the kitchen table. You know there has to be more to it than that."

Terry sighed and looked up at the stars. "He said now that our daughter's older and out with her friends so much, he wanted to work on being Evan and Terry more instead of just Stephanie's parents. He wanted more spontaneity, and he said I treat him more like a second child than a husband."

Now Joe was crossing that conversational high-wire again, only this time he was blindfolded and slightly intoxicated. She did, after all, excel in family micro-management and treated them all like children at times. This was the woman who asked him every single year if he'd packed enough underwear for the trip. But again, now was not the time to even hint at siding with Evan.

"It was probably some midlife meltdown," he said, "and he just doesn't have the balls to come crawling back."

"Maybe." She sniffed and shrugged her shoulders, and the subject was closed. "What are you doing with her, Joe?"

He didn't need to ask who she meant. "I don't know, sis. It started out as some weird mix of curiosity, revenge and nostalgia, but now… Sometimes she's a total stranger and sometimes she's the Keri I loved. And the chemistry's still pretty damn potent."

"She's going to leave again, the second she has what she wants from you, and don't forget it. She's not any better than Lauren."

That was a low blow, but not a surprise. Terry didn't like feeling shitty alone. But dragging his ex-almost-fiancée into the pity party was just bitchy. "She's nothing like Lauren. Keri's not hiding what she wants from me or why she's here. And I know she'll be gone as soon as she has her interview. I'm just enjoying her company until then."

Terry turned to make eye contact with him again. "I didn't like the guy you became after she left the first time, and I still don't think you should be around her."

"For chrissake, Terry, you're acting like a mother hen."

As soon as the words left his mouth he wished he

could take them back. It wasn't the first time he'd ever said them to her, but he couldn't have chosen a worse time.

"Fine, Joe," she said in a low voice. "Get your heart broken again. We can be a matched set."

Then she crossed the playground to her camper without looking back.

Keri was, regrettably, already awake and mentally updating her resume with the covers over her head when Joe slapped her on the ass.

"Rise and shine, babe. Breakfast is at eight and by eight-fifteen Kevin's licking the last crumbs off the plates."

"I don't care." She had just passed the worst night of her life, and a pancake wasn't going to help.

"I'm heading over. If you're not there in a few minutes, Ma's going to send the boys after you. Just FYI."

When the cabin door opened and closed, Keri groaned and pulled the covers down. Camping sucked.

When a subdued Joe had returned to the cabin last night, he'd promptly fallen into a sound sleep. She, on the other hand, had tossed and turned on her foam slab—kept awake by a silence broken only by Joe's unfamiliar snoring and what had sounded suspiciously like a rabid, ferocious raccoon trying to jimmy the deadbolt on the cabin door.

Agreeing to this asinine blackmail scheme had been a mistake.

Looking in the mirror was a bigger one. Even feeling as crappy as she did didn't prepare her for how bad she looked.

And she had no sink. No shower. And no toilet.

Yes, camping really sucked, except for the opportunity to bury Joe's body out in the wilderness where nobody would ever find it.

Keri threw everything she needed for a trip to the bathhouse into one of the plastic shopping bags Joe left lying around, then donned a hooded, zip-up sweatshirt. After pulling the hood as far over her really bad hair as possible, she opened the door.

Flash. "Say cheese!"

No. Strangling. Children. "You and I are going to have a little talk about privacy, Bobby."

"Aunt Terry said to tell you I'm the parazappy."

"That's *paparazzi*, and I'm not them. I'm a journalist, so you can tell Aunt Terry to..." Just in the nick of time, her thought-to-speech filter woke up and smelled the coffee. "Never mind."

"You were a lot prettier yesterday."

"And you were a lot more charming."

He just grinned his uncle's grin at her. "Grammy said the food's going fast and you don't want to go riding on an empty stomach."

"I don't want to go riding at all," she said, but Bobby was already running down the dirt road.

She managed to shower fast enough to snatch a pancake and the last two strips of bacon out from under Kevin's nose. The caffeine flowed freely from the coffeemaker connected by extension cord to Lisa's RV, thank God, and she was almost feeling human when the boys started dragging gear out of the totes in the screenhouse.

"I...have a headache," Keri lied weakly.

Joe took her coffee mug away and tugged her to her feet. "You can ride with me today, to get a feel for it."

"I'd rather not."

"You didn't go flatlander on me, did you girl?" Leo demanded in that booming voice of his. Terry snickered.

Keri may have spent half her life in California, but she was no damn flatlander and said so.

Terry tossed her a helmet, which she managed to catch without breaking a nail. "Prove it."

Joe grinned and leaned into her personal space to whisper, "Just wrap yourself around me and hold on tight, babe. You'll be fine."

"Where's the duct tape?" Terry yelled, and this time it was Lisa who snickered.

Keri shivered when Joe's breath tickled her ear. Between the newly triggered hot flashes and the imminent threats of mud in her hair and duct taped thighs, she was anything *but* fine.

About the Author

New York Times and *USA TODAY* bestselling author Shannon Stacey lives with her husband and two sons in New England, where her two favorite activities are writing stories of happily-ever-after and driving her UTV through the mud. You can contact Shannon through her website, shannonstacey.com, where she maintains an almost daily blog, visit her on Twitter, Twitter.com/shannonstacey, and on Facebook, Facebook.com/shannonstacey.authorpage, or email her at shannon@shannonstacey.com.

To find out about other books by Shannon Stacey or to be alerted to new releases, sign up for her monthly newsletter at bit.ly/shannonstaceynewsletter.

We hope you enjoyed reading

FLARE UP

by *New York Times* bestselling author

SHANNON STACEY

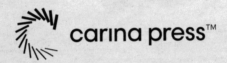

carina press™

Connect with us for info on our new releases,
access to exclusive offers and much more!

Visit CarinaPress.com

Other ways to keep in touch:

Facebook.com/CarinaPress

Twitter.com/CarinaPress

CarinaPress.com/Newsletter

New books available every month.

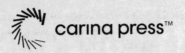

Introducing the Carina Press
Romance Promise!

The Carina Press team all have one thing in common: we
are romance readers with a longtime love of the genre. And
we know what readers are looking for in a romance:
a guarantee of a happily-ever-after (HEA) or happy-for-
now (HFN). With that in mind, we're initiating the
Carina Press Romance Promise. When you see a
book tagged with these words in our cover copy/book
description, we're making you, the reader,
a very important promise:

**This book contains a romance central to the plot
and ends in an HEA or HFN.**

Simple, right? But so important, we know!

Look for the Carina Press Romance Promise and one-click
with confidence that we understand what's at the heart of
the romance genre!

Look for this line in Carina Press book descriptions:

*One-click with confidence. This title is part of the **Carina Press
Romance Promise**: all the romance you're looking for with an
HEA/HFN. It's a promise!*

Find out more at **CarinaPress.com/RomancePromise**.

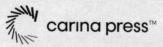

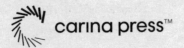

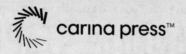
carina press™

Get the latest on Carina Press by joining our eNewsletter!

Don't miss out, sign up today!
CarinaPress.com/Newsletter

Sign up and get Carina Press offers and coupons delivered straight to your inbox!

Plus, as an eNewsletter subscriber, you'll get the inside scoop on everything Carina Press and be the first to know about our newest releases!

Visit CarinaPress.com

Other ways to keep in touch:

Facebook.com/CarinaPress

Twitter.com/CarinaPress

Get 4 FREE REWARDS!

We'll send you 2 FREE Books
plus 2 FREE Mystery Gifts.

Harlequin Intrigue® books feature heroes and heroines that confront and survive danger while finding themselves irresistibly drawn to one another.

FREE Value Over $20

Get 4 FREE REWARDS!

We'll send you 2 FREE Books plus 2 FREE Mystery Gifts.

FREE
Value Over
$20

Both the **Romance** and **Suspense** collections feature compelling novels written by many of today's best-selling authors.

YES! Please send me 2 FREE novels from the Essential Romance or Essential Suspense Collection and my 2 FREE gifts (gifts are worth about $10 retail). After receiving them, if I don't wish to receive any more books, I can return the shipping statement marked "cancel." If I don't cancel, I will receive 4 brand-new novels every month and be billed just $6.74 each in the U.S. or $7.24 each in Canada. That's a savings of at least 16% off the cover price. It's quite a bargain! Shipping and handling is just 50¢ per book in the U.S. and 75¢ per book in Canada.* I understand that accepting the 2 free books and gifts places me under no obligation to buy anything. I can always return a shipment and cancel at any time. The free books and gifts are mine to keep no matter what I decide.

Choose one: ☐ **Essential Romance**   ☐ **Essential Suspense**
                     (194/394 MDN GMY7)   (191/391 MDN GMY7)

Name (please print)

Address   Apt. #

City   State/Province   Zip/Postal Code

> Mail to the **Reader Service:**
> **IN U.S.A.:** P.O. Box 1341, Buffalo, NY 14240-8531
> **IN CANADA:** P.O. Box 603, Fort Erie, Ontario L2A 5X3

Want to try 2 free books from another series! Call 1-800-873-8635 or visit www.ReaderService.com.
